It didn't look like a place where a murder had been committed....

There was no blood, no disarray, just Lundy lying naked, chained to a concrete wall. In the harsh light brought in by the investigative team, I could clearly see the look of agony on the young prince's face.

I lowered the viewer and took a deep breath. Hadrien cast me with a quick review. "Are you all right?"

"Yes," I answered, certain that I wouldn't tell him the truth, even if I weren't. "I've done this work before."

"Yes, so I understand. Do you think you can actually catch this killer using the science of the interplanetudes?"

"I believe it is *we* who must catch the killer, not just me."

"Well, if it is we who must, then I better be straight with you. I have no patience for astrological bullshit. I deal in facts, not interdimensional possibilities."

"I deal in facts, too, Lieutenant."

He chuckled.

✧ THE ASTROLOGER ✧

HEART
------- OF -------
STONE

DENNY DeMARTINO

ACE BOOKS, NEW YORK

To My Mother and Father

This is a work of fiction. Names, characters, places, and incidents either are the product of the author's imagination or are used fictitiously, and any resemblance to actual persons, living or dead, business establishments, events, or locales is entirely coincidental.

THE ASTROLOGER: HEART OF STONE

An Ace Book / published by arrangement with the author

PRINTING HISTORY
Ace edition / February 2001

The Penguin Putnam Inc. World Wide Web site address is http://www.penguinputnam.com

ISBN: 0-441-00807-0

ACE®
Ace Books are published by The Berkley Publishing Group, a division of Penguin Putnam Inc., 375 Hudson Street, New York, New York 10014.
ACE and the "A" design are trademarks belonging to Penguin Putnam Inc.

PRINTED IN THE UNITED STATES OF AMERICA

10 9 8 7 6 5 4 3 2 1

1

As the planet Mercury enters a retrograde period, astrologers believe that bedevilments increase. It's a bad time to sign a contract, to make travel plans and, in general, to communicate and think clearly. When Terrapol Lieutenant Artemis Hadrien contacted me, I was spending MercR doing porridge—serving a period of mourning for the recent death of my husband—and to tell you the truth, I didn't want to get dirty in some police investigation. I was having enough trouble just hiding in the crowd at the Universal Astrology Conference on Maya Prime in the Pleiades Star System. Hadrien had been insistent; the emperor wanted me back on Earth. I'd been booked passage on a space liner leaving for terra firma, and he refused to give me a chance to back out of the coming trouble by running off to some lonely planet on the edge of the galaxy. Why the emperor insisted on me being the astrologer on duty was another mystery altogether.

The fact is, I once considered myself a knowledgeable forecaster of the future. With my ego's shortsightedness, I convinced myself that I could read the logos—the hor-

oscope chart of any man, woman, child, or alien being—
and combined with the science of the interplanetudes, I
could tell them precisely what would happen in their
futures. This confidence surrendered to disillusionment
when in the midst of my fancy-pantsy certainty about
my extraordinary talent, I missed seeing a very important
event. My husband was murdered in a most agonizing
manner, and I was left alone with the realization that I
didn't know Siegfried from Roy about how the interplanetudes determined our destinies.

I left Earth and my services as an astrological detective and hid among those stars that so plagued me. I'd
traveled from system to system, earning easy money by
becoming the Harry Houdini of the astro set. Find an
easy mark—a man or woman who needed to hear nice
words—throw out some cream and pudding about life
challenges, and then fleece them for my fee, pulling a
disappearing act before they could find out that the
charts I used belonged to a long-dead singer named Elvis
Presley. At first I felt bad about this nefarious lifestyle,
but then I convinced myself that if the client wandered
off a cliff I should have warned him about, it was his
own fault for listening to me. My talents might not so
much lie in reading the future as in persuading people
that I could. To be honest, I had no idea what was really
in store for me other than what I told myself about the
upcoming situation. Still, there was Hadrien's big, bold
Uranus opposing my Sun.

I debarked at the World Spaceport in London and
paused at the bottom of the ramp to fluff the material
on my dark blue jumpsuit. This was always a peak travel
time to nearby tourist worlds like Arbutus and Sematia,
but this summer day was humid enough to make a trip
to Dover Beach more preferable than fighting the crowds
of travelers who tried to escape it. I picked up my travel
valise and glanced around, noting the numbers of imperial soldiers guarding the entrances. They silently did

a precheck of baggage, and seeing this, I felt a peck of annoyance surface. Emperor Theo Aurik cared diddly-squat about secrets unless they were his own.

Hadrien waited for me at the end of the ramp, and from the first contact with the policeman, I quickly determined that someone had piddled in his tea, no horoscope chart necessary.

"Philipa Cyprion?" he asked without extending his hand.

"Indeed, that would be me," I answered.

He nodded. "Artemis Hadrien. Nice to meet you, and sorry about the yank from your conference. Couldn't be helped." He pointed to a lonely corridor, the entrance of which was flanked by two sentries. "You'll be bypassing customs today. If you'll follow me."

I let him show me the way between the two men, and they dispassionately ignored us as we entered the hallway. "I see Theo wasted no time securing the routes offworld."

"Yes, but he did it too late. We didn't find Prince Lundy's body until three days after the crime. Plenty of time for the murderer to escape."

"What makes you think he wanted to leave Earth?"

"Let's change that question to what makes me think *it* wanted to leave Earth."

"Alien?"

"That's the way this thing is breaking down." He sighed heavily, picking at the collar of his black jumpsuit. "I thought England didn't get this blasted hot in the summer."

"Ah, yes, it does. And the midgies can be a frightful pain in the arse."

He glanced at me. "Midgies?"

"Mosquitoes. Since that big eco-spill in the North Sea fifty years ago, the stinkers have been a problem. I've suffered through bouts of Vestian malaria three times in the last ten years. It's a good thing they found a way to control it, or I'd probably be shaking and wheezing right now." I scratched at a sudden itch on my thigh.

He grunted, but beyond that, he didn't open his trap. I kept to myself as well, but like I'm given to do, I pasted him with a candid stare.

Hadrien might have been my late husband's age, but taller and far more sturdy and robust. He wore his long, blond hair loose and flowing, and to balance the effect, his short-cropped beard was the same hue as Nile mud. His most striking feature, though, was his suspicious gaze. He had deep-set, dark blue eyes, and even while he talked, he took in the corridor like he expected an assassin to jump out of the recessed lighting.

Hadrien led me to a side exit and a covered parking garage. The moment we left the building, I took a deep breath, smelling the scent of fresh rain and fried kippers. It was good to be home again, even if I wouldn't admit it out loud.

His car was a dented, green sled with a cracked windshield. He paused to open the passenger door for me, cursing when it wouldn't respond. Finally, his code card correctly demagnetized the lock, and he pulled the hatch back. I slid inside, finding myself in a sinking seat surrounded by a moat of trash—food wrappers, tins, plastic cups—all sticky with sugary residue.

Hadrien slid into the driver's seat and started the repulsor engine. It squealed when the antigrav system came on-line. As we rose gently from the pavement, I finally spoke.

"I didn't get any information on you."

"Why do you need any?" he asked, backing out of the spot.

Remember that touch of annoyance I mentioned? Well, it instantly surfaced, and I belched it out. "I want to know who I'm being forced to work with. I didn't ask to come here, and I'm not accustomed to working with a partner."

"So I understand. You've been walking the tightrope alone this last year. Let's see, the way I figure it, you've been running a neat little scam on folks, just enough to seed the cred account and make it possible for you to hit and run." He took a hardy breath before adding, "Strange what grief will do to a person. From court astrologer to star pimp."

"You have me at a disadvantage. You know about me, but I don't know about you."

He turned his attention from the garage to glance at me. "I'm from the United States peninsula of Florida-Cubano."

"Then the heat and the midgies should be nothing to you."

Hadrien chuckled but didn't remark on it. "I was ordered last week to come here. I had enough time to throw my clothes in the back of my jitney before I was driving into the belly bay of a Ci3 North Atlantic transport."

"You must have sterling credentials to be torn away from your tropical paradise by the emperor."

"Yeah, well, I've caught a few murderers in my time, but I don't know bug about Waki'el."

"There aren't many who do." I pumped in a breath before saying what I figured was on his mind. "Still, there are other Terrapol officers who have more experience at nicking aliens. Why you?"

He pulled the sled onto the busy street before building on our conversation. When he did, a hint of a smile smudged into the edges of his beard. "Apparently, a court astrologer who Theo trusts suggested that you and I would be a good match. As I understand it, you were chosen first, and I was chosen second, my selection done to complement yours."

I studied him. "I hadn't heard that." Why the blazes did Theo want me back that badly? I wasn't bothering him. If anything, I was trying to remain unobtrusive by building a reputation as an astrologer who couldn't tell a black hole from a hole in my shoe.

"I suppose you want to know my birth date," he said flatly.

It was issued as a challenge, and I was really in no buggering mood for it. "I don't need to know it.

He pushed a skeptical look my direction. "Why?"

"Because a man's actions speak for him. The stars don't mean a pot full of hot manure when it comes down to who we are."

He leaned forward, wiped at the steam building on the windshield, and whispered, "You better get happy with the stars again, Philipa. Theo is looking for blood for his boy, and I don't think he cares whose red is soaking through the carpet."

"Well, I didn't ask to be brought in on this case, and I'm under duress because he's tapped me cred accounts. It tricks me off. If I get the chance, I'm going to give the little bramble bunny a piece of me mind."

"A piece of *me* mind?"

"And that's another thing. Don't go braying about me accent. I'm from East London. Get used to it."

He grinned but steered the conversation away from my complaints. "I understand you gave Prince Lundy an astrological reading for his sixteenth birthday. You made a prediction that he would become a great leader once he'd sowed his wild oats."

"I said, 'If he survived sowing his wild oats.' Which he didn't." I apparently didn't know what I was talking about, even then. Still, a blind man could have delineated Lundy's logos, because he was a walking casebook. There were aspected planets in his chart that had ensured that he would live until a ripe old age despite temptations and challenges in his early life, and that's what burned my loaf the most. Most things written in the stars took an inordinate amount of free will to change, and people like Lundy had no such power. Their lives usually played out in perfect accordance to their astrological charts. Why hadn't his?

In 2130, scientists finally harnessed zero-point gravity and used it to make deep space travel a possibility. Zero-point gravity is the vibration of creation, the force that keeps the atoms in their tiny, little orbits and the planets in their huge, concentric orbits. Not only had they used zero-point gravity to cross the parsecs of space, but they had also managed to cut through the celestial fabric that wound up the universe, discovering that the material dimension wasn't the only thing containing this potent life force. There were other planes of existence, each as vital as the next, and each like bubbles in soap. They clung together, the skin of one sphere touching another, connecting through the intercessions of the creation vibration. It filled every conceivable point of the universal dimensions and was the building block for all that was or would ever be.

It was this initial discovery that cut loose humanity's ancient dependence upon religious faith. Though much of our information was made on inference, the afterlife had became a quantifiable place, caught firmly within astronomy and physics. The pioneers of this new understanding called this methodology the interplanetudes.

From what we know of the nature of the universe, there is a single vibrational quality that restricts all human physical life. This quality is time. Materiality finds us trapped by these familiar laws of linear motion, but once we die, our life force is no longer constrained to a past, present, and future. We expand back into the creation energy and follow this flow into the next dimension, moving from a universe of heavy gravity and corporeality to a plane comprised of pure thought. Here, time turns fluid, having very little meaning for us after our earthly exit. It only serves as the conduit for our movement between dimensional realities. In other words, time is the element that ignites the stream of the creation force that fills organic cells with life.

Science now agrees with dogma and is so bold as to state that it believes this creation energy phenomenon to be the same for all species in our known galaxy. Though no concrete evidence of life after death has been found, the researchers accept the theory that our discarnate state is a way station for our souls, and while lingering in this ghostly dimension, we are tasked with finding a way back into corporeality by selecting the perfect human body as the physical vehicle. To this end, each discarnate entity who wishes access to the material realm must first attach to a portion of the time continuum that vibrates through the creation energy and then direct the flow to a designated point in this causal plane. It's this span of years, this flow within zero-point gravity that the astrologer measures.

By calculating the time of corporeal arrival into this dimension against the positions of the planets, houses, and signs, I'm supposed to be able to tell what bit of time that person occupies in the flow, what events are likely to transpire in his life, and just when this time stream through the creation energy he harbors will cease. Most people do find it a bit over the edge, and studying Hadrien, I realized I was in for a tussle on these presumed issues.

I started in this interplanetudes business as a minor court astrologer for Emperor Theo. When he hired me, he already had one hundred children, and he was intent upon pumping out another dozen or two before his pecker fell off. It was my job to divvy the days for his new kids—numbers one hundred through one hundred twenty.

I'd seen early dismissals for numbers 113, 117, and 119, but Lundy had a good chance of knocking off his entire allotted time. Something had gone seriously wrong, and now Theo wanted a reckoning. My skin was as a good as flailed.

Hadrien used his right hand to dig into the plastic console between the bucket seats while he maneuvered the car with the other. Finding what he wanted, he tossed me an envelope decorated with the imperial seal. His words were cold as he announced the contents. "This is the murder weapon. It was found lodged in the left upper ventricle of Prince Lundy's heart." He paused, negotiated a turn down a narrow avenue, and continued. "There were no signs of how it got there. No entry wounds. No exit wounds. His sternum was intact as was the heart muscle around the stone."

"That's impossible," I said.

"We don't know what some of these aliens are capable of, Philipa. Personally, I think it was an ironic way to die."

"What does the etching in the stone mean?"

"It's the symbol of the Acu-Sen'Tal, the Waki'el priesthood."

"You are sure it's the Waki'el behind this?"

"That's right. The poopers with the exterior hearts."

"Where was Lundy found?"

"In a bunker beneath the palace."

"Did Lundy have this liaison unbeknownst to his bodyguards?"

"No," Hadrien said. He nodded toward the envelope. "It must have felt like freaking Stonehenge inside his chest."

It had been no easy death, that was for certain. "Have you talked to the guard unit?"

"Can't find the unit commander. Not surprising, given the tragedy that befell his charge. Theo would make sure he was crucified. I have to agree with the fellow—get as far away from this problem as possible."

"The bodyguard could have been part of it."

"Yes." He shut up, so I dipped into the envelope to scrape out a digital photo reader. Placing it to my eyes,

I hit the Play button and the tiny computer showed me stills of Lundy's crime scene.

It didn't look like a place where a murder had been committed. There was no blood, no disarray, just Lundy lying naked, chained to a concrete wall. In the harsh light brought in by the investigative team, I could clearly see the look of agony on the young prince's face.

I lowered the viewer and took a deep breath. Hadrien cast me with a quick review. "Are you all right?"

"Yes," I answered, certain that I wouldn't tell him the truth, even if I weren't. "I've done this work before."

"Yes, so I understand. Do you think you can actually catch this killer using the science of the interplanetudes?"

"I believe it is *we* who must catch the killer, not just me."

"Well, if it is we who must, then I better be straight with you. I have no patience for astrological bullshit. I deal in facts, not interdimensional possibilities."

"I deal in facts, too, Lieutenant."

He chuckled.

"What do you find so amusing?"

"The way you say lieutenant. *Lef-tenant.*"

I ignored his childish observation by reaching into the envelope to pull out a small, delicate gold chain, its beauty enhanced by two glittering gemstones. "What's this?"

"It's a Waki'el heart chain. It was found in his hand."

I slipped the jewelry back into the bag before asking my next question. "Did you visit the crime scene?"

"Yes. There's not much there. No fingerprints. Waki'el don't have them. We found traces of Lundy's blood, as well as a chemical solution that was swabbed into a series of open gashes on his chest. I don't have the breakdown with me. I'm still waiting on the lab report."

I unfurled a new subject. "Tell me. I've been offworld

some time and haven't received reports from home. Have there been others from the royal family to die recently?"

Hadrien stared at me, and I realized he had different levels of suspiciousness. It looked like he believed I was all pork pies—that is, built on lies—until I asked that question. "How did you know that?" he husked.

"Don't be an ass," I answered, using a bit of false dignity. "I'm an astrologer. The science of the interplanetudes works, whether you agree or not. So, tell me. Which dustbin lids were they?"

"Dustbin lids?" he asked.

"Dustbin lids—kids," I said.

The fact that I knew this only served to dish up his intense expression. "Lundy's brothers Prince Tenner, Prince Coran, and his sister, Princess Shelagh. They were killed in a transport accident as they were leaving Delphi. The ship blew up. It was a closely guarded secret. I didn't know anything about it until I was briefed yesterday morning."

I shook my head but didn't reply. Tenner, Coran, and Shelagh. Obviously, I hadn't been wrong about numbers 113, 117, and 119.

2

*Hadrien drove straight to the Terrapol Head-*quarters, cursing when a traffic jam impeded our progress at Piccadilly Square. From his fiery manner, I figure his birth date fell somewhere in Aries or Taurus. It was a generalization, but if true, our relationship was in for some sparks. Being a Libran, we could well have been complete opposites. What crazy astrologer had pasted us together? Probably one who had the same method I did when it came to the horoscope flimflam—the old scientific wild-assed guess. That's all it had ever been for me. I'd stopped denying it shortly after Eric's death.

I was glad when the roadway was stalled with commuters, because I was allowed a look at old London-town, and I will admit, it seemed as alien to me as any other world. Had I been gone that long, or had one planet started blending into the next?

We entered the Terrapol offices via the parking garage, took the lift to the tenth floor, and walked into the investigative unit. Hadrien nodded to the secretary, a perky little puffer who giggled before each sentence.

"Oh, Lieutenant. Chief Albertsone wants you to go to the interrogation cell. It seems that Prince Lundy's bodyguard unit has grassed on their commander."

"Grassed?" he asked.

The puffer glanced at me and giggled. "You know, grassed. They ratted on him."

He smiled, the light of understanding picking up the tone of his expression. "Excellent." Turning, he placed his fingers gently upon my elbow to guide me out the door and down the hallway to the suspect questioning area.

The bullpen leading to several interrogation cells bristled with activity. These detectives stood out proudly among the prisoners, each wearing the same crisp, black cammies and gold armbands. I saw no women, though I saw at least two Sumereks lumbering around the large room with their fingernails painted rainbow colors and their round skulls shorn of the fur that covered the rest of their bodies. As we moved through canals formed by rows of metal desks, we passed in close proximity to one of the aliens, and I saw Hadrien squint. Sumereks were highly trusted by the imperial court, while humans often had to prove themselves. It made for a trying relationship between species. That, and the fact that Sumereks smelled of sour cabbage.

A short, dark-haired detective pointed out the grilling room, and in we went. Lundy, being of the immediate imperial family, was saddled with three bodyguards at all times, but I was surprised to see that the commander of the prince's protective unit was a Corrigadaire. Theo had tried for years to gain the confidence and alliance of the Corrigadaire king, but the ugly old rascal would have nothing to do with him.

The cell was tight, sterile white, and crowded with Terrapol officers. One gentleman looked in our direction as we entered, calling us over with a flick of his fingers.

He studied me openly, and I saw him shake his head slightly.

"Chief Albertsone, this is Philipa Cyprion," Hadrien said.

He nodded, using his gruff exterior to mask his unease. It was a good act, but I felt his discomfort at working with an astrologer. To people like this man, I was no better than a bloomin' Gypsy fortune-teller. Still, he had the smarts not to mention his feelings.

"We found the stinker trying to get out of London by skyrail," he said. Albertstone pointed at two humans who flanked him. Despite their manacles, they did what they could to pull their chairs as far from the alien and his two-inch claws as possible. "You have Warren Enderson and Jaink Fellers. And this smelly sonofabitch is K'ton Koor."

The Corrigadaire angled his face toward the white metal table, but his large, bulbous eyes swiveled neatly in their sockets to take us in.

"Confession?" Hadrien asked.

"You wish," Albertsone said. "No, so far, he's been uncooperative." Pausing, he pulled me into the conversation. "What do you need for your part of this sordid affair?"

"Birth records," I answered, layering my voice with authority. "Month, day, year, time, and place."

"Your science will not work for me," the Corrigadaire growled.

I didn't reply but instead accepted the data strip from Albertsone, seeking out a chair and small table at the far end of the room. Hadrien made himself comfortable at the table with the suspects. He stared at them silently until Albertsone and his men departed the room for some other surveillance spot. When they were gone, he touched a stud on the side of the table, and a small, flat computer rose from the top. He glanced at it before beginning, but while he used the quiet time to frazzle the suspects' nerves, I received the distinct impression that the bodyguards were not the only ones who were being observed.

If I'd had any doubt, I soon discovered that Hadrien was good at toasting the crust on a pork pie, too. "K'ton, I deal with aliens all the time, and from the looks of you, I'd say you set up Prince Lundy."

Koor shook his shaggy head and dug his claws into the table. "I would not do that to the prince." He snorted, flinging his gaze in my direction. "She cannot tell about me. I was not born in this backward star system. Your planets cannot discern my fate."

Hadrien leaned back, and the plastic chair squealed under his weight. He rubbed his beard for a moment before answering. "You seem terribly concerned about the astrologer's presence."

"I am not."

"Don't let him tell you that," Fellers spat. "Of course he is."

"Why?" Hadrien demanded.

"Because she can get the clampers on him."

Hadrien frowned. "Clampers?"

"Yeah, the wristbands they use when you're executed by electro-crucifixion. Theo thinks a lot of astrologers and their talents. What she says might keep us from turning into grease spots."

I smiled to myself. It was nice to enjoy a bit of life-and-death power. "Theo's mother was a court astrologer when she met his father. The emperor loved his mother very much. They were soul mates."

Koor snarled, baring a couple of fangs in a showy performance of bravado. "I am a citizen of Corrigadaire. You cannot hold me. My government will intervene."

It seemed not to faze Hadrien. He sat there calmly, waiting for the alien to work down toward silence. While he did, I entered Koor's personal data into my computer and called up his logos, in particular the chart that told me the placement of the planets when he was born. Scanning it, I realized three things about this being: Mars inconjunct Saturn; Neptune was in his twelfth house, the house of secrets; and Venus squared Lilith, the Dark Moon.

Hadrien glanced at me. "Does this monster have reason to fear your report?"

I pulled a deep breath and thereby donned my courage and my own lie. "Yes."

"How so?"

"Simply put, I see a being who deals in dynamic ways with frustration, denial, and unfulfillment through his personal vision. He aligns with occult doctrines, made more mystical by the disinformation about his species. He also finds expression through the shadow side of love and loyalty. From this quick breakdown, it seems apparent that an astro-profile had not been run on him before he was hired to protect Prince Lundy."

Hadrien scoped in on my statement. "Shadowy side of love and loyalty. We know Lundy had a voracious sexual appetite. Did you pimp for the prince?"

Enderson answered. "We all did at one time or the other."

"Did he give you bonuses for finding him new playmates?"

"Yes," Fellers said. "He liked alien females."

Hadrien squinted at Koor. "And your alienness was a perfect cover. You hate humans, don't you?"

"I respect all species."

"He's lying," I said. "He doesn't want to be among us. We produce a sense of disgust in him."

"Well, I suppose that's natural," Hadrien said. "I'm not particularly crazy about bug-eyed beasties myself." He leaned forward and used his thumbnail to scrape at a piece of dirt on the white table. "These gentlemen claim that you brought the murderer to Lundy."

"I did not. They lie."

"So, you're saying you had nothing to do with arranging this tryst."

"I do not understand the word tryst."

I hit him with a couple of basic generalities according to the placement of his planets. "You have many contacts. You gather wealth from many different sources, though it does little to appease your restlessness. You know many people hailing from different worlds and have joined with them for this sinister game."

"The Corrigadaire do not associate with the Waki'el."

Hadrien stood up, took a few steps my direction, and facing away from the suspects, he grinned at me. It transformed his features, making me blink at how pretty he was when he smiled, but as abruptly as it came, this angelic quality disappeared. He turned away, just as I did. "How did you know Prince Lundy was having sex with a Waki'el?"

Koor was true to astro-form, and at that moment, according to my calculator, his Southern Node transited his Sun in Leo. He hesitated, his eyeballs swinging back and forth in his head, while he obviously tried to think of a creative excuse as well as find the path of least resistance.

Hadrien returned to the table and grabbed the alien by one of his pointed ears. Koor winced and bellowed, but constrained by chains, he could only retreat so far. "How do you know it was a Waki'el?"

The alien rattled his handcuffs, roaring as Hadrien twisted his flesh. Enderson and Fellers tipped their chairs back, hustling to stand, pulling at their shackles in an attempt to put space between them and this nice little drama.

Hadrien continued to press the Corrigadaire. "Come on, Koor. Give it over, and you might just miss being the next bag of meat at one of Theo's crucifixions."

"No!" Koor barked. "It is an affair of the heart!"

With that, he snatched his head from Hadrien's grip

and leaned over his manacled hands. A second later, his salmon-colored blood splattered my Terrapol partner in the face. Hadrien reacted instantly, pushing Koor's face with the flat of his hand. The Corrigadaire offered no opposition, and when he thumped back in the chair, I saw that he had indeed taken the path of least resistance by opening his jugular vein with his fore claw.

3

I remained composed following this grisly oc-
currence, standing up quietly after the suicide and slowly
walking to the ladies' loo. When I got there, I nearly
puked in my boots before I stepped up to the commode,
but I didn't cry, didn't moan, didn't groan. In fact, aside
from the biliousness associated with seeing someone
slash his own throat, I felt nothing. That scared me a
bit, so I hid in the johnnie for a while to wonder why I
was so blank in the brain over watching such a hideous
death.

One thing was certain: This investigation was as cold
as a Saxon's titty on Christmas morning. I could tell by
my new partner's attitude that he didn't think it would
get any warmer any time soon. That led me to question
again why Theo had sent for me. There was nothing I
could do except play with horoscopes, and that wouldn't
solve this case.

As I sat in the cracked leatherette couch in the bathroom, the puffer came in to fiddle with her makeup. She
was a pretty sort, but she had way too many places on
her body that were pierced, and she apparently loved to

show off the parts that might have done better being covered up.

"How are ya doing?" she asked, blessedly without a giggle.

"Well, considering I lost all me breakfast, I guess I'll live."

She nodded, clucked, and then rifled through her canvas bag. "Got some nauseous pills in 'ere somewhere." Her hand finally clamped around the prize, and she tossed me a bottle of dram. "Pop two of those, sister. I keep 'em for situations such as we just had."

I was grateful, and to prove it, I didn't hesitate to take them. After I swallowed the capsules, I decided to use her pleasantness to further my knowledge. "So tell me, what do you know about Lieutenant Hadrien?"

The lollipop smiled brightly into the bathroom mirror. "Oh, he's a real looker, ain't he?" She giggled. "I'd love to get me claws into that one, I would."

"You're right. He is a nice-looking bloke, but what about his background?"

She shook her head and lost her smile. Turning, she came to sit down on the sofa, and forgetting about her hair, she pulled up her short skirt to play with a bangle pierced through the fleshy part of her thigh. "Well, now, if you're interested in that one, you should watch yourself."

"Why?"

"Because he's a junkie."

Being a junkie didn't mean that Hadrien was addicted to a controlled substance. It meant that through selective genetic madness engaged in by Theo's great grandfather, there were a whole host of people out there who had junked-up nervous systems. Hadrien couldn't drink alcohol or take any sort of depressant medication.

The puffer took my silence as understanding, and she nodded. "Yep, that's right. One good stiff drink, and he's comatose for a week. I understand he can't take revs to pull back, either, so if he celebrates New Year's Eve, he doesn't wake up until way late the next year."

"He doesn't sound like the kind of investigator the emperor would want on this case."

"Oh, don't get me wrong. He's one capable bloke. Has a kill record that can't be outdone."

"Kill record?"

"You know—nabs, nicks, arrests."

I nodded. "So, he could get his man if the trail wasn't so frosty."

The puffer pulled around to study me. "How'd ya know that? Did he tell ya?"

"No. It's been a week since Lundy was murdered. They should have some suspects."

"But they don't. It was a dry path from the start. That and budget cuts 'ave made it tough to get the forensics work completed. I figure that 'ill be a half-assed job when the Queen Bitch of the Laboratory gets through. She ain't exactly a lover of the imperial family."

"I don't know many who are."

"Yeah, well, them whistles in the next room are all that stands between us and the crap on the streets. It's right unsettlin' knowin' so many of 'em happily boink the gov they work for."

"A lot of under-the-table tricking?"

"Ain't one of 'em not on the take."

"So a lot of lingering and finagling. That's why they brought Hadrien in. It took three days to make the decision that they needed a different kind of expertise."

She smiled. "You got a lot on the ball, me sister. Whatever ya' do, watch your back." With that, she rose and, picking up her canvas sack, she left.

I returned to find that Hadrien was waiting for me in the holding cell where Enderson and Fellers were locked down.

Enderson was fifty-nine years old and had been born during a lunar eclipse, a sign that made most astrologers wince. It portended a grievous life and a sad ending. Studying him, I could tell that this knowledge was not as esoteric as some would think. He could see his final days with crystal clarity.

Fellers clocked in at thirty-two years of age. He had a boring logos, save for the blip between Pluto and Mars.

I finished scanning their charts on my calculator before trying out the information I had gleaned and a hunch of my own. "Mr. Fellers, did you realize that you have a tendency to make poor choices of self-sacrifice?"

He blinked at me like an old cow. "Excuse me?"

"I mean that you don't choose well. You give your energy and effort to the wrong causes and in that, you continually deface your morality. It's self-sacrifice taken to an odd extreme."

"What do you mean?" he whispered.

"I believe you have given your life to a cause that is described as an affair of the heart."

"You talking about that bunk Koor was mouthing?" Enderson interrupted. He snorted and leaned forward, his cuffs clanking on the edge of the table. "That's alien buggle, that is."

"Why is it alien buggle?"

"It just is."

"You think it's some sort of term for honor, perhaps?"

He shrugged. "Ain't got a clue, Madame Astrologer. I do know that old Koor wasn't above a little shim-sham."

"I take it he was bringing Lundy females for sexual exploitation."

"Yeah. Especially Waki'el females. Old Lundy had a honey addiction."

"Honey addiction?" I asked.

"That's right. Waks got pockets in their throats that delivers up a narcotic effect with their saliva. It tastes like honey and puts a man on cloud nine. Lundy couldn't get enough. I don't know that he particularly cared about

Waks that much, but he sure did like those sweet kisses."

"Where would he find these females?" I asked. "I was under the impression that few Waki'el traveled from their home world."

"They come in once in a while aboard Corrie vessels. That weasel they call a king has allied with Felis Bray'el, the head of the Waki'el Sen'Tal."

"Why do you think he killed himself like that?" I asked.

"Ain't got a clue. Those Corrigadaires are like no other species we've ever run into."

"Why do you say that?"

"Because they synthesize light," Hadrien said, stepping into the room. He sat down beside me and nodded before explaining. "They're creatures who distill photon particles. As you probably know, humans emit photon particles in their electromagnetic energy signature."

"The human aura?" I said.

"That's right. A Corrie can tell if a person is about to die by the absence of this photon shield."

"And that's why Koor had eyes like mince pies," Fellers said. "He could see someone ready to pop off to the next dimension. It was bloomin' weird, I tell you."

"Did he know that Lundy was about to die?" I asked.

Fellers glanced nervously at Enderson. The older man tossed him a curt nod. "Maybe they'll go easier on us."

"Tell us," Hadrien demanded.

"He told the prince that there were more than a few folks in the imperial household who were missing their auras."

"Did Lundy try to warn these people?"

"No. Lundy was bloody callous about it, he was. Talked about having less bodies at the feed trough. It pecked on Koor's nerves. He didn't like this lack of loyalty. Corries are big on the whole allegiance thing, you know. Trouble is, they're mostly loyal to their own kind."

"Did you know about this information previously to the deaths?" Hadrien asked.

"No," Fellers snapped. "You've got to believe us. Koor told us afterward. Lundy's reaction had lowered his respect for the prince."

"Do you think Koor sussed him up?" I asked.

"Sussed?" Hadrien said.

"Yes, it means to set up someone."

Enderson shook his head and hacked a dry cough before answering. "He had to know about it."

"Why?"

"Because he's the one who gave the prince the key code for the bunker room. I saw him do it."

Hadrien slammed me with an expression that had a lot of Scorpio in it: cold and icy. When the prisoner didn't reply immediately, he flipped the same look at him. "Koor knew Lundy was going to die, didn't he?"

Enderson swallowed and licked his lips. On the breeze of a sigh, he responded, "Yes, I think he did, though he never admitted it out loud."

"When he brought the prince females, where did he find them?" Hadrien asked.

They shook their heads. "Koor liked to haunt the Slug Sector in East London. Used to go to a tavern run by a human named Mick Morely. Place called *The Rabbit Hole*. He was doing a little side business with Morely for Lundy, so he said, but I don't know what that was all about. He did find the prince quite a number of bimbs from there, that I'm sure of. But you would only see the likes of them once and never again. This last one we didn't get to see at all. That's the honest truth, it is."

"Did Lundy know you were aware of this situation?"

"Yes, sir," Enderson said. "He forbade us to speak of it. Said he'd cut out our tongues."

Hadrien rubbed his earlobe and wiggled around in the chair. "So, do you think he meant that the prince's death was an affair of the heart? Possibly revenge for some act that Lundy perpetrated against an alien female? Or maybe Koor felt that the prince used him and he'd had enough?"

They both shrugged in unison. "Can't tell for sure. Never heard the term before, but like I was telling this lady here, it's just alien buggle. If you want to know what I personally think, I'll tell you, though I ain't for sure that it happened, you understand."

"Explain," Hadrien barked.

"Well, if Koor could tell when a person was going to die, then he must have seen it coming for Prince Lundy. I figure he just expedited it."

4

Enderson and Fellers apparently didn't know much more than their horoscopes suggested they did. Either that or I was bilking myself into believing that they didn't. It was a shame that their years of service to Lundy would see them executed, but they couldn't deny they were part of a conspiracy to assassinate the prince. With the death of the Corrigadaire, their fates had been waxed and sealed.

Hadrien and I left Terrapol Headquarters and headed off to the Slug Sector. As we skimmed through the streets, Hadrien fought his car's navi-computer while I felt my mood dim to a shadow. Flipping open my logos calculator, I saw that Saturn was transiting my moon in Gemini. That was the reason I felt like a rotten hagas; that, and these were the streets where Eric and I had lived.

Hadrien slammed the console with his fist, making me jump. The navi-computer quacked out the location we wanted to go by displaying a map on the tiny vid screen that popped from the dash. "Finally," he muttered. He set the autopilot and sat back in the seat to study me.

"That was a good interview with those two. I might have to revise my preconceived opinions of you."

"I'm flattered," I murmured. Then, louder, I said, "I suppose you know all about me."

"And I suppose you know all about me. You did have a free hour to collect data while I was trying to wash off the Corrie's sticky blood." I didn't admit to anything, so he continued. "Court astrology can get predictable and boring. I'll bet you don't like boring. And you're fleet of foot, as we say in the business."

"Now you'll have to explain that term to me."

He chuckled. "Well, isn't that a switch? Fleet of foot means you think fast. You're way ahead of the situation and, like a game of chess, you look at the moves yet to be made. Those are all talents that an investigator needs. Your Midheaven must be in Virgo."

All right, my mouth did drop open a tad at his observation, but then I closed it after I realized he could have looked at my birth logos at any time and probably had.

He smiled, stretched his arms, clasping the frozen steering wheel with his hands before he pooted more words into the awkward silence. "So what do you think of the old neighborhood now?"

It wasn't the same. Beings from a dozen different worlds had settled into this workingman's village, turning the place from gray and dismal into a neighborhood of metal that blended with the old brick buildings like a tinfoil lava flow. Evening had come on, and the streets were cast in the blue light of a thousand neon tubes. Garbage cluttered the streets, and strange animals pawed at the filthy water streaming into the gutters. At one time this part of London had steamed under the polluted perfume of the Thames River, but now it had that tainted flavor so overwhelming in the air of foreign worlds. It smelled like the inside of a Sumerek's armpit.

We parked in an alley next to the public house called

The Rabbit Hole where we were certain we would find Mick Morely. My new partner paused before climbing from the car to peg me with a wild stare. "This could get dicey. Are you sure you want to come in?"

"I've been in me share of pubs, old man. I can take care of meself. Besides, I've traipsed about all over the galaxy on me own. No one's buggered with me yet."

He snorted but didn't try to stop me.

"Shouldn't you call in for backup or something?" I asked as we slipped around the flowing metal corner of the building.

"I thought you were my backup," Hadrien said. "You said you could take care of yourself."

I smiled, whipping his answer into a quick comeback. "Just move out of me way if this turns into a bother. I don't want to hurt you."

"I'll make sure of that," he answered.

We reached the entrance and stopped inside the door to take in the patronage. It was an exotic theme park of alien delights: low, red fluorescent lighting for the Corrigadaires, and a section packed with Sumereks lusting after the mood-enhancing high of sage nut. Toward the back where the shadows grew more pronounced, I could make out figures engaged in a little tallyho—a game of alien chance played by Bikarians. Lose a roll and you have to pluck out your pinfeathers. Someone would stroll from this tavern with big patches of raw skin shining through before the evening was over.

Hadrien stepped farther into the crowded bar, drawing looks from several aliens sitting at a nearby table. Humans had no particular rights in places like this, but my new partner handled their scrutiny by focusing on it.

He turned to them, hit the stud in his wristwatch, and displayed a holographic image of his Terrapol badge. Then, properly introduced, he moved in their direction to study them with that dark, menacing look of his. "In about five minutes, my compatriots are going to storm this joint. Woe be he who lingers."

His words effectively cleared the table. It also signaled others that trouble was a shortfall away. Before another human appeared from a back room behind the bar, half the tavern was missing.

I glanced at the man and saw surprise register in his lean face. He squinted at Hadrien before refocusing his glare upon me. "What the buggering hell is going here?"

"Mick Morely?" I asked.

"Yeah. Why'd you run me customers off?"

"They decided to leave on their own," Hadrien answered.

"We need to speak to you, Mr. Morely," I said.

"About what?"

"The death of Prince Lundy," Hadrien said.

Morley stared at him a moment before rubbing his hand across his thick lips. "I don't know nothing about it. What would make you come here, anyway?"

Hadrien stepped up to the bar and casually leaned his elbows across it. "We understand you had a little side business going with Lundy's bodyguard, a big strapping Corrigadaire by the name of K'ton Koor. Is that correct?"

"Yeah, so? I ain't doin' nothing illegal."

"Well, now, that depends," Hadrien said. "If you were pimping bimbs, you can't say you weren't doing anything illegal."

Morely tried to remain calm in the face of these questions, but he started to sweat like Aunt Martha's old mule. "I never did no pimping. No, siree, gov. I wouldn't stoop so low." He stopped chattering his defense long enough to pick up a smudgy beer glass and pour off a stout from the tap. He pushed it toward Hadrien, but my partner pushed it back. "No, thanks, not while I'm on duty. Now, why don't you stop stalling and tell us what kind of business you had going with Koor."

"I'm a mender of broken hearts," he said, after sipping from the beer. "And as far as I know, it ain't illegal to be a mender."

Hadrien narrowed his expression, letting it roll lazily into a scowl. Abruptly, he reached forward, grabbed Morely by the shirt, and yanked him onto the bar. The beer flew out of the man's hand and splattered the end of the counter. Hadrien spoke with him nose-to-nose. "You better tell me something, or I'm going to haul your ass in and whip you up where there's room to lay on the bruises."

Morely hissed at him, drawing back his lips to show off his horse-sized teeth. "You won't get ten meters before someone plugs you in the head with a pin laser bolt."

At his warning, I glanced around, noticing for the first time how two Sumereks were edging their bulks toward the brouhaha. "You better hurry, Artie."

My words made Hadrien flip his attention around. Seeing the advancing trouble, he grunted and pulled Morely clear across the bar. The man barked as Hadrien laid him noisily to the floor. "Stop him!"

I'm a tenth-degree chi expert, and having practiced this form of martial arts all my life, I responded automatically.

The Sumereks charged. I stepped forward. Planting myself firmly before Hadrien and the struggling barkeep, I held both arms out, palms raised toward the oncoming aliens. They came at me, and like a painter slinging paint at a canvas, I grabbed one of the furry beasts by the arm. I used leverage to toss the whacker onto his back while I tripped his comrade. They climbed to their knees, lumbering and slow, which gave me more than enough time to pummel them again. I kicked at groins and then at faces. Before I could finish this highland dance, one of the peckers banged me straight in the kisser. It made me back up. Turning, I grabbed for lumber and smashed him over the head with a chair.

Hadrien must have gotten the better of Morely, because he came to my rescue by pulling his pistol and firing over the Sumerek pestering me. The alien bellowed and charged out of the door. I stood where I was, brandishing a chair leg. What customers remained slid into the darkened shadows, content to sip tiddlywinks and cause no undue trouble.

Hadrien replaced his gun to his shoulder holster, fastened the chain, and then punched Morely to add a little emphasis to his statement. "Now, was all that necessary?" he snarled.

"I ain't done nothin' wrong," Morely barked. He spat blood into my partner's face, and I could tell from where I stood that Hadrien a good mix of Mars and Aries in his chart. He growled and smacked the man again.

Hadrien flung Morely into a chair and then glanced at me. "Are you okay?"

I nodded and dropped the chair leg. It clattered loudly, and it was then that I realized the place was deadly quiet. Instead of joining Hadrien, I went behind the counter and turned on the tavern's sound system. The music was electro-Celtic, and there was enough of it to drown out our conversation with Morely.

Hadrien wiped at the blood on his face and cursed. "This is the second time today I've had someone else's juices up my nose. Do you know what kind of mood that puts me in?"

Morely dabbed at his lips with the back of his shirt. "You just can't come in here and harass me like this."

"Yes, I can," Hadrien said. "I have temporary jurisdiction." He pulled a chair up to the dodger and didn't give him time to think more on the subject. "Now that we have your undivided attention, I suggest you start talking. What is the mender of a broken heart?"

I dragged up a seat and dropped into it while Morely stalled. Finally, coughing up a bit more blood, he hacked an answer. "It's just what it is."

"What? Some kind of mail-order marriage deal?"

"Mail-order marriage?" Morely managed a caustic laugh. "You're some kind of twitter, aren't you? Don't know nothin' about the Waki'el, do you?"

"Not many people do," I said. "Answer his question."

"I mend broken hearts—literally. The Waki'el got those exposed pumpers, you know."

"So?"

"So, they go bad a whole lot more often than a human heart."

What he was saying practically brained Hadrien. His mouth fell open. "You're dealing human organs?"

"Naw. That's illegal. I'm dealing biohazardous waste material."

"Do you mean you're getting the buffy left over from the surgeons' knives at the local hospital?" I asked.

He nodded. "That's right. Bits and pieces; aortas and ruby-red flesh. Even cardiac plaque. The Waki'el use the stems and pieces like grafting material so that the original pumper can repair itself. Don't ask me how they do it, because I ain't got the bummiest about that."

Hadrien cut a look my way and then used the same squint to scan Morely. "How do you get these goods?"

"The prince got them. I didn't." Morely paused to look sorrowful. "Now that old Lundy is dead, guess me business is, too. I was saving me shekels for a chance to move out of the rottin' neighborhood. In case you haven't noticed, it ain't the best part of London."

"Did K'ton Koor deliver these parts to you?"

"Aye, that he did."

"How often?"

"Good and often. A couple times a month."

"And what did Lundy get in return?"

"I got no idea. That deal was struck betwixt him and the Waki'el. I was a middleman."

"Why you? Why didn't Koor deal directly with the Waki'el?"

"Don't know. Didn't need to know. I got paid regular to take the parts from Koor and hand them to the messenger what come from Arif."

"Arif?" I said. "That's the Waki'el home world. Did you meet with one of these aliens?"

"Sure. They were different every time. Always female though. God-awful strange bimbs, them."

"Why is that?"

"They just ain't sociable. They sure don't rabbit like human women."

Hadrien glanced at me for the translation.

"They're not big talkers," I said.

He nodded and picked up the interview again. "Waki'el aren't known for their interest in traveling to other worlds, and they don't maintain their own stellar ships. How do they get here?"

"Aboard Corrie vessels. How else?"

"Who was the last one?"

He shook his head. "I don't know her name. They never tell me. I just get paid, and I don't ask."

"When did the last courier arrive?"

"On the sixteen of the month."

"Did she come here?"

"Yes."

"Did you give her the biowaste immediately?"

"No, I couldn't. I was waiting on Koor. He said he would have a special aorta to pack into the cooler. It was a piece that the Waki'el asked for."

"How long did the courier have to wait?"

Morely rubbed his forehead. "She had a two-day layover. You don't actually think she killed the prince, do you?"

Hadrien ignored his question. "Did Koor ever come by with the heart parts?"

Morely hesitated, and it was enough for Hadrien to grab his collar and slap him.

The barkeep groaned before cowering over the possibility of a repeat. "All right, I'll tell you!" He blubbered and bubbled for a minute while looking for his composure. Finally, he stopped squeezing the cat in the bag. "Yeah, Koor came in."

"When?"

"That first evening."

"Did you find anything odd about him?"

"I always found stuff odd about him. Them goddamned peepers are enough to make me own eyes water."

"Was the female here when he delivered?"

"Aye."

"Did they speak?"

"Aye. I don't know what they said. They were talking some bastard Corrie dialect."

"Did the female leave with him?"

"No. He dropped off the stuff and left. She ate some food before getting off with herself."

"Who is the Waki'el contact?" I asked.

"I don't know for certain."

"But you do have a name."

Hadrien leaned forward in the chair and Morely panicked. "Don't bonk me again, gov. I'll tell you. His name is Dumaka Lant. He's the high priest of the Sen'Tal."

5

Hadrien called for backup assistance and ar-
rested Morely on suspicion of conspiracy to kill Prince
Lundy. The poor rotter wouldn't last long at Terrapol
Headquarters before the imperial manager would have
him taken to the emperor for further interrogation. Like
Fellers and Enderson, he'd probably not be heard from
again.

We walked outside, lingering while the police inter-
viewed the remaining patrons before hauling old Mick
to the nick. The poor sod looked at me with an expression of appeal, but there wasn't anything I could do. I
didn't even care to try.

Once the clap wagon went roaring down the street,
we strolled up the alley to Hadrien's car, and there we
were met by a Corrie. The alien chummed with the shadows, never really showing his face to us. Hadrien must
have decided he wasn't up for another ta-do, and so we
both stayed to the far side of his auto while we had a
conversation with this stranger.

"I know what you were talking about in there," he
said, his voice edged with a growl.

"Now, how could you have known that?" Hadrien said lightly.

"Don't play games. I can read lips. I saw what you were talking about."

"So?"

"So, I might be able to help you."

"For a price."

"Of course, for a price. What do you take me for?"

Hadrien leaned on the top of his car, but from where I stood, I could see he'd draped his arms so that his hand was poised on the grip of his gun. "What do you want, and why should I believe your information to be worth paying for?"

The Corrie swayed in the shadows, and I saw his long hands. He wore a sparkling gold ring on his pinky finger. "After Lundy came up dead, Koor came into that stinking rub-a-dub and was trying to sell off some of the prince's personal items. Said he needed to make up some quick cash to get off the planet."

"Like the trinket you're wearing on your hand," I said.

He moved back into the darkness. "That's not the point. Now, are we going to negotiate or not?"

"What do you want?" Hadrien asked.

"A double pony."

Again my partner looked at me with a questioning expression. "What the hell is he talking about?" he whispered.

"He wants fifty pounds," I answered softly. Then, before Hadrien could wag at him about how ridiculous his request was, I quickly accepted by reaching into my pocket and pulling out a couple of notes. I leaned on the car with Hadrien and flashed the money. "If I don't think your talk is any good, one of these bills goes away."

I could almost see him licking his lips as he tried to decide. He finally relented. "Okay. I expect I'll get them both anyway. Pass one this way."

I stretched over the car top and met him halfway. He quickly retreated back into the safety of the darkness. It took him a minute to get started, waiting as he did on a vehicle to pass on the nearby street. "I can tell you what the Waki'el were paying Lundy with."

"What?" Hadrien said.

"Honey."

"Honey, as in Waki'el spit?"

"That's right. This stuff was almost pure. Must have been pumped out of the females by syringe or something."

"So you're saying that Lundy was a honey addict," I said. Glancing at Hadrien, I added, "Is that even illegal?"

Before he could answer, the Corrie spoke. "Lundy was getting a tremendous load of honey for each exchange of heart parts. He wasn't using it all himself. He was creating demand."

Hadrien squinted. "He was addicting people to honey."

"Yes, yes." The Corrie smacked his lips and it was a loud sound in the quiet alley.

"How do you know this?"

"Because I was one who Koor trusted to deliver the word and goods on the street. By the time someone took Lundy out, he had half of London barked. A lot of them were his own kith and kin."

"Members of the imperial family?" I asked.

"That's right. Word was that he'd even approached his sister about her abilities to create honey."

"Belinda-Agnes?" I asked.

"That's right. The crossbreed. Lundy used her. The stuff she coughed up was called amber. It was gold in color—beautiful stuff. Not only could it addict you after the first time, but it would literally make a man a slave. Koor hated her because of it."

"Why?"

"Because he was an amber addict from the bottom of his big toes to the tops of his ugly eyeballs. He would do anything to get it. Including calling a kill down on Lundy."

6

*We returned to the headquarters and immedi-*ately found Dr. Jolie Purdue in her forensics lab dutifully attentive to her computer and her medical analyzer. When we entered her inner sanctum, she glanced up with an irritated expression on her freckled features. It was all spitballs after that.

"I'm busy; go away," she ordered.

"Hey, you called me," Hadrien said. "We're here about the chemical analysis for the Lundy case." He paused to perch himself upon a stool and then crossed his arms as he waited silently for her next volley.

Purdue aimed her evaluation toward me. "Who are you?"

"She's my partner, Philipa Cyprion," Hadrien interrupted. "She's cleared for this information."

"Well, jolly, lolly, lolly," she answered. Purdue brushed at her plum-colored tresses and then keyed in a command to her computer.

What was it with people, anymore? Was having some scientific idea about the reality of life after death a license to be a shithead during physical incarnation? Eric had started to become the same way toward the end. Knowing that life was a cyclical package comprised of many returns to the physical dimension pecked off a lot of folks who preferred not to take a seat on the carousel again. I, for one, could wait my turn in the next go-round, but it didn't turn me into a bloody horse whipper.

Rather than call the tech on her rudeness, I decided to take a stroll about the lab while she fiddled with her machine and our time.

It was a junk-strewn place. Old boxes of dinnertime take-away decorated the specimens counter, recessed lighting affixed over the examining area were missing their concealing panels, and soiled gloves had been carelessly tossed into an open waste bin. Inside, I saw the shiny edges of several syringes, bloody gauze, and a cracked beaker. Leaning toward this mess, I smelled the heavy odor of urine. It was enough to plow my insides with a furrow of biliousness, making me realize that I'd not eaten since having landed on this planet. I backed away, and my stomach suddenly grumbled about cruelty and inattention, so I sat down in a chair beside Hadrien to impatiently await the verdict on Prince Lundy.

It came about two minutes later. Purdue stood, stretched, and then patted the pockets of her white lab coat, finally fetching a piece of paper from her pocket. She checked it prior to speaking. "Your wonderful Prince Lundy was a real, stinking knacker, he was. If you ask me, he deserved to be diddled to the last."

"Why?" I asked.

"Well, for starters, he had a number of social diseases." She named them by counting them off on her fingers. "Cibulana virus; herpes simplex oh-three; gonorrhea, and crabs."

"So he was a walking factory of ooze and redness," Hadrien said. "Given his lifestyle, I'm not surprised. What else?"

"If you'll let me finish," she snapped, "I'll tell you."

She checked her paper again. "Whoever killed Lundy knew he was also infected with amilleas fumagante."

"What's that?" I said.

"It's a very old fungi genus that has been found throughout this arm of our galaxy. It's a bacteria that survives in a dormant state for thousands of years, and this ability has enabled it to spread throughout space. Scientists are about one hundred percent certain that amilleas fumagante originally came here via ancient meteorites. A subgenus of this spore here on earth is known as aspergillis fumagante. It was released when ancient tombs were opened for excavation, and several hundred people have died from it."

"How does amilleas infect a person?"

"The spores are transmitted through the air. The host breathes the junk into his lungs, where it hatches and feeds on the soft-organ tissue until it completely consumes its food source."

"How could he catch such a disease?" I asked.

"How, indeed? That's a question you'll have to answer. Lundy may have gotten it from his female friend."

"You're referring to the Waki'el who was present at the murder scene?"

She smiled sweetly, and it made me shiver. "Not necessarily that friend. Lundy has had the infestation a long time."

"How bad was it?" Hadrien asked.

"When we did the autopsy, we discovered that he had already suffered severe damage in his lower left lung."

"Were there any indications that he was taking drugs to relieve his discomfort?"

"Yes. Phenyldolomide."

"Which is?"

"A prescription analgesic, but according to my inquiries, no one on the imperial medical staff had prescribed the medication. No one will admit to it, anyway."

Purdue stepped away to a dripping water tap to fill up a soiled foam cup. She slugged it like a tavern lass used to accepting favors from drunks willing to buy her a drink. Finished, she burped daintily. "I don't think he was visiting a medic about any of his problems."

"Why?" Hadrien demanded.

"Why? Use that lump on your shoulders there to figure it out."

"He had too many problems that could have been solved through medical intervention," I said.

"That's right," she answered. Purdue poured off some more water before hitting us with the cricket bat. "The compound that had been swabbed on his chest contained a substance that appears to be a version of the aspergillis fumagante. It has an unusual structure though."

"How so?" I asked.

"Each molecule of this fungus has a magnesium atom at the center of the cell. When a photon strikes this atom, it releases a high-energy electron. I believe the fungus charges in sunlight and then stores energy within the atomic structure once it's ingested. This keeps the fungus active so that it can feed on the host."

"What about the yellow juice?" Hadrien said.

"That is a stabilizer used on heart patients. It will keep the heart beating during a cardiac arrest. That stuff has saved a lot of people."

Hadrien winced. "So what you're saying is that Lundy lived a while after the stone was placed in his heart."

She nodded, and a hint of cruelty played about her thin lips. "I'm saying more than that. Lundy was alive and awake. Someone wanted him to suffer, Lieutenant. They were efficient in their manner of his execution."

"What about the stone?" Hadrien asked.

The tech shrugged. "What can I say? Its placement caused an aneurysm in Lundy's chest. I can't get a look at the inside of it, if that's what you want to know. I can tell you that it's encased in ceramic with some sort of magnetized central core. It doesn't open, and reflects any attempts at getting a look at with the microscope. I'd say that it's definitely of alien manufacture, and there's no equipment in this pitiful excuse for a lab that will adequately analyze it."

"Did you find evidence of a substance known as honey in his system?" I said casually.

She turned her critical eye upon me like one of my boobs was higher than the other. Purdue wet her lips, tossed the cup into the sink, and then walked back to her stool. "There was evidence of something."

"Meaning?"

"Meaning I don't know what it is." She stopped to plunk Hadrien with a stare. "What is this honey you're talking about?"

"It's a Waki'el substance, so we understand."

"DNA analysis couldn't place it."

"What else did it show?"

"A number of compounds that directly affect the serotonin levels in the brain. There was one other interesting thing about it, too. It also looks like it might affect the temporal areas of the brain, in which case it might cause hallucinations similar to the classic opium dreams experienced by people living in the late nineteenth century."

"Would that substance cause a person to lose control if he didn't get it on a regular basis?" Hadrien asked.

She leered again. "Oh, yeah. The withdrawals might cause you to take your own life just to get away from the pain."

Hadrien trilled a low whistle and touched me with his intense gaze before shaking his head.

Purdue dropped the rest of the bomb. "I'd say that if Lundy was high from this substance, then he probably didn't even need to be chained to the wall like he was. He would have let his murder happen."

7

After our visit with Purdue, Hadrien and I re-
turned to our lodging for the night, where we were met
at the lobby door by two of the emperor's soldiers. We
were then escorted to my room for an audience with
Theo himself.

I stepped into my suite ahead of Hadrien, and seeing
the runty rat of a man, I felt my expression squeeze into
a scowl. In times past, Theo had terrified me, but since
losing Eric to the same kind of violence the emperor
impressed upon the world, I felt no fear at all. I dropped
my bag of take-away chicken on the dresser and turned
to stare at the emperor.

He sat in one of the straight-backed chairs wearing a
pair of black slacks, a black shirt, and black boots. His
hair had long since turned white, and the contrast with
his mourning clothes caught and held my attention. Did
he even know which one of his sons Lundy had been?
The answer probably lay more in political maneuvering
than it did in a cause of love and concern. Theo always
had to look good in front of his adoring public.

Hadrien stumbled into the room and barely held on to

a gasp when he saw who our visitor was. He came to attention and saluted, remaining there in his official capacity as one of the protectors of the realm. Theo ignored him to focus upon me.

"Since your arrival this morning, things have started to happen," he growled. "I knew I could count on you to put this into perspective. Unfortunately, you haven't checked in with Chief Albertstone, and so I do not know everything that has occurred. You were ordered to contact my office when you found out anything. As usual, Philipa, you defy me at every turn."

I gave him one of my best google-eyed stares, and then I let him have it no holds. "I defy you at every turn, governor, because I don't like you."

I do believe that Hadrien gurgled, and for a moment, I thought it was a death rattle. Glancing at him, I checked to see if he'd swallowed his tongue. He watched me, wearing a pleading expression. I flipped back to Theo to snare him in my sights again. "Why don't you do Lieutenant Hadrien a favor and let the old man stand down."

Theo flicked his chin at him. I heard Hadrien drop his arm, but the vibration he threw off was none too relaxed.

I brushed my fingers through my hair, grabbing at stray locks before shaking my head. "I would have a better perspective if you'd put us up in a decent hotel. I'm not accustomed to sharing the floor with Sumereks and Valdinis." I paused and sat on the foot of the bed. "They smell."

Theo frowned but then smiled. "You've not learned any manners, Philipa. None. And I don't believe you when you say you don't like me."

I slid into my astro-routine, sure this geezer was ripe for the curing. "I don't need manners. The stars always speak the truth, and I'm always talking about the stars. What do you want, Theo?"

Hadrien whined at my familiarity. I ignored him, not taking my eyes off of the emperor.

"It's been a long time since I've had a life reading, Philipa," Theo said. "Since you left court to pursue your investigative duties, I've not trusted any of my advisers to competently interpret the interplanetudes for me." He leaned forward to peg me with a blue-eyed squint. "I want you to do this for me. Now."

"I don't do interpretations for free," I said.

"You are too goddamned insolent for your own good!" he roared. "I own this world. You are a legal citizen of this world. Therefore, I own you."

"I don't give a Friar Tuck what you think you own. I'm not like Eric. You can't intimidate me. It has no effect, because the thought of death has no effect on me. Now, I told you that I would work for you to help you clear up the matter of Lundy's murder. I didn't say I would spread meself thin by giving every rotter I come up against a free reading of the future."

By this time, Hadrien cleared his throat loudly, and it made me dash him a look. "You have something to say?"

"With the emperor's permission?" he croaked.

Theo nodded curtly.

"We don't have that much information yet. There's nothing for us to go on at the moment."

The emperor studied him and then turned his gaze back on me. "I do own you, too," he said quietly. Sighing, he let it signal his defeat. "Grief has undone you, Philipa. Eric's death has made you rash and rebellious."

"We learn as we go."

"All right," he said, tagging on another sigh. "What do you want?"

"Twenty thousand gold-standard credits deposited into me savings account on Atrion."

Theo waved a hand toward one of his soldiers. "Inform my secretary of this transaction." He turned back to me. "You'll have your money in about an hour. I expect to have a very good reading."

"Have a seat at the table, please." I rose and headed for my valise as Theo motioned for my new partner to join us.

I smiled to myself. Hadrien made no remarks about the way the emperor had called him *left-tenant*.

"I want to know your thoughts on my son's murder, sir," Theo ordered.

Hadrien jumped at the command and immediately slid into a chair at the table while the emperor fiddled with the cheap lamp hanging above it. When he finally coaxed out more light, I took my place between them with my calculator and my cards.

Many people find it odd to use cards when working with the calculations of specific science as mandated by the interplanetudes. There was a time when I put my whole shim in this sham, and by that I mean I literally believed the prophecy I called out. I actually thought I was blessed with a sixth sense that was there to help mankind, but after missing so much of the obvious, I realized that I probably needed more help reading the future than most people.

My talents of interpretation are firmly fitted into my intuitive thinking, and they have always been so. To help me understand what I am seeing in a particular logos, I invented a series of fifty cards, each representing a portion of the zodiac and manifested emotions associated with it. The supposed accuracy of this system allows me to be belligerent to emperors and still command a high price for my services. I do not deny, however, that the accuracy just might come from blatant generalizations.

"Do you think that my son knew his killer?" Theo asked Hadrien.

"It's hard to be certain at this time, sir. But I don't think they were acquainted."

"Then, do you believe it was just an aggravated assault that went too far?"

Hadrien winced. "No, sir. With the stone in his heart, we've concluded without a doubt that he was assassinated with a purpose in mind. He wasn't robbed, and aside from the obvious struggle to escape a pair of handcuffs, his body didn't show any signs that he had been forcibly coerced into that particular situation."

The emperor brushed his hands along his cheeks but kept his attention to the tabletop. As I set up my calculator, I threw him the all-important question of this session. "What's really bothering you, Theo?"

He raised his head and flashed me a look as hard as leftover plum pudding. "That's what I want you to tell me."

I nodded and set about to oblige him in his desire, explaining as I went, more for Hadrien than for Theo. "These cards represent harmonic aspects, such things as impassioned life, happiness, fear of failure, success. Theo has drawn from these cards before to establish a baseline for further readings. Each card represents a planet or the Sun and Moon as it appears in a certain house of his birth logo."

"So, each card determines the emotional value of the planet," Hadrien said.

"Very good, Lieutenant." I paused to shuffle the stack. "And knowing that should give us a good idea of the concerns and objectives present in his life at this time."

I imitated a card shark in Old Las Vegas by spreading the cards facedown across the table and giving Theo a hard-boiled look of my own. "Pick five, please." He pointed to cards quickly while I pulled them from the stack. Before turning them over, I took a minute to consult his logos on my computer.

Theo had his whole life locked up in his twelfth house of Capricorn. His Sun, Moon, Mercury, Venus, Chiron, and Northern Node were trapped within this constellation, giving him a deep-seated indecisiveness about matters of substance: riches, property, and possessions. Yet the twelfth house meant much more because it contained a person's sacrifices and secrets. In the science of the interplanetudes, Theo had chosen a difficult transition into life, one of court espionage and intrigue and one of being able to see both sides of the same button. This discord was the reason that so many political prisoners found themselves dangling from a skinny rope. Theo relied upon a standard punishment to a predetermined set of parameters. He veered neither right nor left for fear the scales would bang together and he would be flattened like a slave trying to wedge that last stone atop the Great Pyramid.

I glanced at Hadrien. He sat back, his face hidden in the shadows created by the yellow bulb. Smart bloke, he was. Showing emotion of any kind might make Theo angry, and we really didn't have time to deal with an imperial sussing.

"Well?" Theo asked.

I turned the cards over as he had chosen them, stringing them into a sentence as I did. "Anger and sorrow unite to defeat objective."

Theo blew his hot breath on me. "I suppose I should have expected that."

"Anger is controlled by the planet Mars. The objective card is the face of Saturn. Both of these planets were in Scorpio when you were born. Saturn represents boundaries, caution, discipline, limits of vision." I stopped to tap the card for emphasis. "It also contains the elements of loss."

"My children?" he husked.

"That and more. Mars causes things to happen. It is the impetus for action. Saturn is conjunct, meaning that this anger feeds your vision, bringing more and more frustration because Saturn squeezes the exertion. There's literally no place for the steam to go." I sat back and studied him a moment. "Feel like you might explode, do you, Theo?"

He snorted, sitting back himself. "You're right, Philipa. There's no way I can release the pressure."

I nodded. "That's because when you designed this incarnation while cooling jets in another dimension, you forgot to fashion a steam valve to eject the tension. There are no planetary complements on this configuration. It's as though you chose a life hindered by political hardship."

"Yes, you've told me this before. What do the cards mean?"

"Theo, you know I would never lie to you."

He froze at my statement. I could read the terror in his eyes, and it made me sing with happiness deep down inside. "I know this," he murmured.

"What I'm about to tell you is not going to please you."

He leaned forward into the gentle glow from the lamp. "You don't have to worry about repercussions. You know that. Tell me, now."

"When you were born, Neptune was in Libra, the house that represents balance and justice. The defeat card contains Neptunian elements."

"What are you saying?"

"I'm saying that your anger and your sorrow are going to cause you to lose your throne if you don't do something to change it. My advice would be to change it soon."

Hadrien gasped, catching it too late. Theo glanced in his direction and snarled a command. "No word leaves this room. If it does, I'll personally cut out your tongue."

I have to hand it to the wanker from the tropics—he held his own. Following his hard intake of air, Hadrien pulled on a bland expression that didn't betray his fear. "Yes, sir. Nothing leaves this room."

Theo swiveled to eyeball his guards. They stood at

strict attention, gazing into the middle distance. He shook his head and flapped a hand in their direction. "Brainless. I don't have to worry about them." Turning back to me, he touched the table with his knuckle. "Continue."

"You see conspiracies all around you, don't you?"

"Yes. From every quarter."

"Is there one involving Lundy and his unfortunate siblings?"

"You tell me."

"You suspect it. Why are you hiding information from us?"

This statement forced a frown from Theo, and he grunted. "What makes you think that?"

"Uranus is in Cancer, your sixth house. This planet is associated with your cruelty to your children. We've talked of this before."

Theo stood, ran a sweaty palm down the front of his pants. He walked a tight circle not far from the chair and then, suddenly, he stopped to motion to his guards to leave. After we were alone in the room, he confronted us with the news. "Another child has died. Belinda-Agnes, my fortieth daughter. She was very special to me. I loved her mother a great deal."

"I'm sorry for your loss, but you must tell us, Theo. How did she die?"

He shook his head while leveling his gaze at the floor. "She was found in her apartments in the imperial compound. Her heart was ripped from her chest."

"What?" Hadrien said, forgetting his manners at addressing the emperor. "When did this happen?"

"Apparently this evening. Investigators are still at the crime scene."

"We should be there," Hadrien said.

"As soon as we're done here," Theo answered.

"Had she been alone?" Hadrien asked.

"No. Apparently, she'd had a male caller."

"Let me guess," I said. "There's no gate confirmation."

"No."

"Well, that is interesting. If there is indeed a conspiracy, then one thing becomes evidently clear."

"What's that?" Hadrien asked.

"Whoever is killing the siblings has no regard for species," I said.

"Belinda-Agnes looked much more Waki'el than she did human," Theo murmured. "She had the breast ridges that make her species so well-known, and she had an external heart."

"And she didn't feel as though she fit in anywhere," I added.

"No, she never did. But my daughter wasn't promiscuous, so the assumed circumstances of her death are questionable."

"Leading you to a conspiracy theory?" Hadrien asked.

"Yes, Lieutenant."

"Have you rounded up your daughter's staff?" I asked.

"Yes, but no one saw or heard anything."

"We need to talk to them, sir," Hadrien said.

Theo nodded. "Imperial police are holding Belinda's handmaiden in custody at the compound." He paused to rub his chin thoughtfully. "Answer me one more thing, Philipa. "Will I survive this latest incursion against my house?"

"Do you mean will you keep your throne?"

"Yes, exactly," he said.

I pretended to really care as I studied the logos and the cards. The truth was, I had no frigging idea. If the answer was right there before me, I couldn't see—or maybe I didn't want to. I let the little peckerhead swim in his own juices for a few minutes.

"Well?" he demanded. "What does it say?"

I took a deep breath for emphasis, and then I lied. "Everything looks like it will work out fine. You'll keep your throne."

8

We arrived soon after at the Imperial Compound,
an impressive, domed structure that sat on the old site
of Buckingham Palace. This bubble complex surrounded
several smaller domed buildings and, sitting at the gate
waiting for a pass, I noticed that the bombproof skin
shone in the orange glow of floating streetlamps. Though
we were invited by Theo, it still took forty-five minutes
to clear us, and when we finally gained access, I gained
entry to Hadrien's thoughts.

"I was born April 1, 2264," he said. "Seven o'clock
in the A.M. in the province of Miami, on the peninsula
of Florida-Cubano."

I smiled but didn't glance at him. Instead, I focused
my attention upon the plethora of guards inside the compound. Each held a military assault laser and all wore
riot gear. There seemed to be no civilians, no bright-red
staff uniforms to spoil this crowd of black jumpsuits.
"Why do you tell me your birthday now?"

"Because you impress the hell out of me," he said.

That did it. His statement forced me to study him to
see if I could find the beginnings of a con starting on

his part. His expression was unusually tense, and I found that I didn't know him well enough to read him. "You're impressed because of me relationship with the emperor?"

He shrugged slightly, turning the steering wheel in the direction of a signaling sentry. "I guess I'm more impressed by your power. I didn't think an astrologer could wipe my nose in it. You opened my eyes by your deductive reasoning and no-nonsense, gumshoe honesty."

"Gumshoe honesty? You've got to be rudders, old man."

"What do you mean?"

"If you're talking about the flapdoodle I just handed Theo, then you're way off your mark. I don't believe what I'm saying half the time. I can swing through generalizations as well as any other supposed psychic."

"Then you can't read the future in those cards?"

I hesitated by taking in the view of the cracked dashboard. When I didn't answer, he called my name gently. "What's wrong?"

"Nothing. I guess Theo was more right about me than I was about him."

"How so?"

"I'm supposed to be this great astrologer with all this deductive reasoning, and I never even saw me poor husband's murder coming. Now, I ask you: How good at this forecasting could I be?"

"Once in a while, things are hidden from us."

"I thought you didn't take in all this metaphysical bunk."

"I just think that the obvious can be right before our eyes and yet, because we're not supposed to know, the answer never manifests itself." He smiled at me, and I was suddenly pleased he aimed it in my direction. "And yes, I think Theo might have been right about you. Grief has made you rebellious. It sounds like you're fighting to find your balance again."

"What? Are you some sort of trick cyclist or something?"

"Excuse me? Trick cyclist? What's that?"

"You know, a shrink, a canner, a psychiatrist."

He laughed. "No. I'm sure if all is said and done, I might be a client someday."

If he waited for me to answer, he didn't remark on it. He dropped the subject as we angled into a parking space in front of the building where Belinda-Agnes kept her apartment.

I pushed my way through the clutter of trash on the car's floorboard and climbed out, leading the way into the dome's lobby area. It was a palatial entry, draped in antique Victorian fabrics and weighted with heavy, dark furniture. The white marble terrazzo floor was so polished that it looked wet, and I took my time about putting my moccasins on it.

Hadrien pushed in behind me and grunted, murmuring loud enough for me to hear. "A goddamned Sumerek."

I glanced at the alien at the entry counter. It was a female, her long sand-colored fur looking faded in the halogen glow of the wall sconces. Her mouth was large, and she had a considerable number of crooked fangs. She nervously pulled a fallen lock of hair from her almond-shaped eyes before nervously patting at one of her drooping breasts.

We approached the desk slowly. Halfway there, I gathered a whiff of the creature's body odor. Having not gotten to eat my take-away chicken, I paused a moment to fight an onslaught of biliousness.

"What is it, Philipa?" Hadrien asked, stopping to touch my shoulder.

"Sorry, mate. Feeling a tad bit queer. I'll be all right. The emperor interrupted me evening meal."

He nodded, but rather than waiting on me, he stepped forward to introduce us and to begin interviewing the Sumerek. "What's your name?"

"Xeac Took," she growled. "I was not on duty when Princess Belinda-Agnes was murdered. I can tell you nothing."

"Did you talk with the princess?" Hadrien asked, ignoring the alien's profession of ignorance.

"Well, yes. I am the major domo three days a week. I take care of all problems and correct all inconveniences in this particular dome."

"So it's your job to keep the princess comfortable. Did she have many male guests?"

"She had very few. She was very strict on that account. She did not like human males. I cannot say that I disagreed with her." Xeac Took studied Hadrien before taking a step away from him. She slid onto a stool sitting next to the wall. "I have told the other investigators. I know nothing about this. You should interview my assistant."

"Apparently, your assistant can't be found. That doesn't look good on your staff or your association with your staff."

"I did nothing," she said flatly.

Hadrien leaned on the counter and tried to paste on a pleasant face.

"What about female visitors?" I called out.

Xeac Took stared at me. "She had quite a lot of those."

I stepped forward. "Did they sign a register before proceeding to the princess's apartment?"

She reached under the counter and produced a small data chip. Shaped like a large button, it looked strange in her hairy hands. "This is everyone who came by in the last twenty days, but I was required to dump all information to the police security computer. There is no backup of this file, so I cannot tell you who came and who went." She stopped to lick me with her look. "Nevertheless, you will not find intruders during my duty hours."

"Did she get any Waki'el visitors?"

"Only her mother, Mann Re. She came twice while I was on duty."

"Do you know why?"

Xeac Took snarled before answering. "That is not my business."

"Did Mann Re bring anyone with her?"

"Her daughter Ne'el Zara accompanied her one time."

"Did Prince Lundy come through here?"

"The prince came frequently," she said. "They were quite sociable. The princess held genuine affection for him."

"Did he sign in?"

"He is not required to do so."

"Who else is not required to do so?"

"All members of the royal family have this privilege." She glanced around nervously, rubbing the large, dark knuckles of her fingers.

"What's wrong?" Hadrien asked.

She frowned and stepped back. When she did, I was overwhelmed by a sour cabbage smell that made me dizzy. I stumbled for a chair and sat down heavily, taking a hard breath to keep my stomach acid from rising up my esophagus. Hadrien seemed not to notice the smell or my difficulty.

"What's wrong?" he growled at the Sumerek.

Xeac Took took a large inhale herself before leaning toward him and speaking in a conspiratorial tone. "It was an incident that occurred in the lobby about three standard weeks ago."

"Go on," Hadrien pushed. "What happened?"

"Mann Re was accompanied here by Prince Lundy. As they arrived, the executioner was leaving."

In Theo's world, the executioner was one of the highest officials of the imperial state. He served as a chief warden over all criminal activity, whether real or supposed. In the emperor's cracked-up logic, he made the executioner one of his prime diplomats, stressing whenever questions arose that Cornelius Paul wielded his title like a sword. He garnered the attention and respect of alien societies that had their own means of dealing out swift judgment.

"Did the executioner somehow challenge Lundy?" I asked.

"Yes, he did. He told both Prince Lundy and Mann Re that they were not allowed to approach the princess."

"Was she ill?"

"I do not know. I saw no medical staff enter or leave that week."

"How did Lundy and Mann Re react?" Hadrien said.

"Not kindly. Mann Re demanded to see her daughter. She accused the executioner of disrespect and told him she feared for her daughter's safety."

"What did Lundy do?"

"He attempted to defend Mann Re, but the executioner called his guards to have them removed."

"Did they come back after that?"

"No. The princess had not left her quarters since that time. At least, not while I was on duty."

Hadrien backpedaled a few steps, and I found myself wondering if Xeac Took's ripe odor had driven him away. He didn't mention the offensive smell, and he did take a deep pull of polluted air before going on with his questions. "Did you ever see Lundy and Belinda together?"

"No, sir. He would go to her apartments. She would not come downstairs with him."

"Did Prince Lundy come to visit Belinda shortly before his death?"

The Sumerek twisted her mug into an expression that might have been dismay. "He came to see her each day since the first of the month."

"How long did he stay each time?"

"Only a short while. Perhaps thirty standard minutes."

"Did he look any different when he left?"

"Different? I do not understand."

"Did he look inebriated?"

She shook her head. "He did not stagger or make rude noises as most humans do when they've had too much alcohol. I really cannot say for certain. I am no expert at identifying the behavior."

"Did Cornelius Paul come through here after the big blowout with Mann Re and Lundy?" I asked.

"Yes. He was here only a day or two before the prince was found murdered. I did not speak to him, and I have no idea of why he visited."

"When was the last time you saw Prince Lundy?" Hadrien said.

"The night he walked out with princess's hand-maiden." Xeac Took scratched her ear. "He liked Waki'el females. At least, he seemed to like her."

"How could you tell?"

She leaned forward. "I saw them touch lips on several occasions."

9

We walked upstairs past the police cordon and into the palatial apartments of Theo's fortieth daughter. I had expected a conglomeration of Waki'el artifacts but instead found myself stepping into a warm, inviting home filled with mauve tones, lavender flowers, and contemporary Earth art. As we moved farther into the living room, we spent a moment enjoying a trickling waterfall designed as a quiet jungle pool. The delicate sound filled this understated space, complementing it by giving it that Zen feel. It would have been a wonderful retreat had the circumstances been better.

Hadrien whistled. "Nice joint. I live in an orange crate compared to this. In fact, I'm pretty sure I still have the rotten oranges in the crate."

I smiled, despite the seriousness of the situation. "I don't even have a place."

He stopped walking to turn his stare directly on me. "What do you mean?"

"I mean that I'm used to alien flops that go for two pence a week."

"After that little bilking of the emperor I just saw, I

would have assumed you had a nice seashore chalet somewhere."

"A seashore chalet? Well, I suppose that covers the field from mountains to beach. No, I don't have a house. I did, but I sold it after Eric died."

"Oh," he said, nodding. "Too many reminders, huh?"

"Not really. Eric was rarely home long enough for his vibration to settle into the carpet, if you know what I mean. Unlike this place." I stopped my explanation to wave a hand around the room. "I never met Belinda-Agnes, but this apartment seems to speak of her presence. It's odd."

He frowned. "Have you been on many crime scenes?"

"No."

"Well, then, that feeling you're homing in on is not Belinda-Agnes's presence. It's her death." With that, he walked across the room, leaving me trailing behind, wondering just how hard-hearted my new partner could be. I was not long in finding out.

There was a clot of uniformed imperial police standing by the bedroom door. One of these men broke away to introduce himself.

"Captain Jon Farnham," he said, extending his hand. "We've been expecting you."

Hadrien introduced me and then quickly jumped into the questions. "Any damning evidence so far?"

"Very little, governor," Farnham answered. "This way."

He led us down a short corridor to a back bedroom dressed elegantly in beige silks and crowded with cops as well as forensic techs. There, lying on a big, round bed was the bloody remains of the princess. Her heart had, indeed, been ripped from her body and lay in its own juices beside her. Blood spread dark across the taupe-colored comforter. The princess's head was propped on a pillow, and her hands were crossed at her throat. Her skin had lost the classic sparkling blue of the

Waki'el species, having turned a deep plum shade. If I'd thought the Sumerek smelled bad, I was in for a treat with the corpse. Her stench reminded me of kidney pie gone rotters. Hadrien, as though he knew what to expect, dug through his pocket to pull out a clean, pressed nose hanky. He handed it to me while he focused his attention on the crime scene.

"Fill us in on the parameters," he ordered.

Farnham nodded, running his hand through the greasy strands of his thinning black hair. "The body was discovered by the princess's handmaiden at approximately four P.M. standard time today. According to the front desk, she had no visitors, and the handmaiden was not in the quarters all afternoon. Her heart appears to have been forcibly torn from her chest. Examination of the sternum ridges reveal several of them have been cracked, indicating that a thoracic separation tool was used."

"Was the body disturbed?" Hadrien asked.

"No. The handmaiden claims to have found her in this position. She swears she didn't touch her."

"It would appear that she didn't struggle."

"Yes," Farnham said. "I don't see how, though."

"Fingerprints?"

"Nada. We scraped the carpet but came up with a zero on footprints, mud, and telltale fragments. Whoever did it knew what they were doing."

Hadrien nodded, threw me a quick look, and then wove his way through the clot of techs working around the bed. Tapping one of the boys on the shoulder, he asked him for a latex glove. After he slipped it on, Hadrien began to probe the body up about the poor woman's bread loaf.

"What do you expect to find on her head?" I asked from behind my hanky shield.

He didn't answer immediately. Instead, he gently moved her fingers out of the way so he could scan her neck. Another minute clicked by before Farnham got in on the act.

"What are you looking for, Lieutenant?" he asked.

"Well, to be specific, needle tracks," Hadrien said.

"In her neck, gov? Why there?"

Hadrien shook his head but didn't give up any more information. It was Farnham who did.

"If you find some, I don't know that we can link that to the murder."

"Why?" I asked.

"She was undergoing medical procedures, according to her secretary."

I grunted beneath the rag. Medical procedures actually meant painful experiments. It made perfect sense that if the honey was extracted from glands in the mouth, a suction needle would have been used. Given her "medical procedures," she might have indeed been able to hide the evidence.

Hadrien finished his examination, stripped off the glove, and conveniently changed the subject. "Where's the handmaiden? I'd like to talk to her."

Farnham pointed down another hallway. "In the kitchen."

Hadrien thanked him and, placing his hand on my shoulder, he steered me through the crowd to the corridor.

"Did you see anything in her jowls?" I asked quietly.

"Yeah. Doesn't look like she was trying to hide it. I'd say she'd been poked a number of times. This makes me wonder just how deep into the imperial medical staff Lundy's dirty little secret flows."

The hallway widened into a room made of black marble counters and recessed lighting. There was a restaurant-sized stove that used natural gas, a rationed product that had placed reserves in Theo's pocket. A large butcher block table made from oak took up much of the floor space, and there, sitting at the far end, was the Waki'el female whose name, Nata Atane, loosely translated as *speaker's daughter.*

They are such ugly creatures. They have too many points, too many sharp edges, too many things to bloody a person.

I sat down and studied Atane, wondering why those beings without tear ducts bothered me. She should have been weeping over the loss of a benevolent benefactor instead of sitting calmly in the midst of turmoil and death.

Hadrien ran off the coppers milling about before closing and barring the door. He hadn't quite finished swinging the lock into place when he started talking. "Nata Atane, you have been charged with conspiracy to assassinate Princess Belinda-Agnes."

"I am innocent," she said in a raspy voice. "I could never have done such a thing."

Hadrien spun around to take one of the chairs like he was swinging onto a horse. He frowned, rubbed his dark beard, and spoke in a husky tone. "We know you were having a physical affair with Prince Lundy," he lied.

Atane sat forward and arched her back slightly so her skin picked up the iridescence from the lighting and her sternum ridges looked imposing. "What does it matter? The princess was the one murdered."

"So, you admit to having sex with the prince?"

"Yes."

"Did you introduce him to any other Waki'el females?"

"Yes."

"Why?"

She stared at him defiantly but didn't reply.

"We know about the substance called honey or amber," I said.

She turned her rebellious gaze on me. "Then you know why Lundy had sex with Waki'el. He was a pig. He couldn't get enough of it."

"What did he give you in return for sex?" I asked.

"He gave me nothing but his time, his grunts, and his sweat."

"Then why did you do it?"

"Because Princess Belinda-Agnes ordered me to."

"She ordered you, and you did it?"

"Our alliance was of commandment and obedience. I had no choice but to obey. She was Basira and I'm N'galia. It was not for me to refuse."

"Now why would Belinda want you to accommodate her brother?" Hadrien asked. "Was he paying her?"

"I don't know."

"How did Belinda feel about Lundy?"

"Feel? I don't understand."

"You know—did she like him or despise him or just suffer him?"

"Their relationship was inadequacy versus fruitlessness."

We both stared at her. Hadrien paused to rub his ear. He frowned and then tried on what was, for him, a pleasant expression. "You're going to have to explain that concept. We don't understand why you term it as inadequacy versus fruitlessness."

"We have alliances, associations you would loosely term as friendship. A single concept holds us bound to another individual, except in the case of a blood clause, where there are a variety of concepts that may come into play."

"What do you base these alliances on?"

"Birth. We have many castes on our home world of Arif. Each must pay respect to the other and not invade the boundaries of a social level that does not concern them. The princess was Basira. I am N'galia. I am, forever, her servant."

"Is a Basira Waki'el a species different from N'galia, or are you the same?" I asked.

Atane's iridescence dimmed at the question, and I

found myself squinting. "We are a subspecies of Basira Waki'el. All of my kind are."

"Basira Waki'el are in charge of your world, then," Hadrien said flatly.

She turned to stare at him. "As I said, they are the dominant species on my planet. They rule because they are more aggressive. That's only logical."

"You look exactly alike," he murmured.

"Well, we are not."

Hadrien nodded before launching his final volley. "Do the Waki'el have a concept for what is known as an affair of the heart?"

She hissed, and it was a very mean face, indeed. "That is corruption at its most high."

"What kind of corruption?"

"There is only one kind of corruption. Anything that goes against the views of the Sen'Tal."

Hadrien sighed. "That leaves a lot of maneuvering room."

"Yes, it does."

This frustrating development didn't deter my new partner. He switched gears like an old-fashioned vath car—with a grunt. "How long have you been on Earth and in the employ of the emperor?"

"Since childhood. I was indentured early on. I've never known my home world."

"Why were you indentured?" I asked.

She flipped me a hard look. "To repay the cost of having my father's life being saved by the Acu-Sen'Tal."

"The Acu-Sen'Tal," Hadrien said. "They're a religious sect that broke with the traditional Sen'Tal on Arif."

"That is not correct," Atane stated.

She took a deep breath. When she did, I noticed that her sternum ridges separated ever so slightly, and I was granted a view of her exterior heart. The moment of disclosure sickened me again, and I closed my eyes for a few seconds as I pushed down the nausea.

"Why isn't it correct?" Hadrien demanded.

"Only Basira and Tus may be members of the Sen'Tal. All others are members of the Acu-Sen'Tal."

Hadrien nodded and then somersaulted through the rest of the interview. "When was the last time you were with Prince Lundy?"

"Three weeks ago. Shortly before he was murdered."

"What did you talk about?"

She paused, looking thoughtful. "We talked about his pain."

"Pain?"

"Yes, he was dying, and he knew it. He wanted to end his days with dignity, but it was too late for that."

"What did he want to do?"

"He wanted to give his heart organ to the princess. She had a bad pumper, so I understand. It's not uncommon for the Waki'el. But he was so infected with disease that she could not have used it. He knew it. He just didn't want to believe it."

"Did he go so far to arrange for this transfer of organ material?"

Atane glanced at the table. "I don't know."

I leaned forward and touched her hand, feeling the tendons strain as she braced herself at my intrusion. "Are you certain?"

"I wasn't the prince's confidant."

"Surely he did a little bragging," I said. "I know that he would."

"How would you know that?"

"I was his personal astrologer. It's in the stars, you know."

Atane quickly flicked her attention toward Hadrien and then back to me. "All I can tell you is that he was afraid to die."

"Why?" Hadrien asked. "Everyone around this place

seems to believe in the plausibility of the interplanetudes. Lundy appeared to be the type to be comforted by the science."

"He believed," she said. "But he wasn't comforted."

"Again, I ask—why?" Hadrien said.

Atane took a deep breath and then shook her head sadly. "I guess it doesn't matter. I'm doomed to head for the emperor's dungeons to await my execution."

I wondered if Hadrien thought fleetingly of disputing this. "Then you need to tell us what you can so the killers can be brought to justice," he said.

"What I know. I know from Lundy's bodyguard, a Corrigadaire by the name of Koor. He told me. Koor could read Lundy's photon field, and he said that there were big tears occurring. Each day, there were more photons displaced by some unknown action. At first, Koor thought it had to do with Lundy's health, but the manner in which the displacement occurred startled him. It appeared methodical. Disease doesn't produce such an effect in a person's energy field."

Hadrien stood up, his expression intensely dark. He was openly uncomfortable with the implications of what she said. "Did Koor think that someone was killing Lundy slowly?"

Atane nodded. "But how could that be? Even Koor couldn't understand it."

10

When we returned to Hadrien's car, I slid inside and breathed a huge sigh. Traveling by zero-point gravity gives you space/time lag, a headache, and sometimes, the shakes. I had all three pinned atop an impossibly long day that had reunited me with my planet and my saddest memories.

Hadrien's hard expression softened when he noticed my difficulty. From there, he used his own intuitive abilities to zone in on my problem. "Too much death for one day, huh?"

I fumbled through my pocket for the hanky and passed it back to him. "Thanks for the nose-wipe back there."

"My pleasure," he answered. "Those things can really rush up and hit you in the head, especially when you come out of a zero-point trough. Interstellar travel always makes me feel pretty low for a couple of days." He paused to prime the choke on the engine and start the car. "Let's get back to the hotel and get some sleep. We could both use a few hours away from imperial problems."

We floated through the guard checkpoint and were once more on the lonely streets of a Londontown that seemed strangely alien. From my vantage point, none of the familiar spires seemed to be there: no Big Ben or Westminster Abbey, no signs that this city had been inhabited by humans for centuries. Perhaps it was a racial memory that I missed, because from the time of my birth, none of these things had ever existed except in history books. In 2035, a shifting land mass beneath the Arctic Ridge caused incredible earthquakes across Britain and Europe. Spain was inundated when the sea came crashing in, and Germany developed a number of crumbling sinkholes. Places like Amsterdam disappeared completely, and jolly old England crumbled like me mum's Yorkshire pudding crust. London turned into a seaside resort, and the Thames emptied into the sea miles from where it had originally.

It took years to repair the damage that occurred across the world. And not much of it had gotten done until Theo's bold and bloodthirsty ancestor decided to unite the planet under his singular domination. True, there was not much left of the world after the crack-up, but he took what there was and fixed it like a bad watch.

When zero-point gravity provided a stellar gateway to other systems, the new city of London underwent even more modifications as aliens flocked to the planet. Earth was a blooming paradise compared to most worlds out there, and the Corrigadaires, the Sumereks, and the Ehar-re were slowly refitting the place in their own images. Theo encouraged this influx, giving the aliens squatter's rights where no human could get them. It was one of the things that I hated about Theo. Enough with the open arms; it was time to put the snick on the snack and close the door to the overwhelming immigration.

As though reading my mind, Hadrien asked a question. "You lied to the emperor, didn't you?"

He was good. I had to hand it to him. "Yes. Will you tell him?

"Do you really think I'm such a shnook?"

I laughed. "Shnook? Now I'm confused."

He grinned but didn't answer. Instead, he manually negotiated a turn down a new street.

"Lieutenant," I said slowly, drawing out the word so it sounded like *loo-tenant*.

"That's lef-tenant to you." He chuckled and then sobered quickly. "I wouldn't dream of giving up the secret. Theo is crazy about those electro-crucifixions of his. If he takes a disliking to you, he burns your butt."

"Yes, I know."

It must have been the way I said it, because he double-checked the autopilot status before turning his full attention to me. "I have a feeling you blame Theo for your husband's death."

Was this information in my personal file or something? "How do you know that?"

"I'm a very good cop."

"You don't need to know the circumstances."

"You know I'm a junkie," he said flatly. "Don't deny it. Why shouldn't I know about you?"

I studied him for a moment, realizing that he was far different from Eric. And I needed his refreshing change. "You must be the manifestation of conjunct aspects between me Mars and Chiron."

"Chiron? What's that?"

"It's an asteroid named after the mythical creature, Chiron the Centaur."

"The half-man, half-horse fellow?"

"That's right. Chiron represents our search for truth, no matter where it may lead us. He's also the wounded healer and identifies areas where we must discover our weaknesses and learn to strengthen them. Mars and Chiron conjunct in me first house, making this an active learning game between us."

He leaned in my direction and smiled. "*Me* first house. I catch myself when I hear you say things like that. Those me's make *me* pay attention."

I was abruptly aware of the heat from his body, and it caused me to wiggle in my seat. He didn't notice my anxiety surfacing.

"Do you always hide your true feelings behind the interplanetudes?" he asked.

Why deny it? "As often as possible," I said stiffly.

He leaned back and faced the windshield. "I think I deserve to know why you lied to the emperor. It has something to do with your past associations. If you don't tell me, I could be the one swimming in the moat. I don't think I'd appreciate that. So, do you blame Theo for your husband's death?"

I shook my head but told him anyway. "Eric was a researcher on the emperor's medical staff. His duties were to investigate alien organisms. He probably knew more about the known galactic races than any other human on this world." I paused, gearing myself up to speak about it all. "Eric discovered a genetic permutation that identified similarities between two species separated by thousands of light-years."

"What species?"

"Humanity was one, but I never got to find out the other."

"What does it mean? Why is it so important?"

"It means that humans are related genetically to an alien people on a world far away. Maybe more than one. It gives credence to the possibility that humanity was seeded through the influence of a nomadic species."

Hadrien frowned. "Sounds like a lot of supposes. This worried Theo?"

"According to Eric, he felt that this knowledge out in the open would make humanity vulnerable in many ways. He feared for the safety of our species. I don't know specifically what concerned him, but concerned he was."

"He silenced your husband and his work."

I shrugged. "I believe so. One night, Eric didn't come home. The police found his body a day later lying in the muck of some greasy back alley here in London. He'd been electro-crucified. It was a bad job, too, made to look like some petty thug strung him with wire and tortured him before turning on the juice all the way."

"What makes you think Theo was behind it?"

"Because it's clearly marked in his horoscope. He's capable. There was a glitch that corresponded to a pattern in me own logos, which matched Eric's completely."

"So they were star-crossed?"

"Yes. Their incarnational karma was joined at the hip, so to speak." I ladled in a sigh. "It was me own fault for not having noticed it. Missing something like that puts you in your place, too. I realized right then and there I was not some grand sorceress capable of reading the future. I certainly wasn't capable of changing any of it."

Hadrien tapped the steering wheel. "I wouldn't have believed you this morning, but after seeing you in action, I think you're brutally hard on yourself." He paused and asked what was really on his mind. "Do you think we'll be the ones to bring Theo down?"

Three months ago, I might have said otherwise, but now? There seemed to be a real possibility of collateral damage from this investigation. What was the mood of the people on Earth? I couldn't be sure, because I'd lost touch with everything human after Eric had died. Turning in the seat, I studied Hadrien, hoping I could trust him. "The truth? If there is any way I can be part of bringing Theo down, I will."

11

In the science of the interplanetudes, it can be quite clear when associations have been formed between physical incarnations. In fact, it's as obvious as Cupid tripping over your feet as he stuffs his arrow in your arse. Each party in the relationship knows it, and each denies it.

That night, after Hadrien dropped me off at my hotel room, I compared our charts. Our planets cross the same paths at the same time, bringing us together for victory and defeat. I could tell immediately that we were old incarnational acquaintances destined to travel this lifetime's road together for a very long stretch. Saturn and Venus were conjunct for us, meaning that limitations as well as sorrows would surface in a relationship of love. I wasn't happy with what I saw. Yet sitting there, I kept telling myself that I was feeding on dog chow. Reading the chart didn't give me any secrets that I hadn't already sensed. Therefore, I was wasting my time trying to carve out a confirmation through the stars.

The simple truth was that Hadrien felt the relationship in his groin already. I, on the other hand, wouldn't admit to taking a hard blow for him, even though I piddled on the truth. When I'd been freed from marriage, I'd vowed not to do another stupid thing like taking a hardy sniff of male pheromones. So much for resolve.

The next morning confirmed my suppositions. There was a definite shift in Hadrien's manner, starting with the fact that he'd cleaned the litter from his automobile and had bought me breakfast.

He slipped into the car and proceeded to open the lids on steaming plastic cups of tea. "You looked like a woman who'd taken one to many dives in the well yesterday," he said. "Kind of green around the gills. Thought you might want to nosh on a bagel."

I opened the white bag he offered and peered inside. It wasn't a bagel but a Corrigadaire popover known as a black hole. The bread was so dense, it was jokingly said to scrape in all the light. Pulling it out, I broke it in half and gave him a piece. "This ought to keep us to the next star system." I paused, took a tiny bite before adding, "We are leaving for the Pleiades Star System straightaway, aren't we?"

He snorted. "How did you know that? Your cards?"

"I got a message from the captain of the *Kourey*."

He grinned. "Well, I got another one. We don't leave until this evening. Some holdup in the shipping lane or something. A zero-point accident."

The emperor had made a decision the night before to place us aboard one of his outbound diplomatic corps ships already bound for Arif with a delegation. It was a ride designed to cut Theo's travel expenses, but it also placed us in the middle of the usual intrigue of the imperial court. It made me feel like the old bastard was buggering us from behind.

"Any idea why the delegation is running off to Arif?"

Hadrien started the car and revved the engine. "Presumably to appease Mann Re about her daughter's death. I couldn't get any word out of Albertstone this morning. I don't think he knows. I suppose there are some apologies to be made as well as some questions to be asked."

I took another bite, chewed until my jaw hurt. By the time I had enough spit mixed with the bread, I was too tired to eat anymore. It took me an impossibly long time to swallow the doughy hunk, but pass it onward to my stomach I did by melting the rubbery consistency with hot tea. Once more master of my mouth, I asked, "Where are we going now?"

"To see Clarissa Emory. She's Albertstone's aunt. She's supposed to know a little bit about the Waki'el. Apparently, she did some anthro-work with them years ago."

He didn't say much else as he thoughtfully chewed on his half of the black hole. By the time we arrived at the expert's house, he was wiping away crumbs as I endeavored to feed him the other part of the alien dough ball. He stuffed it into the glove box for later, and off we went to Emory's quaint little flat in New Piccadilly Place.

It was a place of Victorian chintz curtains, hooked rugs, and ecru doilies. Mrs. Emory sat amid crooked antiques collected from that long bygone era, but she wore her hair in a bright red tint that she highlighted with her gaudy yellow pantsuit. So the effect of staid knowledge was instantly erased by flamboyance. The moment she spoke, I had a feeling that Hadrien had been grassed by one of the boys at Terrapol.

"Come in and have a seat, you two," she trilled. She pointed to a lumpy-looking couch before shutting and bolting the flat's front door. Following us deeper into this museum of a living room, she joined us by sitting daintily in a deep-back leather chair. "I understand you wish to know about the Waki'el."

"Yes," Hadrien answered. "We have some specific questions, especially about Waki'el society."

"Oh, their society is a closed community."

"Meaning?"

"Meaning that they keep secrets." She stopped to flick a piece of dark lint from her jacket. "I have studied them for years on an anthropological basis, and I still haven't scratched the surface. Of course, now that there is a little more openness between their planet and ours, we may have a further opportunity to enlighten ourselves."

"Can you tell us how they organize their society?" I asked. "We've had one Waki'el claim to be a subspecies of the Basira Waki'el. She referred to herself as a N'galia."

Emory nodded. "Yes. They are a subspecies. Did you know that there are over three hundred and sixty-five Basiran subspecies?"

"That many?"

"There certainly are." She leaned forward and pegged me with a blue-eyed stare. "They don't teach this in the university, and they really should. Waki'el are expanding through the galaxy. I've noticed the influx in this stellar arm alone. They like our warm sun, you see. Arif is a dying world."

"Their primary is a red dwarf," I said when Hadrien gave me a confused look.

"And it's cold," Emory said. She added a fake shiver for emphasis. "The air is cold, the ground is cold, the people are cold."

"They don't like humans much, do they?" I asked.

"It's hard to say," she answered. "I do know they don't like the cold. Do you know it never snows on their home world of Arif? It frosts. Nothing grows except for stubby grass and cacti. They've had problems for decades with food consumption. Like it or not, they've had to ask for help from other planets in the Pleiades."

Hadrien opened his mouth to ask another question, but she droned on, interrupting him before he could take a breath.

"I understand the Sen'Tal is petitioning the emperor to establish a religious colony on Mars—a nice summer place, you might say. I did mention that Arif is a very chilly place?"

Hadrien steered her back to the initial question. "Do the Waki'el base their society on subspecies like humans used the birth caste system in the past?"

"Oh, yes. They have three hundred and sixty-five of them. Did I mention that?" She flicked at another piece of lint, this time on her trousers.

"Are there any real differences in the Waki'el species?" Hadrien asked.

"As far as I know, there are biological differences, mostly found in the way the brain activates."

"How the brain activates?" I said. "I don't understand that."

"Well, you're not alone, Ms. Cyprion. Only the Waki'el know what that means for certain." She sat back and patted her hair. "They are delicate creatures with a short life span. Fifty years is considered quite aged. I do know that." She laughed. "I'd be like Methuselah compared to them."

"Which leads me directly to another question," Hadrien said. "Have you ever heard of an operation whereby the Waki'el fix damaged hearts using cast-off material from human heart surgery?"

"Ah, yes. Menders of broken hearts. They have apparently been popular among the Corrigadaires. The Big Eyes provided the Waki'el with organs from their own kind, but when they discovered us, they saw a bright new source for repairable heart material. And how awful can it be? Heart surgery is a laser snip here and quick tuck there. Routine beyond routine. In and out in one day. Why not give off the odds and ends to the Waki'el? I've had my ticker fixed three times and donated organs."

Hadrien rose and stepped to the small window overlooking the back patio of the walk-up. His expression registered as dark as black Darjeeling tea and standing there in his crisply pressed cammies, I had the immediate sense that he could be a very dangerous man. "How do you think Princess Belinda-Agnes fit into this Waki'el relationship?" he asked.

"Belinda-Agnes? Well, she's a crossbreed, an experiment. I believe the birth alliance that her mother had with the emperor was one of interference spurs completion." She stopped, screwed up her face, and then said, "Yes. Did I mention that Arif is dying?"

"Yes, ma'am," I said. "Can you tell us how these alliances are chosen?"

"Each relationship can be defined by two single emotional factors. How they are chosen is a mystery to most humans. I'm one of them who doesn't understand it. Never did. I guess I have too much humanity in me." She cackled, obviously pleased with herself.

"Are certain alliances constrained to certain subspecies?" I asked.

"All subspecies have such constraints, even the Basira Waki'el."

"Is there a definite rhyme or reason to the types of alliances? For instance, are the Tus confined to relationships of anger and sorrow only? Are the Basira Waki'el subject to other alliances?"

"I don't know the alliance ranges," she answered, shrugging her shoulders.

Hadrien stepped back to the sofa and sat down. He ran his hand across his lips before speaking. "What do you know of the Waki'el concept of an affair of the heart?"

Emory scowled. "That is a taboo in their culture. Very bad. They don't talk about it." She sighed, put on a thoughtful expression, and then slid in one stunning fact. "I do know that it has something to do with life after death."

12

When Hadrien and I stepped on board the Kourey that afternoon, I had a feeling that my Sun and Moon were about to collide.

Hadrien led me down softly carpeted corridors toward our suite. The *our* part of the scenario bothered me to no end, but the ship's purser explained that the accommodations had been made at the last minute, and it was the best he could do. There were no other females aboard for me to bunk with, and he certainly couldn't ask one of the delegates to double up. Our accommodations fell out as a two-room cubby, so for that, I was grateful. I could at least lock Hadrien out of my room, if necessary. I just wished I could lock out my memories along with my growing distaste about being manipulated.

We found our cabin and, once inside, I was struck by the alien feel of the room. It was decorated in salmon colors, smeared with gold and silver. The furniture was oversized for the space, and we were forced to squeeze by plump floor cushions to reach our sleeping areas. Once there, we were treated to Asian carpets, heavy brocades, and a frightful amount of maroon. Whoever had put together this garish shipboard hostelry had absolutely all of his taste in his mouth. My dear old, blind granny could have done better.

Hadrien drawled in an East London accent. "By gov, you'd think the frigging ships wouldn't be decorated like a petal."

I harumphed, unimpressed by his effort and certain that he did it to taunt me. "It's a real flowery dell, all right."

He questioned me with his eyes, but I smiled, enjoying the moment of superiority before pushing on to my own sleeping compartment.

Hadrien hoisted his duffel bag toward one of the flimsy hatches, changing the subject. "Not bad for three days. At least we have a sitting room and the potty is between the sleeping chambers."

"Oh, that's very important. I'm sure you get up several times a night to relieve yourself."

He glanced at me with a hard expression. "I drink a lot of fluids. How did you know that?"

"Fluids. That's a funny one."

"What are you talking about?"

"I'm talking about your logos. You're generally a pissed-off personality, what with your Uranus aggravating Pluto in Sagittarius. It's a combination that leads to frequent urination." With that, I headed for my own little closet and swung my valise onto the bunk. A moment later, he proved me right by entering the loo and aiming his whiz so the sound tinkled into my space.

"You know what concerns me about this whole imperial mess?" he called.

"What would that be?" I asked.

"We have no motive." There was an interruption in communication until I heard the vacuum sound of the toilet, followed by running water. Hadrien walked from the bathroom as he dried his hands on a bright green

towel emblazoned with the imperial seal. He turned to
his cubby and before he finished his statement, he
packed the glad rag into his duffel sack. "We don't know
if Lundy was tricking someone off with his honey deals
or if someone in the Sen'Tal had him bagged because
he was getting in the way. And maybe it has nothing at
all to do with this alien drug."

"Are you inclined to think it's something more?"

"The drug seems like a convenient cover. The fact
that Belinda obviously participated makes me think the
problem runs much deeper." Hadrien walked into the
johnnie and picked up one of the small bottles of hand
soap. He aimed it at me like a pointer before storing it
into his carry-on luggage. "I hate it when I can't figure
a clear-cut motive."

We each incarnate with a specific inspiration in mind,
this inspiration being the spark that we wish to manifest
and eventually learn from. Thus the physical law of like
attracts like is the first precept of the science of the interplanetudes. We choose what families we will be born
into based on what patterns they can bring us to help us
determine our growth during our period of corporeality.
If, for instance, you return to transform futility into pleasure and success, then you might pop into this dimension
under a limiting Saturn in your ascending sign. Your
family might be comprised of a bunch of crude beggars,
maggots, harlots, and assorted vermin who are intimate
with futility, cruelty, and sorrow. If the interplanetudes
are applied, then the situation of such a rotten birth can
be a cosmic gift, because your family feeds you up with
these negative patterns to give you something to conquer. Without knowing adversity, you can never know
when you've stumbled upon the moment of transformation.

The law of attraction works with friends, associates,
relatives, acquaintances, enemies, and murderers, so a
reason to kill could be a preconceived notion that defies

the term *motive*. Fortunately, passionate living always provides a corporeal reason for any event.

Still, like Hadrien, I wasn't sure what I was looking at. Worse than even that, I couldn't figure out why Lundy's and Belinda's patterns had drawn Hadrien and me together. I craved solitude like it was a balm for my blistered soul, but something that I'd agreed to in a former incarnation prevented any possibility that I might be a fence-sitter or a nun. I kept it to myself, but those thoughts frosted my brain more than any ideas I might have about the investigation.

Joining Hadrien in the sitting room, I set up my astrology equipment on the small table in front of the full-length observation portal. From this vantage point, we could watch dock operations as the ground crew prepared for liftoff. Loaders floated provisions into the ship's belly, and farther down the ramp an official-looking black car spat out a mysterious individual wearing a hooded blue cape.

Hadrien watched him climb into the lift that would take him to the ship's grand lobby. "I wonder who he is?"

"He's the emperor's executioner, Artie."

He flipped his gaze at me and for a minute, I was trapped by his endearing expression of surprise. "Are you serious?" he said.

"Absolutely."

"We need to talk him."

"Why don't we go right now?"

"Don't tell me you know this guy. No introductions necessary from the captain of this crate?"

"I've known Cornelius Paul since he rose to his current rank."

"And what do you know about him besides his position as official imperial butcher?"

I shrugged and dialed up the database on my computer. "Let's see."

Hadrien chuckled. "Do you have the goods on everybody in the imperial court?"

"Do you know the old saying: Cover your arse?"

He snorted. "Yeah."

"Well, I wear a silk blanket over me bum, and I intend to keep it there." Pausing, I selected a file, called up Paul's logos, and was reminded why this man was not to be trusted: He was cruelty from stem to stern.

Paul wore his ferocity like a heavy chain about his neck. On this hung medallions of deceit, jealousy, disappointment, and strife. Mars, Pluto, and Venus formed a grand trine of aggravated assault with a deadly weapon. If anything truly could be said for Paul, it was that he deserved to win his job. He'd come to this dimension to be an executioner.

"He's got a charming logos—for a killer," I said.

"And a special talent for electro-crucifixion," Hadrien murmured.

"That's for a fact. Watch him, Artie. He'll wiggle and squiggle you, and then when you least expect it, he'll hook you up to the execution table."

"Do you have any idea about his relationship with Lundy?"

"Adversarial."

"Why?"

"Because that's the way Paul is."

"Doesn't this bastard have one redeeming quality?"

I nodded. "He's breathing."

"Great. So, he'll force-feed us a lie if we talk to him."

"Quite likely. But then there is always a flip side to a pork pie."

He glanced at me, squinted, and then smiled. "Porkies are lies, aren't they?"

I winked at him. "We might learn ya to communicate proper-like yet." Scanning Paul's logos, I found that little resource I'd hoped he had: His point of fortune was strategically placed Libra. Killer though Paul might be, he still suffered a gram of guilt when he put innocent men to death. It was not because he felt shame but because this specific little astrological calculation burdened him with a sense of justice. And here, he found his greatest successes, even if he would never admit to it. "Let's go have a blow with this old fart and see what he has to say."

After another scrap with the purser, we were escorted to Paul's cabin, a luxurious suite of rooms that had, unfortunately, been decorated by the same designer who'd done our quarters. It was like walking inside of a can of salmon. Paul's attaché, a buck-toothed fellow with a limp, protested our visit immediately.

"I can't let you through. His Excellency is having a private moment before we lift off."

"We just want a few minutes of his time," Hadrien said. "It's not like we're going to be here all night."

"I can't interrupt him," the attaché said. "He would kill me."

"Literally?" I asked.

Before he could answer, Cornelius Paul walked into the room, shaking his head. "Samuel, that's enough. Let them through."

Samuel groveled and headed for the wet bar to make himself useful with the ice bucket.

Since his arrival, Paul had removed his hood. He stood in a pair of wrinkled black cammies while siphoning a drink through the end of a straw. He studied us, and I had the feeling that he wore his innocuous expression with a great deal of difficulty.

"I was wondering how long it would take you to seek me out and grill me like a some common criminal," Paul said in a voice full of smooth stones.

I took the part of the mouthpiece. "It's been a number of years since we've spoken, Cornelius. You're looking well."

He snorted. "My hair has fallen out into my hands,

my buttocks are sagging to the floor, and no manner of silk and gold lamé can hide the fact that what was once powerful and sleek no longer carries a hint of ferocity or feline grace."

"Ah, well, then perhaps it's your reputation that looks so good to me."

He smiled sardonically. "That is closer to the truth, I'd say." Glancing at Hadrien, he threw him a curt nod. "Theo said you would be aboard. He said he's granted you diplomatic protection while you're on Arif." Paul stopped speaking again to sip at his drink and turn slightly back toward the view of the dock. "I'm the senior diplomat on this trip. Are you planning to cause me trouble?"

"It might happen," I answered. I plunked down heavily on a fat, stocky chair and sank farther into the seat than I'd intended.

"Take care, you two. Arif is a wild place. It's not prone to treating tourists nicely." He pointed at Hadrien and jutted his head toward an empty couch. Once we were both trapped by the velvet chairs, he called to his assistant. The man rattled to attention from behind the bar, silently waiting for his orders. Paul studied us before remembering his manners. "Would you like a refreshment?"

"Tea for me," I answered. "Ceylon black."

"I'll take a Sumerek rainbow," Hadrien said. Then to start the interview in earnest, he forged ahead with a new question. "Please tell us your relationship to Lundy."

Paul didn't answer the question but instead asked, "Did you know that the Waki'el have a drink that is made from the spit of their females?"

"No, I didn't," Hadrien said.

"Yes. The females carry a substance in gland pockets in their mouths. Mixed with a stabilizer and allowed to

ferment, it makes a hardy drink—one that will inebriate
you in ways that alcohol can't."

"You know Lundy had a hard time with the honey,
didn't you, Cornelius?" I asked.

"Yes, I was aware of it."

"Was Belinda supplying him?"

"No, Belinda was supplying the researchers." He held
his hand up in surrender. "Please, don't ask any more
probing questions on that matter. I'm not at liberty to
divulge classified material."

Theo and his paranoia waltzed in to cut off that line
of inquiry, so I taunted Paul with what I knew was the
bloody truth. "You didn't like Lundy, did you?"

Paul cleared his throat. He coughed, then slid into his
answer. "I couldn't stand Lundy. He was a fool of the
worst sort. Atop that, he would bugger the *Mona Lisa*
if he thought he could get some life out of an inanimate
object."

"Was he all that bad?" I asked casually.

"You don't think so, Philipa? Do your precious interplanetudes tell you something different?" He sneered.
"Was Lundy bound for big and grand?"

"Promiscuity doesn't necessarily make a person bad."

He sat back, swigged on his drink, and thought about
it for a moment. "Where does promiscuity end and per-
version begin?"

Hadrien downed his Sumerek rainbow before asking,
"What does that mean?"

"Lundy was a perverse individual. Personally, I believe he was mentally unstable, and that is the thing that
eventually led to his downfall. He had a honey addiction,
and he was starting to draw in a whole host of unsavory
characters. It was behavior not fitting a member of the
imperial household."

"And Princess Belinda-Agnes?" I said.

Paul frowned. I had the feeling that beneath that crust-
iness, he held even more antagonism. It took him a sec-

ond to prove it. "Belinda-Agnes," he whispered. "Ridiculous name for a Waki'el, don't you think?"

Hadrien picked up on Paul's emotional reconfiguration and pushed on it. "We have evidence that the princess may have been murdered because of her association with Lundy."

"No," Paul snapped. "She would not have willingly played advocate to that walking worm factory who called himself her brother."

"So she might have participated in something unwillingly," Hadrien answered. "What?"

Paul narrowed his eyes and then carefully placed his glass atop a coaster on the low table. Halting, he studied Hadrien intently, giving him a look as if he measured my partner's head to see if it would easily fit into the metallic embrace of the guillotine. "Let us get one thing straight. Princess Belinda was not suspected of entering into any illegalities. None. She had the mark of a saint who endured a lifetime of agony. If nothing else, Belinda was compassionate about the plight of others. It was a lesson she'd learned well living here on Earth. Besides, her sacrifice became the basis for an alliance between our peoples."

Hadrien took a chance by snorting his derision. "You'll pardon my blatant response, sir, but aside from some signatures on a piece of paper, there is no alliance. We are no more friends with the Waki'el than we are with the Corrigadaires or the Sumereks. We go at each other's throat when no one official is looking."

"There are very few humans on the Waki'el home world," I added. "Relations between us are cool, to say the least."

"There are many more humans on Arif than you think," Paul said.

"What is your mission, Cornelius?" I asked. "Are you going to recement our connections to the Waki'el and smooth it all out by troweling on the condolences to Mann Re?"

He chuckled. "Troweling on the condolences? You were always one to turn a phrase." Paul pulled a deep breath, then shook his head. "You are right. As the man responsible for life and death on Earth, the Waki'el see me as a person of great power. Mann Re gave her child to be raised and cared for by Theo. Her murder has symbolized a breach in this contract."

"So, atop this unfortunate event, Theo's oath has gotten him into trouble with the high and mighty of Arif," Hadrien said.

"In a word, yes."

"Do you think Mann Re had anything to do with Belinda's death?"

"No, I don't."

"What about Lundy's death?"

Paul scowled. "Your line of questioning has lost its cohesion. Mann Re had nothing to do with Lundy's murder. That is preposterous."

"Lundy and she were friends."

"That's not true. Whoever told you that was lying."

"What kind of relationship did Belinda have with her mother?" Hadrien said.

"Belinda regarded it as compassion seeks strength. I am unaware of the particulars of their relationship."

"What do you know about the Waki'el concept called an affair of the heart?" I asked.

It took him no time to contemplate the question. "I know nothing." He picked up his drink and stood. "I have an appointment within the hour to discuss a few things with the main delegation members. You really will have to excuse me." With that, he called for his attaché and we were abruptly shown the exit hatch.

"Do you notice that every time we bring up that subject of affairs of the heart, we quickly run into a brick wall?" I said.

"Yes," Hadrien answered. "And since I'm generally a pissed-off person, it's starting to play with my figs now. I don't like it one bit. Our butts are dangling over the fire, and something is going on that could save us from a terrible blister."

We turned off down a lonely corridor, ducking low when we reached a ladder to the next level. It was a tight turnaround with a lot of liquidly drawn metal decorating the access tube. A bit busy for my likes, but then most alien architecture is.

Hadrien stepped on the landing, and I followed him, lingering a moment to look down the central staircase. It was fifty levels in height, and the red glow from the exit lights displayed above the hatches appeared to form two long, contiguous rows that reminded me of a laser bolt fired from a rifle.

In the next moment, Mars transited Mars in my house of fortune, and karma intersected that fanciful thought to form realization. Someone shot at us.

13

Hadrien pushed me to the deck with such feroc-ity, you would have thought that a rhino were charging straight at us. I rolled to the protection of the bulkhead and tried to squeeze out of the line of pink laser fire coming from below. Hadrien used his own body to shield my bum from the stabbing precision of the energy volleys. With a quick snap of his wrist, he yanked out his side arm, returning the shots. He used a punch pistol, old-fashioned but effective, the ammunition of which de-livered little warheads of disruption beads. If he hit his target, the beads would activate into the victim's flesh to send out electrical impulses that interfered with the proper firing of the nerves, rendering the attacker help-lessly paralyzed.

Laser fire slammed past him to knock a chunk from the overhead. Melted metal pelted us like silver hail, and we both dropped flat to the deck. Hadrien grabbed my head as well as his own in a desperate attempt to deflect falling debris. I smelled smoldering fabric and, checking my new partner, I saw his uniform arm smoked. Risking movement that might draw fire, I tried to brush off the molten beads. He grabbed my hand, tossing me a quick look before he twisted to shoot at the panel that controlled the lighting.

We fell into a gray darkness and the firing stopped. Hadrien used the opportunity to pop over the railing and return a couple of quick shots, an action that obviously pushed our assailant into a fit of anger.

More volleys sang around the landing. Hadrien flopped down beside me, but the marksman kept us pinned against the tile by working the laser gun's trigger continuously, aiming at the blistering hole growing over us.

What the bloody sam hill was going on? Suddenly, I'd been made a live target at a skeet-shooting contest and, for whatever reason, the person with the rifle was going to see to it that I was broken apart like a clay pigeon.

Alarms started screaming around us, echoing up the tube until I thought my ears would burst from the noise.

The laser fire stopped. Crewmen streamed into the corridor with weapons drawn, holding us at bay on the landing while they communicated with their superiors. Hadrien tried to talk us out of their gun sights.

"We were the ones who were under attack! The shooter is at least five levels beneath us."

A young lieutenant stepped from the crowd of weapons to protect us from fast trigger fingers while Hadrien stood up. He tried to holster his pistol, but the officer held his hand out.

"It's against regulations to discharge a power weapon aboard a space transport," he said stiffly. "You will surrender your weapon."

Hadrien tested the waters of his defiance by ignoring the lieutenant's request. He replaced his gun to its leather nest and snapped the chain across it with a definite flick of his fingers. He then held his hands palm out in submission before taking a step forward. When he was within a quarter of a meter from the man, he stopped, judged his height and weight against the officer, and then used it for menace. "You're lucky I don't pitch your ass over the railing." He paused before laying on more sorghum to the waffle. "I'm telling you, *Lef*-tenant, we were under attack. The person with the laser rifle is wandering around freely in this ship. You need to contact your captain to tell her that there's walking death on this trawler. And I don't mean the executioner."

The lieutenant backed away, nodding to a sergeant standing close by. "Signal Verena."

"No need."

It was a commanding voice, spoken on a growl. We turned our attention toward the end of the corridor and saw Captain Verena swaggering our way. She was a woman of big hair—it flowed around her, adding more wheat color to the taupe tone of her skin and matching uniform. Surveying us with obvious disdain, she growled again. "Damn it! Will someone delete that Klaxon?" She waited impatiently, studying the melted hole in the bulkhead. After a minute, the alarm stopped wailing, and she asked her question. "What happened here?"

Hadrien shook his head and muttered a curse, turning from this belligerent attitude to pull me to a stand. He must not have been giving me much more than a thought during this altercation because he cleaned up my dark blue cammies by nonchalantly using the flat of his hand to scrape the dirt off my backside. Before I could even squeak, he'd spun back to face Verena.

"Don't you think you should seal the ship?" he demanded.

"It's already been done," she answered. "The moment we detected the energy signatures of your weapons, the ship was placed on Alpha Con One. No one leaves this ship until we dock again, and then only those whom I authorize." Verena marched by him to inspect the hole in the overhead. "Did you see who fired at you?"

"No," I answered, realizing my shattered nerves had made my reply quiver. I swallowed and glanced at Hadrien. "Did you see anything?"

"No. Whoever it was used the ladder and the shadows to hide himself."

Verena forgot the ceiling damage and took a few steps away from us before asking another confusing question. "Why would someone try to shoot you?"

"Why wouldn't they?" Hadrien said. "We're here trying to catch a killer. We're making someone very nervous and, like it or not, it's become your problem, too. Why don't you pause in the liftoff schedule to find this would-be assassin?"

"We can't," she answered. "We're already under way. If we abort the sequence, we'll be delayed by another day until we can bring everything on-line again."

"Aren't you concerned about another attempt?" Hadrien pressed. "It might not be us this person aims at."

It was time for me to speak up. "You have a security problem, Captain Verena. Don't you think you should be attending to it?"

She glared at me for half a minute and then stalked away with the lieutenant.

We waited for the crew to leave the area before Hadrien touched my shoulder. I thought he might inquire after my health, but his words stunned me. "Please tell me that you've used the interplanetudes to calculate the hours of our deaths. Tell me that today won't be the day we make the great big leap into eternity."

For some reason, I was disappointed that he didn't pause to place a little comfort between us, but I brushed away my emotional reaction to the stress of the situation.

In reality, I had no idea of our dismissal times. Who in their blinking right mind would want to know when they're checking into the ethereal realm? Certainly not I. Still, I experienced a moment of perverse pleasure.

"Yes," I lied. "I know when we're going to die."

"So?" he asked, masking his thoughts in a concerned frown.

I took a step down the corridor, before calling back over my shoulder. "So, you should make every breath count."

14

Traveling through zero-point gravity always kicks up my nightmares. A doctor once told me it was because the gravity flux in the creation energy disturbed the chemical balance of the brain. Apparently, it wasn't such a rare occurrence in intergalactic travelers. Still, my sleep is severely affected. So the night of the assassination attempt, I had a particularly frightful night of being chased, pillaged, and killed. When I awoke lying in a puddle of my own juices, I saw Hadrien standing in the doorway of my sleeping cubicle, wearing nothing but a pair of silky black britches. He studied me with a curious look upon his handsome face, and as much as I don't like to admit it, I panicked a bit upon realizing that I was attracted to him.

"You called out in your sleep," he said quietly. "Your husband's name."

I sighed, started to climb out of bed, but paused to check if I'd slept in the raw. No, I had on a pair of socks. "Would you mind closing the door and giving me a minute to find me Dicky dirt?"

He squinted, then smiled. "Dicky dirt—your shirt?"

"Yes." I flapped a hand at him. "I'll be along in a bit."

He chuckled to himself, pressed the stud on the wall control unit, and turned away before the slider snapped into place. I rose, dressed, and met him in our sitting room, where he had two breakfast trays heating under their own power.

The interesting thing about being an astrologer is the fact that subtle nuances are so rarely hidden. In the time before I'd given up on my own talents of interpretation, I'd relied on the clarity provided by the interplay of planets. Now, charged again with having to look within at myself, I wasn't sure I read anything right because I was *sure* that nothing was particularly on target where I was concerned.

Still, I've always been one to make sweeping suppositions. Hadrien had a strong planetary configuration in Cancer, a zodiac house that speaks of home and nurturing. Eric had no planets in this house, and his Venus, that planet overlooking love energy, rotated in icy Scorpio. It made him come across as cold and uncaring much of the time. While we were married, I chalked up the distance he placed between himself and the rest of the universe as his need for creative solitude. But standing here with Hadrien, I knew that Eric's problem had cheated me out of years of tenderness and consideration. Worse than that realization was the next one that came: I had let it happen.

"Thank you for checking on me," I murmured, sliding into the seat opposite Hadrien at the table. "I had a restless night."

He smiled gently, and again I had to fight a breezy attraction to him. "We're partners," he whispered. Then, louder, he added, "And it looks like we're going to have to protect our backs." Before I could say anything, he continued, launching into his ideas about the case. "I did a little reading last night and discovered that the Waki'el planet, Arif, is made of mud, stones, cooking smoke, and a millennium of fungus. There's some research that's been done by an independent corporation on Maya. This company claims that humans with respiratory conditions are often adversely affected by the presence of this fungus. It's been known to create illnesses similar to amilleas fumagante, though that's not been verified by any other sources."

It was my turn to smile. Hadrien had his own ways of processing his understanding of the world, just as I did with my astrology. His way was based on logic combined with more earthiness than I possessed. "So you think Lundy contracted the disease from actually traveling to Arif?"

"It could be, but I think it was his desire to peg pretty young Waki'el females for their honey." He squinted, and it drew me off the next question to ask another one.

"You find that offensive, don't you?"

He frowned and studied me. An unbidden swell of yearning pumped through me so badly I thought I was in deep curry from exposing my true thoughts. Hadrien didn't remark on any wiggling I might have been doing in the chair. "I think that humans should mate with humans. I'm a purist, and I don't deny it."

I didn't much care for the idea of alien sex myself, but rather than giving away my own desires, I nodded and tried to think of another subject. It was too bad that my brain refreshed my oath about getting involved with any more men.

Hadrien stopped his data flow to pull back the foil on our instant breakfasts. Steam lazily escaped, and I smelled the odor of eggs and sausage. He pushed a tray toward me along with a plastic fork. "It's not the Ritz, but it will do."

"The Ritz?"

"Old American slang." Hadrien speared a potato and popped it into his mouth, talking while he chewed. "I found out something interesting while I was reading."

I grabbed a sausage link with my fingers and took a bite. "What?"

"Lundy and his sibs shipped out for the Pleiades a month before everyone came up brown bread. The trip included his brothers and sisters who were killed in the accident as well as Belinda-Agnes."

"What was their destination?"

"Maya. Supposedly."

"So, you think the records have been doctored?"

"I believe it was major surgery." He took a bite of egg before laying on another big theory. "The fungus found on Arif? I discovered that the substance works quite well as a biological agent. Highly toxic. Sounds like something our government might want to have a handle on."

His assertion put a whole new corner on the edge. Theo had several nasty arguments with different planets and different governments. It was a fact that had driven Eric's work. Theo's requirements of secrecy fed my husband's desire for adventure and power through clandestine acts. Because he had no planets to balance this compulsion, he had become remote during the last year of our marriage.

I was about to speak, but the buzzing intercom interrupted me. My partner leaned back and hit the button on the bulkhead unit. "Hadrien."

"This is Dr. Omar, chief physician."

"Yes, Doctor. What can we do for you?"

Omar's answer came in true British fashion: dignified, calm, and commanding. "I need to see you and Ms. Cyprion immediately. I have a situation in the medical lab of which you should be apprised."

"We're on our way," Hadrien answered.

"Tell no one," Omar said before cutting the communication.

We forgot our breakfasts and headed for the ship's infirmary, where we found Dr. Omar huddled over his desk. I was stunned to discover that the *Kourey*'s head physician was Corrigadaire. He glanced up at our entrance to peg us with those huge eyes, and I saw that his mincers were bright blue with a yellow pupil. In his white lab coat, Dr. Omar was a strange artifact indeed.

He studied us silently, forcing Hadrien to speak first. "What is so important, Doctor?"

"Before I tell you, I must know something," he growled lightly.

"What's that?"

"Are you working with the executioner?"

"Paul?" Hadrien shrugged. "Is that even a possibility?"

"Do you report to him?"

"No," I said. "We're employed by Theo. Whatever you want to tell us will stay among us."

Omar rose carefully from the human-sized chair, which was when I noticed how big this alien really was. He towered over Hadrien by at least a half meter. Turning from us, he waved his enormous hand before stomping toward the steel door of a medical refrigeration room. He stopped at a cracked plastic counter, flicked two surgical masks our way, and pointed to our mouths. Once we were appropriately attired, he cycled the lock on the hatch, entering without further word. We followed and, guided by the comforting glow of blue neon tubes running the length of the box, we came to a halt before a covered examining cart. Omar yanked back the sheet to expose a dead Waki'el.

Hadrien whistled, and I saw his breath mist in the cold air. "Now, where did he come from?"

"Not he, Lieutenant," Omar answered. "It is a female, approximately twenty-five Earth standard years old."

"Is she supposed to be aboard this ship?"

"No. There is no Waki'el mentioned on the *Kourey*'s passenger list."

Hadrien gave me a hard look before turning his concentration upon the body. "Tell us everything you know."

Omar stepped away from the Waki'el to sit down in a plastic chair. "I was called by an underling who was scrubbing the decks in the engine room. He found her in an equipment room closet. I asked the engineer not to speak of this, and he has agreed, though I can't be certain that he won't renege on his promise and tell the captain. Therefore, I must contact her after we conclude our visit here."

Grabbing the sheet, I pulled the cover completely away, dropping it on the frosty floor.

The normal iridescence that marked this species had faded to a dark cranberry, and the bony body appeared almost brittle. I delicately touched one of the points on her sternum ridge and the tip broke away. "How long do you estimate she's been dead?"

"Not long. Perhaps a day at most."

"But the body is in serious decay," Hadrien said.

Omar crossed his legs at the knees, shaking his head as he did. "Not uncommon in Waki'el. Arif is a dry world. Waki'el evolution has become such that once the organism dies, it separates back into the environment in only a few days. In another twenty-four hours, there will be very little left of this specimen."

I glanced inside the space of her sternum ridge. "She has no heart."

"That is correct. It appears to have been ripped from the body."

I winced. "Murder?"

"Perhaps."

"What else could it be?"

"Suicide."

His response made us turn to stare at each other. Hadrien wore a wild-eyed expression that immediately proclaimed his discomfort with the idea of a person having the wherewithal to tear her beating heart from her body.

"This might be our shooter," he murmured.

Omar filled in any problems we might have had in drawing our own visual conclusions. "Once the heart is ripped away, the Waki'el bleeds to death. It takes approximately nine minutes for death to occur." He swallowed, and I watched his huge Adam's apple flicker in his throat. Then, he added another startling fact. "It is amazing that this female could actually use a pair of thoractic expanders on herself. There should have been excruciating pain."

"Perhaps Waki'el don't experience pain like we do. What about the amount of nerve endings in the area?"

He shrugged. "They have a sophisticated neural system. Waki'el physiology provides them with a natural chemical compound secreted by the brain that alleviates pain. It's the only way I can see something like this happening."

"Maybe someone obliged her," Hadrien said. "A little help on the hari-kari, if you get my drift."

I plopped back into the conversation. "Can you tell if she was Tus or Basira?"

"N'galia, I believe. She carries the sign of the Acu-Sen'Tal on her arm."

Sliding my gaze along her hand, I found a tattoo of flowers girdling the alien's wrist. Inlaid within the painting was a strip of dots and dashes. Omar saw me studying the Morse code and offered an explanation.

"That represents a house delineation," he said. "I did a lot of identity work for the Waki'el when the Uranci attacked their planet. They lost many people in that short little war, and then to add insult to injury, the Uranci decided they didn't really want Arif. They went away like thieves in the night, leaving the Sen'Tal to put the world back together again."

Hadrien was obviously not in the mood for a history lesson. "What does it mean?" he growled.

Omar seemed not to notice his impatience. "According to the pattern, she hails from the family of Felis Bray'el. He's the high administrator on Arif and the head of the Sen'Tal, but I believe you already know that. There is one long dash on the underside of her wrist that delineates her as a servant of Mann Re."

"Mann Re?" Hadrien whispered.

"She had no chest ornaments for further identification," Omar added. He stood, drawing our attention. "There is one other thing you should be made aware of." The doctor stomped to a steel cabinet and pulled out a rod-shaped instrument. He took a large step toward me while he flicked the stick to life. It glowed a lovely lavender shade. "Because my species is sensitive to photonic activity, I noticed a peculiar pattern beneath this Waki'el's hide." He aimed the rod over her arm and down her chest toward where her heart should have been.

He was right. There was a strangely beautiful, zigzag pattern beneath the skin. Under the light, it glowed pink.

"What is that?" Hadrien asked. "A tattoo?"

"It's not a tattoo," Omar answered. "I took a biopsy of the area. The pattern runs through all the layers of dermis and into the fleshy part of the muscle."

"What is it then?" I said.

The doctor shrugged. "I cannot say. I've never seen anything like it before."

15

Hadrien and I stayed close to our cabin during the rest of the trip. My new partner didn't say a dicky bird to me during our hours of confinement together. Instead, he used the quiet between us to hunt through databases for information that might help us to find Lundy's killer.

I spent the time pretending to be consumed by my logos readings, but the truth was, I actually spent the time running into the past, reviewing again and again delicate little pieces of my marriage to Eric. I had avoided this part of the grieving process until Hadrien's arrival in my life. My attraction to this enigmatic man undid all my logical attempts to deny my growing desire for comfort from another human being. When had I given up on expecting this comfort to come from my own species? Why had I run to the scaly, hairy, spindly arms of nonhumans? What had happened deep inside me that had forced me into this mad dash? Whatever it was, my horoscope was giving me no evidence about the source—not that I could interpret it all that well if it did.

Once we arrived on Arif, we soon discovered that

we'd been diplomatically stonewalled by Paul. He refused to grant us permission to interview Mann Re and also shot down our request to talk to anyone who had anything to do with her house: servants, relatives, or lovers. That left only her enemies. It was not a sound place for two Earthers to start on a murder trail.

So, three Arif days later, we exited the old spaceport in the Arifian city of Nald'eken, leaving behind everything that spoke of humanity. This place was was as alien as chicken livers in a Sumerek shepherd's pie.

Many planets in the Pleiades share two or more stars, making them all but uninhabitable except to certain species. Arif was a bit different in that it orbited a red giant, a sun that was, in stellar age, quite old. It bathed this world in a gentle pink hue, and while lovely to human eyes, it did nothing to improve the degraded conditions of urban sprawl.

The city was slung together with thick mud brick, dry thatch, and smooth stone. Glancing down, I saw old, cracked clay gutters channeling raw sewage down a gently sloping incline. The streets were unpaved and dusty, and there were no fueled transports other than Waki'el lugging large sacks on their backs. They did have the wheel, though, because I noticed a person pushing a rickety wooden cart down the busy thoroughfare.

"This is a progressive society?" Hadrien said. "Looks like Miami after the Fidalian War."

We took a short stroll down the street, pausing to glance behind us when we stepped into the long shadow of an enormous stone ziggurat. The rock used to construct the pyramid gleamed in the sun like fool's gold reflected in the eye of an ignorant miner. Strands of white and blue prayer flags flapped in the breeze, and at the top of the ziggurat there was a large metallic carving hoisted on a sturdy pole. The symbol was shaped like the mathematical sign for infinity and shined brightly— silver against the pyramid's gold.

The natives gave us scowling stares as they passed, but other than that, they were silent about our presence. For a moment, I thought it wasn't necessarily a bad thing, but I revised my thinking when boulders began dropping out of the sky.

The rocks, some larger than my fist, thunked around us. Glancing up, I saw a Waki'el female hanging from a third-story window, pitching these lethal bombs our way. I pushed Hadrien forward toward the relative safety of a deep, dark doorway, but not before he was grazed on the noggin by one of these well-aimed orbs. He staggered at the impact, grunting as we wheeled up under cover to watch the stones hit the street like a granite hailstorm.

"All you all right?" I asked.

He sighed and wiped at the blood trickling from his forehead. "I'll live. Thankfully, it didn't hit me directly."

"We should get back to the ship so Omar can have a look at you."

"I'm fine," he growled. Then, sighing again, he said, "Do you get the feeling the Waki'el don't care for humans?"

"Quite the contrary."

We both spun in the small space of the covered porch to see that the wooden door to this den had opened and we stood face-to-face with a wizened, cranberry-colored Waki'el male. He held a storm lantern in his hand, and in the yellow light, I saw that his home was a single room filled with hand-hewn wooden furniture and a bunk laden with a straw mattress. To top off our introduction, we were greeted with a bloody awful stink issuing from the hovel.

The Waki'el studied us and took special interest in the fact that Hadrien smeared the blood on his head by wiping his sleeve across it. Perhaps seeing my partner's injury had softened his heart. Instead of putting his boots to our bums, he stepped back and invited us to enter.

We quickly obliged him. He silently placed the lantern on a small table, checked the meter on the battery pack, and then returned to his open scrutiny of us.

We remained standing while Hadrien rifled his pockets, looking for a handkerchief. Finding it, he held it to the rivulet running into a dripping waterfall over his right eye. His actions finally brought more words from the Waki'el.

"Will you sell your life force now that it has drained into your hand?" he asked.

"Why would I do that?" Hadrien asked. "I can always make more blood."

The Waki'el squinted but didn't comment.

"I'm called Philipa, and this is Artie."

"I'm Yana of the N'galia Waki'el." He frowned. "I have heard that humans are a wasteful lot."

"You would keep your spilled blood and sell it?" Hadrien asked. "Who would buy it?"

Yana shrugged. "The person with enough money."

"What do people do with blood?" I said.

"Form blood clauses mostly," he answered. "That is important and expensive. If you have blood, you can specify alliances." He paused, raised his bony fingers to his sharp-edged chin, and studied the rag Hadrien used to sop his wound. "I don't know how much human blood might fetch."

I stepped to the tiny window and tried to look outside, but the glass was made milky by its own thickness. "Why did that Waki'el throw rocks at us?"

"Foran is Tus. The Tus don't like the Basira, nor do they like the alliances the Basira has formed with humans. N'galia don't join with aliens any more than do the Tus, but we don't care what the Basira do. We're so far down in the caste system that our desires are never heard or acted upon, so we have no reason to protest about propriety and false civility."

I moved back from the window to face him. "What

kind of clauses can you form with blood?"

"You can strengthen the surrender of life by synthesizing unity. That is perhaps the most important one."

"Maybe I got conked on the noodle harder than I thought," Hadrien muttered. "What does all that unity stuff mean?"

"It is a true and spiritual alliance," Yana said. "It symbolizes a pact of allegiance. Such clauses can become very powerful. Plus, it helps to have many people you can count on when necessary."

He nodded to himself, turned on his heel, and walked to a small cabinet where he pulled out a round loaf of bread and two yellow globes of fruit. Pointing to a couple of straight-backed chairs, he fell into a bit of alien wheeling and dealing before he busied himself with preparing a small meal. "I have one hundred tambers that I can offer you for the cloth there. Two tambers equal one imperial Earth guild piece. So, that is a good and fair payment."

Hadrien finished swabbing the deck of his forehead and handed off his handkerchief to the alien. "Here, you can have it as a gift for saving our lives from the lady upstairs."

Yana smiled and took the rag. He carefully placed it in the cabinet from which he'd removed the food. Returning to the loaf, he broke off several pieces, passing them around. "You should not walk about during the day. I'm surprised you weren't told this by the captain of the transport that brought you here."

I took a bite from the bread. It was a reminder of sawdust and sand, but I was suddenly hungry and took another swallow, making Hadrien ask the next question.

"Why shouldn't we walk about during the day?"

"It's against the tenets of the Codex of Sentient Species," he answered. "When we first made contact with other planets, our leaders were concerned. We are a people who naturally segregate ourselves. Only Basira and

Tus are allowed to move about during the daylight hours without fear of interference by the authorities. After nightfall, everyone else is permitted to be on the streets and to go to the temples. The leaders felt that humans and other species rated below the caste of Tus, and they should walk about after dark with the rest of us. Recently, though, more and more aliens have marched down these roads during the time of high sun. Because the Basira are in charge, the Tus feel that there has been a violation of the codex and that they are directly responsible for this problem. It's a sign of disrespect to them. That's why my neighbor threw rocks at you. A form of protest; nothing personal."

"Sure doesn't feel impersonal," Hadrien griped around his piece of bread.

"Are you a member of the Sen'Tal?" I asked.

Yana laughed, and when he moved, I saw his beating heart, long and leathery-looking, through the opening of his sternum ridges. "Only Basira and Tus may become members. Everyone else is Acu-Sen'Tal." He stopped speaking to plant his fingers deeply into one of the globes. It cracked apart like a soft-boiled egg, spilling orange innards that reminded me of a creamy yolk. The odor wafting from the fruit was heavy, like the sweet scent of an orchid. Unfortunately, the fragrance was only a temporary delight, because Yana began licking the thick juices from his fingers with a tongue that was at least fifty centimeters long. This spectacle stopped Hadrien in midbite. He blinked at our host and then said lightly, "You know, I can touch the tip of my nose with my tongue, but I've never seen anybody who could reach their toes."

Yana rolled up his taster, made a sucking sound, and a second later a small bulge protruded from his throat as the extra length of the organ settled into a resting pouch there. He smiled. "I have heard that most humans are physically dysfunctional."

"Is that implying the Waki'el are superior?" Hadrien said.

"Probably."

"Well, it seems that without human hearts, Waki'el have their fair share of limitations."

Yana pushed his fingers back into the fruit to pick out the meat. "That is very true. We are not as long-lived as humans, but while alive, we are vitally efficient."

"We're trying to find a Waki'el by the name of Dumaka Lant. He apparently mends broken hearts."

Yana nodded, chuckling. "He's a surgeon. The word *'fil'enkan'i* doesn't translate well into Intergalactic."

"What kind of surgeon is he?"

"The kind who fixes broken hearts. He is a wonder for our people."

"Why? Is he that skillful?"

"Yes. He possesses great talent and dexterity. Yet his true worth isn't on the surgeon's table but with the fact that he was N'galia. He crossed castes, something few Waki'el ever manage."

"How did he do that?"

"I don't know. There are stories. Gossip. Talk of new inventions."

"Dumaka Lant is an inventor?" I asked.

"Yes. He was adept at mathematics and science. A genius, perhaps." Yana scraped up the fruit and placed it atop two new slices of bread. He handed Hadrien and me each one.

I ignored the nagging warning that alien foods can give you a bad turn. The odor lusted after my nostrils and dragged my mouth into the affair. Once I'd tasted this concoction, I was sure that a case of disappointment would follow this unauthorized pleasure. Still, I couldn't bring myself to stop. I was glad when Yana continued the conversation.

"I'm not sure what Dumaka Lant invented, but it must have been a powerful thing. The Basira never break caste rules of association to take in a Waki'el in a caste below them. Inbreeding problems were the only reason they include Tus in their convictions of superiority." He grinned. "Dumaka Lant has made us proud. He became a Sen'Tal high priest, an accomplishment that has never been won by a Tus, much less a N'galia."

Hadrien took a chance. "What can you tell us about a Waki'el concept known as an affair of the heart?"

"It has to do with the afterlife," he answered. "It's not wise to speak about it to anyone."

"Why?" I asked.

Yana glared at me, and for a moment I was sure he was going to pitch me out on my ear for being so insolent. Instead, he spoke in a low voice. "Heart affairs bring great peace, but they also interfere with the gain of clarity." With that, he changed the subject to include a warning about his neighbor and the box full of rocks she kept by the window.

16

We visited with Yana for a few hours, but he would not or could not answer many of our questions. He played the part of an ignorant servant, content to be counted as one of the lesser beings in the universe. His concern was about how much rain Earth received annually as compared to the amount of moisture the terraformed planet of Mars received. During this time, Hadrien grew a little knot on his forehead, but he displayed no signs of concussion, so I took him off my worry list. Unfortunately, the bigger the bump became, the more his mood matured into ferocity and the more impatient he became to be about his business. When we finally left to go to the temple for a visit with Dumaka Lant, he carried around a chip on his shoulder as large as my bum. And he was just waiting to throw it at someone.

I'll admit, it secretly thrilled me to be around such passion. Eric had little to begin with, and by the time Theo was done with him, he had none at all. As we walked down the street, I found myself lagging a step behind for fear my reaction would turn to full-fledged interest in Hadrien.

Arif had thirteen satellites, seven of which were now visible. Their rusty glow transformed this city into a place of burnt colors and sepia shadows. Front stoops were decorated with iron braziers stoked with small fires; door lintels shone invitingly beneath torchlight. Though the people of this world were burdened under the chilling effects of a dying sun, they obviously had a collective soul that ran hot.

I took a deep breath and exhaled like Saint George's dragon trying to blow off steam. The smoky air dragged up a dry hack and, pausing, I snorted at the grit building in my sinuses. Hadrien spun around to stare in my direction before slowing his step to stay even with me. He said nothing but took my arm to guide me down the street.

I did entertain thoughts of pushing him off. The problem was that I didn't want to. So I allowed him to hang on, compromising a moment of emotional bonding by thinking about Eric and how he rarely took my arm or my hand while we had walked about in public.

"I thought only a few humans have visited Arif," Hadrien said, saving me from myself. "Judging from the number of folks on the street, I'd say that statement was a bit of propaganda."

He was right. The boulevard was crowded with a makeshift bazaar that catered to all manner of aliens— everyone from smelly Sumereks to the leafy-looking Vonaishians—and in between this mess a number of humans lingered. A screaming brawl abruptly broke out in the center of this market, the chilly breeze causing the noise to doppler past us. In moments, the guttural voices were accompanied by a pounding drum, adding a harsh, thrumming countermeasure to the argument.

We continued on into the center of the marketplace until we came to a doorway guarded by a zero-p baby.

They were often called balloon heads by those less enlightened about their circumstances. In the years just after the discovery and application of zero-point gravity, scientists undertook experiments to see how a human fetus would form while stranded for nine months within the creation energy. They also wanted to see how a birth would take place and how a child might grow during the formative years. It was a project that changed the course of history and gave Theo's ancestor another avenue of human exploitation.

An interesting effect of the creation energy was to make the brain bigger and its intelligence capacity fifty times stronger. The rest of the body was a different matter. Zero-p babies were small, puffy, and as white as the glaze on Devonshire china. They had stumpy little fins for feet and hands, and their spines ended in a long, frozen, pointed tail.

Theo's father, John the First, saw the potential in breeding these brain factories and had made a legion of people who were geniuses but belonged nowhere in our dimensional space. He used them as slave labor, cranking out answers to theoretical problems that made John the leader of a technological revolution unlike any Earth had ever known. The zero-p babies complied for the first generation of their captivity, but then they revolted, breaking away from John's fat, grubby fist. They lived their lives peacefully in colony capsules hidden in time pockets within the creation force and rarely accessed this dimension. Yet here on this frosty, dry world, there seemed to be a bloody awful lot of balloon heads.

Hadrien decided to stop, and I was certain it was to harass this particular zero-p baby. He managed to surprise me, though.

"I have a friend who builds custom skimmers," he said, pointing the floating chair that contained the bloke's emaciated body. "You look like you could use a new one."

The fellow snorted, tugged at a few strands of his thin, dark hair, and threw Hadrien a pitch of his own. "I don't need this chair."

"Why is that?"

"I have help."

As if to punctuate his statement, two female Waki'el appeared in the doorway behind him. Their skin glistened in the orange light, and gold chains crossing their sternum ridges glinted with their movements.

"They aren't cheap," the balloon head announced. "But they are worth the price of a guild piece. They know how to service humans." With that, he turned his cockeyed stare onto me. "They aren't particularly open to human females, though."

"Why is that?" I asked.

He shook his head. "Just a peculiarity, I suppose."

Hadrien jumped into this fellow's game like an old dog used to sniffing skirts on the streets. "I might be interested in your ladies. What's your name?"

"You can call me Ross," he answered with a toothless grin.

Hadrien nodded, sized up the duo, rubbed his beard, and then sighed. "A guild piece, huh? That's high. Even for the both of them."

Ross motioned one of them forward and patted her thigh. "Look here. They've got some ham and eggs. Very good pleasure makers."

Hadrien squinted as though he was carefully judging the merchandise. "A half-guild piece, and you throw in some information."

Ross pulled on a pained expression but after a moment, he nodded. "I'll spit you some juice once I've seen the cold metal."

During our stay with Yana, Hadrien had cashed in some Earth credits for local change. He reached into his pocket and pulled out one of the disks, flipping it to

Ross. Satisfied, he tilted his big head in my partner's direction. "What do you want to know?"

"Well, for one thing," Hadrien said, "I want to know why there are so many zero-p babies around here."

Ross scowled and, despite his decrepit position, it made him appear dangerous. "Why not? We have to live somewhere. These folks are open to my kind. We share a mutual alliance of ascension."

"Ascension?" I asked.

He glanced at me. "That's right. We're the true children of the creation energy; real flesh-and-blood beings who can come and go as we please between the gravitic planes. The Waki'el want to one day be able to do the same. We share knowledge about our lifestyles." He paused, put on a thoughtful face, and then pasted on the stamp that delivered the authenticity of his cause. "We are ageless people. Despite our physical limitations, we alone can say that living a thousand years is nothing."

"That's only when you remain in zero-p flux," I said.

"So?"

"You age normally in this dimension."

"Why would you leave a colony to come here?" Hadrien asked. "Pimping hookers for a guild piece isn't going to make you rich—unless, of course, you have a whole house full of them."

The tramp slipped loose from Ross to enticingly run her fingers along the curl of Hadrien's neck. I studied him to see if there was a wince, a twitch, a nostril flare of alien bigotry, but he remained perfectly calm and seemingly unmoved by her exotic, Waki'el mating ritual. He aimed his attention stiffly upon Ross. "Are you a desperado among your own people? Is that why you are here?"

"I told you why I'm here," he answered crisply. "I'm brilliant. We're all brilliant. We've been invited here."

"By whom?"

"By the Sen'Tal, of course. Who else? They run the

place, after all. Felis Bray'el and his kind are the whole show. Everybody bows down to them. Even zero-pointers like me."

"Does the Sen'Tal give you some sort of stipends?" I said.

"When I do work for them."

"What kind of work do you do?"

He shook his head. "Now why would I tell you that? Especially for a crappy guild piece."

Hadrien received the message loud and clear. He ripped out another coin and tossed it to this snide little arsehole. "What kind of work do you do?"

"Theoretical analysis of interdimensional amplitude," he answered.

Hadrien just stared at him without understanding. I, on the other hand, realized immediately. "The Waki'el are working on some scientific application of zero-point gravity," I murmured.

"They've got me writing out formulae by hand, using old-fashioned graphite pencils," Ross answered. "I know it sounds strange. It would be much easier to do it by computer, but they shun the things. They like to work with real flesh-and-blood beings." He shrugged. "I think they are simply intellectually curious. They wonder about the afterlife, too, now that they've been introduced to the existence of the creation force. Their god, Un-ashal, is a vindictive sort. I suppose it's how they justify their short life spans."

"Have you ever seen evidence of any significant higher technology?" Hadrien asked.

"A few times. Don't make the mistake about gener-alizing the Waki'el according to this city. They've got their technological complexes. They just don't show them off in this dung heap of a city."

"You would think that this place would be a showcase for the Waki'el," I said.

"The Waki'el aren't concerned about impressing anybody. Nald'eken is kept this way for a reason."

"And that would be?"

"That would be to serve as a reminder. They nearly lost everything when they were invaded. They want this city to represent the struggles they've had with outsiders." Ross stopped, rubbed his right eye, and added, "Besides, this shit hole makes a good tourist trap. People come here because they've heard how rustic it is."

As if on cue, the other Waki'el female slid from her place inside the door to join her companion, who was already getting cozy with my partner. The moment she did, I nearly lost my teeth. In the light provided by the moons I noticed the jagged pattern running up her right arm. I reached out to her, but when I touched her shoulder, she hissed and snarled at me.

I took a step away, and the altercation gave Hadrien the time to disengage from their lurid embraces. "What is it, Philipa?"

"She has the tattoo," I said.

Hadrien grabbed the Waki'el's arm roughly, swinging her about so he could get a better look in the firelight cast off by the brazier. "Where did you get this marking?"

She played dumb, so he turned his attention toward Ross without releasing the female. "Where?" he barked.

The balloon head jabbered to her, and she spat back. Turning slightly in his chair, he took a minute to study Hadrien. Then, as though he'd made some grand decision, he spoke in a grave tone. "She was warned never to speak of it. She refuses to explain further."

17

Ross dismissed us, claiming that he'd given more than two guilders' worth of info, and unless he saw more stash, his girlies were done, too. We walked off, leaving the balloon head to his own sordid deeds.

Hadrien wiped at his neck with his sleeve and screwed up his face in displeasure. "I think I'm going to puke."

"I was beginning to worry that you'd taken a bad turn with that rock to your bread box. I thought you might actually be enjoying their wicked advances."

He ignored my comment. "Do you think we can bull our way in to see Dumaka Lant?"

"Since you are a generally pissed-off person, I don't see why you couldn't push a little attitude and get us inside."

He grinned and then shivered as he swiped his sleeve across his neck again. I glanced away, fighting down a moment of desire by telling myself I was clinically dead to emotions. Besides, it was neither the time nor the place for indulging in such whims. According to my logos, I had days to prepare myself for a close-proximity relationship with Hadrien. But the fact that assailed me was more than simple: I didn't know how to get ready for an intimate relationship. I'd let that go the same time Eric had passed away.

We finally reached the temple and stood at the bottom of the deep tier of steps that were decorated with regularly set torches. The stairs led to a plain, windowless building plopped atop the ziggurat. It was brightened by a small bonfire and the pearly orange color of the three moons rising over it.

The temple was a busy place, and the steps were crowded with Waki'el as well as other aliens. We worked our way through the havoc, avoiding spiny reproaches from natives who obviously thought my presence was an irritant to their god.

When we reached the pyramid's apex, I wheezed like an old mule. Hadrien stopped to stare at me with an intense expression that asked the question without voicing it.

"I'm okay," I whispered. "The air—it's dusty and hard to breathe."

"It's a trifle richer in composition than that of Earth, too. Do you need to rest?"

I took a big swig of tainted air and tasted something sour when I did. "No, let's get this interview over before we're suffocated by this foul atmosphere."

We strolled into the building, finding it as ugly as the rest of the city. Square columns made of brown stone blocks rose at odd intervals, supporting a soaring ceiling that had been painted with garish colors and molded with pieces of bright glass. The heavy aura of sweet incense added weight to the already oppressive tone. The only light came from burning torches perched in clay pots that reminded me of umbrella stands. A large dangling mobile cast in thin sheets of bronze-colored metal turned slowly on a golden line suspended from a sizable timber bisecting the roof. Several Waki'el gathered around this floating piece of art, each person pitched forward in a posture of prayer.

This did not mean that we were left unnoticed. No more than a minute had passed before a large Waki'el male approached us, pointing at me and hissing his discontent. "She is not allowed inside the Sen'Tal temple. She must leave!" He stomped up to me and used the end of his finger to poke me in the chest, with enough force to push me into Hadrien.

"Hey, you moldy son of a bitch!" I barked. "Get your filthy fingernails off of me."

"You must leave!" Again, he emphasized himself by pushing at me until both Hadrien and I took steps backward.

I am normally a mellow pearl, a real love-and-kisses sort of person, not prone to doing another injury, but I can honestly say I don't like to be provoked into a fight. When that happens I turn into a prancer. It was no different with this current offense. Instead of obliging this foolish alien, I grabbed his forefinger and pinky with both my hands. I snarled, twisting his paw around until I heard a sharp snap.

Who knew a Waki'el could bellow so loud? The fellow let out a shriek that puckered my eardrums before he sank to the floor, blubbering and wailing.

Temple visitors turned their scrutiny on us, deadly silent amid the screams coming from the injured. I felt indignant but knew it wasn't the time or the place to express my displeasure at being considered a female pariah, so I let Hadrien drag me out the front entrance.

"I have to admire you," he said. "But that's going to get us in trouble."

I was about to blow him a story on how much I disliked being touched by strangers. Unfortunately, I was cut short when a large Waki'el female emerged from the temple to stand before us.

As the species goes, she was a real stunner. The low

orange light picked up the glitter of her hide, the sleek-
ness of her form, and the sparkling gems woven into her
black tresses. From my vantage point, I saw the delicate
design of luminescent tattooing flowing across her bare
breasts and along her sternum ridges. She wore a netting
of golden beads across the opening to her heart.

"You are from the Earth delegation ship," she said.

"That's right," I answered.

"Someone should have informed you that human females are considered too powerful to enter a Sen'Tal
temple. You disrupt the energy field surrounding this
place of worship. The Sen'Tal has forbidden your kind
to enter for this reason."

"What kind of energy do I disrupt?"

"You carry a piece of creation within you. That makes
you dangerous, and it displeases Mankor'a, our god of
the sky."

I glanced at Hadrien. "Do you know what she's talking about?"

He shook his head and then faced her. "We didn't
mean to offend. We're just trying to get an interview
with Dumaka Lant."

"I know. The whole city knows who you are."

"Well, just who are you?" I demanded.

"My name is Premian Ti'ha." She paused, took a
quick look-see over her shoulder. Then, lowering her
voice, she added: "Dumaka Lant will see you tonight in
private. Not here at the temple."

"Why not now?" Hadrien asked.

"It wouldn't be wise for him to be seen in proximity
of a human female. He'll meet you in the palmpiset in
three of your Earth hours." Premian Ti'ha turned on her
heel and started to march off, but Hadrien stopped her.

"Where is this palmpiset?"

"Ask your friend Yana. He knows." With that, she
smiled and walked away through the crowded plaza.

18

That our movements were being intensely mon-itored was knowledge that brought home some nasty memories. When Eric worked on Theo's secret projects, I had this same feeling of being surveilled. It made me check behind us, around us, and over us, expecting any moment to be swept up by the Waki'el peacekeepers. There was nothing we could do but go back to Yana and ask for directions to the palmpiset. The moment he found out we were going to meet with Dumaka Lant, he escorted us himself. But try as we might, we couldn't get him to spill the oats about who was keeping their mince pies focused on us.

He herded us through his hovel to an exit that led to a dark, dusty, smelly alley. We turned down a lonely back street where only a few braziers smoldered by the door stoops. The glow from hearth fires spilled through thick glass windows casting shafts of light at odd angles to the shadows created by the moons.

After several hundred meters, the road intersected. We swerved right, descending a short incline until we came to a neatly trimmed park of black sand. Granite monoliths stabbed upward through this volcanic earth and held the enormous weight of carved capstones. It would have been a Druid's delight, now that Stonehenge was a misty memory, washed off the Salisbury Plain when the tidal wave came through.

I stopped within the circle of stones and studied the sparkling veins of silver running through the rock. Perhaps it was just my Neptunian nature influencing my imagination, but I was sure this place was built at the headwaters of an energy vortex. I could feel it rise through my feet and singe my bums on the way toward my heart.

I dashed a look toward Hadrien, wondering if he sensed a change in the atmosphere. He moved purposefully behind Yana, yet from his furtive glances, I could tell he was more concerned with our getting mugged.

I should have been more bothered about our safety, too. In the next instant, I started laying myself out with the old Hobson's choice—you know, that little bit of a nagging voice that buggers you into submission? Arif was an exotic world, but I needed to remember that I was human and not here on holiday.

"What is this place?" Hadrien whispered.

"It's a Sen'Tal prayer circle," Yana answered. He padded on without further explanation, halting when he came to the center of the park. Here he pointed to a hole in the ground covered by a heavy door made of dark, polished wood. "This is the central palmpiset. You should wait for Dumaka Lant inside. It's where he will come to meet with you. Would you like me to remain here to signal you of his coming?" Before we could reply, he pushed his finger through a socket in the door and pulled it open. The second the trap was sprung, I heard the growling sound of a generator kick in nearby. Yana climbed onto a wooden ladder, disappearing under the lip of the hole. A moment later, lights came on inside the bunker. We followed the Waki'el into the pit and found a simple mud-brick room containing a small table and chair placed strategically beneath a hanging flourescent shop light. The lamp buzzed, and the light sputtered before settling into a harsh, uninterrupted glow.

"What's this place used for?" I asked.

"To record the palmpisets," Yana said. "The Sen'Tal come here for reflection and to gain spiritual enlightenment. They transcribe valuable information onto parchment, which is turned into a book of study. This is Dumaka Lant's private chamber."

"How do you know that?" Hadrien murmured.

"It's not a secret."

Hadrien took a turn around the room and then hit Yana with a hard look. "Let's have you stay right here with us," he said, a growl underlying his tone. "I'm not entirely comfortable with this situation."

Was it his astrological twelfth house of secrets and suspicions causing him to have a twitter of distrust, or was it too many years spent tracking down the slimy remains of criminals? Whatever it was, I suddenly felt glad that he relied upon it, because truth to tell, my markers were up, and I was fretting about a coming battle.

Yana was about to answer Hadrien, but a sound from upstairs drew him off to glance at the opening. A few seconds later, another Waki'el entered, climbing slowly into the chamber, coming to stand next to him. I felt Hadrien stiffen as Yana immediately kissed the dirt, groveling like his grovel meter had been set on high. The visiting Waki'el stopped short of stepping on his worshipper's fingertips, but he ignored Yana to study us with a hooded expression.

"I'm Dumaka Lant," he announced. Stepping by Yana without another thought, he sat heavily in the available chair and adjusted the lamp a little lower to the table. "What do you want?"

I studied him for a moment, figuring that he might

have been considered beautiful and powerful among his own kind. He definitely had an overbearing air about him. Brisk, to the point, and haughty—he could have been an Englishman. His attitude seemed to have no effect on Hadrien, who used his own brashness to make sure the conversation went his way. "We're here trying to thwart all diplomatic ties with Arif by entering temples and houses uninvited. We thought demanding to see the chief heart surgeon might piss off a few folks and get us noticed some more."

Dumaka Lant squinted at him, rubbed a finger across his top lip, and then smiled. "Ah, an attempt at humor. I might have missed it if I hadn't been paying such good attention." He fixed Hadrien with a dark gaze. "Your precious emperor has sent you to do this for him personally. The man has no morals and no respect for other cultures."

"That's quite true," Hadrien said. "Still, he's our leader, and we're sworn to obey him as you are sworn to obey Felis Bray'el. But judging from your superior attitude, I'd say that doesn't fit with you, either."

"Felis Bray'el is—how do you say on Earth—he is an ass."

I chuckled, forgetting for a second where I was. Were all supreme leaders filled to overflowing with the same kind of shit?

"We believe that a Waki'el was responsible for Prince Lundy's murder," Hadrien said. "I'm sure you've heard the news about that."

Dumaka Lant nodded. "Yes, I heard. Do you expect me to care?"

"No, not care. All we need is your help."

"I'm not sure I can give it."

Hadrien took another turn around the room, showing his back to the Waki'el, a deliberate action to provoke the priest. From what Yana had told us, it was considered bad form to turn away during a conversation. "We are also wondering if a Waki'el didn't have something to do with the death of Princess Belinda-Agnes."

"Belinda-Agnes was an abomination. She's better off dead." Dumaka Lant turned his neck as though it was gear-driven, and when he'd cranked it far enough around, he studied me. "You are an abomination, too."

They say the Brits are a stoic lot, not given to exercising their tempers. Well, I'm not one of them. I took a step toward the Waki'el, noticing how big he was but not letting this realization give me any problems.

"I'm tired of being called such a crude name," I said. "By calling me that, you label millions of human females. That is not diplomacy by any means. I demand an apology."

The alien remained unruffled. "To us, every human female is an abomination; you are no different. I have no reason to apologize. Any creature who carries a live fetus within its body is considered an abomination. Those species who have attacked us have been like you—mammals." He said the word with such vehemence, I thought he might spit his teeth out of his head.

"Humans have never attacked you," Hadrien said.

"If we let our guard down, you, too, will try."

"Why? There's nothing on this godforsaken world humans would want. It's a dying planet. You place too much importance on the glory of this ball of dirt."

Dumaka Lant stared at him but didn't answer. Hadrien stepped over to me. Touching my shoulder, he steered me a meter away from this large, impressive male.

Dumaka Lant ignored my partner the same way he ignored Yana and focused directly upon me. "Belinda-Agnes should not have been born. She was created only to serve your Earth scientists, and Felis Bray'el complied with your emperor's wishes to see if our species could mix."

"Well, you don't seem all that concerned about using biowaste scavenged from humans," I said.

"You are referring to the organs and tissues I use to reconstruct hearts? Well, your emperor had to make a deal for Belinda-Agnes and Mann Re. That was it."

"Not as we understand it. We hear that Prince Lundy made a deal with you to send heart parts in return for Waki'el honey."

"You are mistaken."

"You were going through Lundy," I said, adding a little weight to my sentence by dropping my voice an octave. "We know you were using Mick Morely and K'ton Koor as middlemen."

"You are mistaken."

"We got the confessions, old man," Hadrien said. "You can't wiggle on this one."

Dumaka Lant scowled. "I told you that I didn't have any deal with Prince Lundy. All these affairs were taken care of through Felis Bray'el's house. I receive the tissues from a courier sent through him. I don't know where the organs come from, and I don't care."

I switched the subject. "Then tell us about Mann Re and the relationship she had to her daughter."

"I don't know what relationship she had. All I know is that Mann Re has suffered greatly for the cause of this Arif-Earth alliance. Her own people spurn her, and now that her daughter is dead, she has no one who will come forward in her behalf except for humans."

"Are you saying she has no power or influence?"

"I did not say that. Stop putting words into my mouth."

"What kind of power does she have?"

"She has her own alliances and her brother has given her charge over his household. That would put many people at her command if Felis Bray'el approves her actions." He leaned forward in the chair. "That doesn't mean he gives his approval often."

Dumaka Lant chuckled and sat back, feathering his

finger across his cheek. "What else do you want to know?"

"How long have you been working with balloon heads?" Hadrien asked.

"A long while. We accepted them when their own human counterparts refused to have anything to do with them." He stopped, took a long pull of air, and then spewed out more condemnation. "I don't understand why humans create only to destroy. It's not like zero-point children are not of the same flesh and blood. We wouldn't do that on Waki'el."

"No, instead you have a caste system designed to keep most of the population in a submissive state," I said.

"That is life on Arif. We don't deny they are Waki'el, though."

"Tell us what kinds of things our zero-point buddies have been helping you with," Hadrien demanded.

"Our zero-point friends have helped us to understand the use of the creation energy. We've always known it exists; we just didn't know how to apply it."

"How do you apply it?"

Dumaka Lant dropped his hands and motioned with his chin. "Many ways. Mostly we're trying to discover a way to save this world."

"It can't be done unless you recharge your sun," I said.

He smiled. "Maybe we're planning to do that. Whatever the solution, it's not my area of expertise."

"We were told you became very powerful because you invented a machine that has changed the fabric of society," I said. "What did you invent?"

The alien stood. "Nothing that would have any bearing on your investigation."

I took a step to intercept him as he headed for the ladder. "How about humoring the abomination?"

Dumaka Lant stopped, placed his hands on his hips, and then sighed. "If you must know, I invented a pacemaker for the human transplanted heart," he said. "What I do saves lives. It doesn't take them."

Hadrien reached into his pocket and fished out the small blue stone that had killed Lundy. He flipped it to Dumaka Lant. "This is our murder weapon."

The Waki'el studied it and then handed it back to Hadrien. "That's Acu-Sen'Tal from the mark upon it. Talk to Zebrim Hast." Turning, he mounted the first rung of the ladder before pausing to consider us. "It's a well-known fact that Zebrim Hast is Mann Re's only friend. Their alliance is one of forgiveness and brotherhood."

19

We left our meeting with Dumaka Lant not much wiser than we came in. Hadrien complained about a headache, so we called it a night and returned to the *Kourey*, where we visited Dr. Omar to see what his huge eyes could see.

I sat in a hard, uncomfortable plastic chair in the examining room while the Corrigadaire used his alien talents to detect any serious injury with Hadrien. Omar studied his bumped head from all angles, relying on the Corrigadaire hypersensitivity to photons to show him any problems. He finally grunted. Gazing past the doctor, I looked at Hadrien, whose expression scrunched into a worried frown.

"Am I going to live?" he asked.

"A headache is normal after having been beaned by a rock," Omar answered. "Yes, you will live. I see no evidence of brain dysfunction or cerebral swelling. You bled profusely because the capillaries in the scalp are numerous and close to the surface. It appears that the wound is already healing, but I'll suture it for you to guard against infection. I know how easily humans are prone to viral complications."

"And I imagine there are more than few on this world," I muttered.

Omar spun around, glanced at me, and then turned to march to his equipment cabinet. As he rifled around inside of it, he answered me. "There are many things on this world one should avoid. Asking the wrong people certain questions can do you more damage than a rock."

"Have we talked to the wrong people?"

"Dumaka Lant is dangerous."

"Now, how did you know we met with Dumaka Lant?"

He smiled, obviously pleased with himself. "I didn't. It was an educated guess. Did you ask him about the Waki'el female we found aboard ship?"

"No. He wasn't much for giving up the goods on anything. What do you know about him?"

"He's risen to power like your human compatriot, Waldemar Hoven. Do you know the one I mean?"

"No."

"He was one of the doctors who followed Adolf Hitler and who committed crimes against humanity by trying to create a superrace for Nazi Germany. He experimented on Jews and other captives of the Third Reich at the Buchenwald Concentration Camp."

"And you're saying that Dumaka Lant falls into the same category?" Hadrien said. "What kind of things have you heard about him?"

"He's not above experimenting on aliens. Apparently, he used the war to further his efforts, selecting POWs at random. His surgery always killed, but it was done in the name of survival."

"So that makes it right?"

"No. I'm not defending him. It's the way the Waki'el feel about it."

"How does butchering aliens promote survival?" I asked.

"Dumaka Lant is intrigued by the bilateral possibilities of species absorption."

Hadrien scowled. "What?"

"He believes he can increase the natural life span of the Waki'el people by using alien parts. I understand he has a program whereby he screens potential candidates—usually prisoners or those deemed too old to perpetuate the species."

"And do you think the Earthers helped him find the suitable material for his research?" I asked.

"Well, of course. The emperor has designs on maintaining the status quo. What better way to do it than by creating a circumstance of debt with another government?" Omar stepped from the cabinet and brandished a small laser suture. Flicking it on with his thumb claw, he aimed it toward Hadrien's head. "Sit still, please. Wouldn't want to suture your eyelid shut by mistake." He paused and smiled, obviously pleased with his little try at medical humor.

I didn't distract him by replying. It wasn't so much because I didn't want him wanking Hadrien but more because my brain had swerved into overdrive like a Rolls-Royce driven by a spoiled princess. My thoughts flew back into the past and covered old ground where Eric and his secret projects were concerned. Had my husband's claim that humans shared a genetic heritage with another species separated by thousands of light-years given the emperor food for thought? Had he instituted some relationship with the Waki'el that involved a shared genetic permutation? Could these aliens be related to us in the ways that made it important? Sitting there watching the Corrigadaire glue up Hadrien's cut, I found myself trying to catalog the differences in physiology between Waki'el and human species. The differences glared at me, and the similarities frightened me.

I came around when Omar finished ministering to Hadrien. The suture looked good from where I sat. He probably wouldn't even have a scar to embellish with stories of daring adventure.

"Have you heard the news?" Omar asked as he turned off the laser unit.

"What news?" I answered.

"Cornelius Paul met with Felis Bray'el."

"Felis is the head of the Sen'Tal. Who else would he have met with?"

"Felis is Mann Re's brother by the same father."

Hadrien climbed off the table. "So?"

"So, Paul presented him with an imperial decree naming Mann Re's son, Ji'am, a sole and legal heir to all properties once owned by Prince Lundy. He then announced that Mann Re's daughter, Ne'el Zara, heir to all properties once owned by Princess Belinda-Agnes."

"Why?" I asked.

"Who knows? Perhaps Theo feels guilty. I understand that is a common human affliction. The death of Belinda-Agnes has caused quite a stir among the aristocracy." He paused, eyeballed me, and added: "And then again, he might not feel guilt. It might be some contractual matter that he needed to honor. That seems more appropriate for the emperor."

"By aristocracy, I'm assuming you're talking about the Basira and Tus castes."

"Who else?"

"There was to be a new alliance treaty signed," Hadrien said. "At least, that's what I heard before we left Earth."

"There is something that's not so well known," Omar said quietly. "I doubt that the executioner will tell you about it."

I rose and stepping close to the two, I murmured, "What secrets are you privy to, Dr. Omar?"

He blinked, an action that seemed to take longer than

a second. "Mann Re was brought aboard the *Kourey*. When we lift off, she's going back to Earth with us."

"Well, is that uncommon? She's made many trips to Earth, so we understand."

"Mann Re was brought to me yesterday for a physical exam to determine whether she is fit enough to undergo another pregnancy."

"So Theo wants more children," Hadrien said. "From what we understand, Mann Re is a social outcast for her association with Earth people. Don't you know that human females are abominations and the mother of a dead half-breed princess is no better? Why should she be opposed to having another child?"

"Because Mann Re has her own measure of power on this planet. Rather than being an outcast, she is feared. Don't believe everything these people tell you."

"Felis Bray'el isn't giving her a chance to change her mind," I said.

"It's not that. It's more like he's getting her out of the way."

"Out of the way of what?"

Omar shook his head, and it was a ponderous movement. "I don't know, but this action will condemn her to death if Theo makes her pregnant."

"Why?" I asked, my voice squeaking on its own.

Omar turned his tin lids onto my partner, studied him, and then shook his head. "Mann Re is forty-two Earth standard years old. That's too old to have more offspring. She's near the end of her life cycle. If she hatches another child, it will kill her."

20

The next night, Hadrien decided we needed to wet our whistles, and so we sought out a back-street tavern that catered to the alien tourists. The rub-a-dub was a rustic place of cold, gray stone and peeling metal beams supporting a tin roof. A fireplace cranked out heat and smoke, and a variety of sharp smells laced the thick air. It was crowded with folks, many of whom were human. As we walked inside, I heard the distinctive accent of an East End boy, so we ordered a couple of cups of tea and invited ourselves to his table. His name was John Trainer, and he sat there with three other people: his wife, Mary, and her brother and sister-in-law, Randal and Nina. They were all approaching seniors age, and all looked quite disgusted by the Waki'el accommodations.

"First time here?" I asked pleasantly.

"Yeah," John said. "It will be the last, too."

"It's the travel brochures," Mary said, patting at a white curl. "Right bit of fraud there, I'd say."

"Wait until I get me 'ands on that travel agent what

booked us," John added. "I'll tear his head off and shove it up his Khyber Pass."

I smiled and glanced at Hadrien. "Translation needed?"

He grinned. "Nope."

"I was really expecting more than this," Nina piped up.

"Well, you wanted a goddamned frontier experience," Randal barked. "You got one—for a whole friggin' week. Let's just hope we don't get killed before the ship leaves."

John was more interested in us and so stopped complaining long enough to demand our life stories. "What are you doing on this smoky dust ball?"

"We're here looking for the murderer of Prince Lundy," I said.

It gathered everyone's attention, so we huddled about the crooked metal table to see what the tourists knew.

"I heard Theo sent an astrologer to work on the case," John said. "That would be you?"

"Aye. It's me."

He leaned close and spoke in a haughty tone. "I don't believe in any of that bunk. It's all wank, as far as I'm concerned."

"Pish," Mary hissed. "Don't mind him none. He's a silly fig when it comes to science. Now, *I* believe in the interplanetudes."

"Crackie, Mar, you believe in ghosts, too," John snapped. "That proves a whole hell of a lot."

"Well, obviously the emperor thinks enough of it to send this here girl."

"Theo thinks he's friggin Charlemagne."

John's statement drew a chuckle from Hadrien, who tried to cover it by sipping at his mug of tea.

"You'd be the hard-boiled detective," Randal said, eying my partner with a squint.

"That's right."

Randal took each person in with a moment of scrutiny before he said in a conspiratorial tone, "Have you ever seen so many bobbies in one place, going about their trade like it weren't nothing?"

Bobbies was short for Bob Hope which rhymed with dope. I didn't need to translate for Hadrien. He understood immediately. "Have you met many drug sellers since you've been here?"

"Have we? We've been here a solid four hours. We must have run off six of the pissers. All female."

Nina popped into the conversation with a voice that cooed like a pigeon. "Did you notice that they think human females are buggers? Not a nice thing to have to deal with when one is on vacation."

I nodded at her observation but pushed down the same dusty road as Hadrien. "What kind of dope were these females pushing?"

"I don't know," John said. "Some alien shit. Said it was as sweet as honey."

"Where did you meet the females?"

"They were hanging around that pyramid they got here. Look in any shadow, and you'll find one."

"They don't look none too healthy, either," Mary added.

"How do you know that?"

"I read somewheres that when their hide changes from bright blue to dusty blue, they aren't fit."

"More crap," John grumbled.

I pegged Hadrien with an idea. "Milking these cows might do damage to their systems."

"Shorten their life spans, perhaps?"

"It just might. In which case, someone is openly giving them permission to sell out."

"Maybe someone is forcing them."

"Well, someone is definitely making money on them," Randal said flatly. "They want two ponies for that stuff.

It'd probably kill a human, but I did see that the Corries like it."

"Corries?"

"Yeah," Mary answered. "They're tight with these blokes. They slurp up that honey shit even before they pay the bill."

"It's as bad as horse, if you know what I mean," Nina said. "Me nephew was addicted to heroin, and it killed him, it did. This honey stuff seems a lot more powerful. At least to humans. I'll betcha it drives 'em to commit thievery and rape. That kind of stuff always does."

Hadrien blew out a hard breath and sat back in his chair. "How would you like to go on a little adventure, John?"

"Depends on what you have in mind."

"We need someone to set up a meet for us. It seems that the pushers are avoiding us. We could use a tourist as a go-between."

"Well, hell, if he don't want to do it, I will," Randal piped up.

"You will do no such thing, you old goat," Nina barked.

Randal backed down, his enthusiasm smoldering into smoky anger. I could see immediately who wore the trousers in that household.

John played hard to get. "You're doing this to find Prince Lundy's killer. I don't give a pence for the imperial family. They should all go rotters as far as I care."

"What about helping us?" Hadrien said. "If we don't bring in a warm body, Theo will punish us."

"How so?"

"Let's just say it's a life-and-death situation for us, too."

"Crackie," he muttered. "Can't have that. We poor blokes have to stay together." He glanced at Randal. "Stop being a pansy and letting the duchess there tell you how to live. Or die."

Hadrien came up with a quick solution. "Randal, why don't you stay behind with the ladies? I don't think they should be left alone without a male escort."

"Listen to him, Randy," Nina said.

John glanced at Mary. "All right by you, me treacle tart?"

She patted his hand. "Go help 'em. They're working stiffs like we were."

John slugged off his drink and rose, waving us into action. "Follow me."

We finished our tea with a couple of slurps and slid out behind the old guy. He walked with a limp, but he still managed to barrel down the street, bumping through the crowds of pedestrians until he led us around the corner and up the hill to the base of the ziggurat. Barging into a clandestine meeting in the shadows, John shooed off a prospective honey buyer. The Waki'el female growled something in her guttural language, but John remained the dominant male. "I got you a bloke and lass who would like to sample your product. They'll give you extra wonga for information, too."

The female stopped her chattering to glare at us. Her features were set in a hard sneer. Yet, after a moment, she smiled pleasantly. We joined them in the shadows, and the moment we did, John made his good-byes, striding away down the boulevard before we had a chance to thank him. Hadrien didn't waste a moment to dally with the female.

"We'd like a sample of your best honey," he said.

"It costs one hundred Earth sterling for one gram," she said.

Hadrien slowly rifled through his pocket, but he never took his attention off of her. "Where does it come from?"

She cackled. "From me. Where else?"

"Do you work alone?"

She ignored his question until he had a sterling note in his hand. "I belong to the sisterhood."

Hadrien flicked the money at her. "What's the sisterhood?"

The female followed the paper with her eyes. "It's a group of N'galia Waki'el." She made a grab for the money, but Hadrien was fast and crumpled the bill in his fist, making her pop more info before he'd give it up.

"Why N'galia Waki'el?" he asked. "Why not Tus or Basira?"

She laughed again. "You don't know much, do you?"

"That's why I'm asking."

The female studied him and then reached into her shoulder sack to produce a small, clear packet of golden liquid. "Do you want honey or not?"

"I want the honey, but I want some answers, too. For this kind of money, you owe me more than just a gram of junk."

She sighed impatiently and leaned against the wall of the ziggurat. "N'galia Waki'el are servants to the Basira and Tus. It's our duty."

"I would think you would be a prized commodity and not out here on the street hawking your wares like common dope pushers."

"We are prized for our juices. We are told to work, too. There are very many of us. I'm nothing unusual. There are those who can make the amber, though."

"Amber?" I said.

She glanced at me. "It is so refined in the system that the Basira males will kill each other to get it."

"Are there many amber makers?" I asked.

"No. Only a few."

"Are they N'galia by birth?"

"They are N'galia, but they are usually born into Basira clutches."

Hadrien grunted at that bit of news and fished in his

pocket for another paper note. "Does your sisterhood have a leader, official or unofficial?"

The female studied him before grabbing the money and throwing him the packet. "Yes, unofficial. She's the overseer of our shop."

With that, she started down the street, pausing only long enough to wave at us to follow.

21

The honey seller moved as quickly as John had, weaving through the people who flooded the city. There were so many different aliens here that it looked like Mardi Gras on Fat Tuesday. I counted Corries, Sumereks, Pheronians, Gabshali, and humans, all celebrating something that we didn't know about.

"Is it like this all the time?" I asked, catching up with our guide.

"Yes. Tourist trade is big here. People like the city. We offer pleasures to aliens."

"Such as honey."

"That, and more. It's degrading to N'galia, but we understand the need to entertain tourists."

"What need?"

She didn't answer. Instead, she loped off, and I found myself hard-pressed to keep up the pace with the ragged air buggering my every breath. By the time the female halted before a plain stone house with a thatched roof, I thought my lungs might explode and my heart might burst through my sternum. I paused before taking the stone steps up to the door, sure I couldn't climb the short riser. Hadrien saw my difficulty and boldly slid his arm about my waist. I tried to slip free, but I wasn't going anywhere, bound as I was by the lack of breathable atmosphere.

Hadrien didn't ask after my health. He literally picked me off the ground and swung me up the steps. Once inside the house, we were greeted by a cool interior lit by a hundred white wax candles. A naked female Waki'el, who looked as old as the proverbial hills, sat on a mass of floor pillows, admiring some kind of parchment book. She glanced up at the interruption and frowned until the dope pusher knelt before her and presented the paper money.

"These humans have need to see you, Rash'nal," she said. "They have paid well for the interview."

Rash'nal regarded us with a suspicious expression, and when she did, I was reminded of the evil eye my grandmother professed to use on her enemies. It was strikingly similar, and I shivered. My movement made Hadrien drop his arm from my waist. He gave me a quick once-over, decided I was fit enough, and turned his attention toward the Waki'el females.

Rash'nal took the money, crinkling it between her long fingers. She dismissed the honey seller with a wave of her hand and invited us to her counsel by pointing to a couple of floor pillows situated next to her. We did as she silently commanded and watched while she carefully folded the book and tied it with a string. Then, picking up the volume, she paused to kiss it before setting it onto a low table beside her. Turning a fierce stare upon us, she spoke. "What do you want?"

I stepped into the conversation ahead of Hadrien, my voice husky from a dry throat. "We're here trying to find the killer of Earth Imperial Prince Lundy and the killer of Princess Belinda-Agnes."

"I have seen your Prince Lundy before."

"Where? Here?"

She shook her head. "No, of course not. I'm N'galia. I'm not permitted to meet with the royal caste. Your Prince Lundy has been to our world many times. He was always in search of amber." Rash'nal smiled. "Males in most species are—once they taste it."

"How do you know Lundy was searching for amber?" Hadrien asked.

"Because Mann Re sent her servant to me to fetch what I had to offer."

"You're a N'galia born to a Basira clutch?" I said.

"Yes, I am. Does that surprise you?"

"No. The fact that Mann Re came to you does. We understand the circumstances of her birth are the same as yours. That would make her full of amber, too."

"Age will make you produce less and less until it stops. Amber is only available during the peak years of egg production. She's near the end of her life cycle and most certainly at the end of her birthing capabilities."

Hadrien adjusted his position on the pillow. His movement made me glance in his direction. I could have sworn to the queen of England that he was suffering discomfort at this conversation about female biological issues. I took charge of the interview.

"Did you give the servant what she requested?"

"For many months," Rash'nal answered.

"All of this was destined for Prince Lundy?"

"No, not all. I understand Mann Re needed it for the creation children."

"Creation children? Are you talking about zero-pointers?"

"Yes."

"Were they using the amber?"

"No. They were experimenting with it, trying to synthesize the compound."

"Were they successful?"

"I don't know. Mann Re stopped requesting it through me. Perhaps she had another source, or her balloon heads figured out the problem. It was none of my concern. I was just glad she left me alone. My life has been a tragic sorrow because of her."

"How so?"

Rash'nal rubbed her hand across her lips before answering. "Mann Re's lover was given permission by Felis Bray'el to experiment on me. All in the name of Waki'el survival, so he said."

"Who was Mann Re's lover?" Hadrien demanded.

"Dumaka Lant. He's a butcher. He proved it on me. When I die, I'll be a ghost, unable to return to the etheric dimension, because of him."

"What did he do?" I asked, wholly aware that my voice cracked with the question.

Instead of replying, Rash'nal rose and turned slowly, showing us her back. A long, jagged scar paralleled her spine on the right side. After we'd had a good peek, she spun around and sat down again. "My heart failed several years ago due to the constant milking of my pouches. This substance keeps our health in balance. Without it, we are prone to many types of illnesses and weaknesses. Dumaka Lant knew I was one of the few who gave up the amber, and so he replaced my heart to keep me alive."

"What's so bad about that?" Hadrien said. "He saved your life."

She puckered her lips and then nodded. "It saved my life. Or maybe I should say he saved *this* life. But what about my other ones?"

"What exactly are you saying?" I demanded.

"When he transplanted my heart, he changed the exchange of creation energy within me. It's now so confused that it can't connect with my manifestational source in the next dimension. I've been cut off from an afterlife."

22

Rash'nal ordered one of her girls to take us to see a Waki'el who had at one time worked with Dumaka Lant. Her name was Emia, and she lived in a mud-brick hovel that was as gloomy as every shack we'd been inside so far.

Emia was young, if her skin shade was an indicator. She could have been attractive, too, but of that I wasn't certain. There was one thing for certain: Beneath the linen shift she wore, there was a person who hated the universe.

The only reason she spoke with us had to do not with finding a killer but with her own reputation.

She steered us to a torn love seat. After we were marginally comfortable, she paraded before us, pacing from one side of the smoky, dark room to the other. "I used to have power, but Dumaka Lant changed all that."

"Are you Tus or Basira?" I asked.

"I'm Tus," she answered. "And I was wronged by a N'galia. It wouldn't have happened before the war. N'galia knew when to keep their places. Everything has changed since we fought off the invaders."

"Why has it changed?"

"The Sen'Tal has changed. It makes the rules and it breaks them. The priests nowadays do not believe in the permanence of the life force. They think they can manipulate the creation energy and not upset the balance of things. They are wrong, and they've condemned many of us to dying in horrible circumstances."

"How so?" Hadrien asked. "Does it have something to do with zero-point gravity?"

"Zero-point gravity. That's an Earther term. It makes no sense, this terminology."

"Then tell us how Waki'el perceive it," I said.

She smiled, obviously delighted to have a female sparring partner. "You introduced yourself as an astrologer. You believe that the vibration inherent in life comes from within the creation force. Correct?"

"Yes. We refer to it as the next dimension. A causal plane of pure thought that uses zero-point gravity to propel these impressions into the denser dimension of corporeality."

"We believe in an afterlife that is similar. We've used this power for centuries." Emia gently touched her chest. "We understand that this force keeps our hearts beating. When it stops, so do we."

"The same thing happens for us," I said.

"But not in the same way. You think of this energy as being contained by your physical body. How do you say: 'carting the soul around'?"

"And sometimes it gets damned heavy," Hadrien muttered.

Emia laughed. "Well, we don't have that problem. We are light, light, light. No heavy souls."

"Why is that?" I asked.

"Because we are at the manifestation side of the material equation. We are in constant contact with the dimension of pure thought because the vibration continually flows to us through the canal of creation energy. There are no discarnates in our plane of death. Our souls blend back into the one force, the single whole from which we are extended."

This Waki'el said nothing that hadn't already been said by humans in one form or the other. "So, what's the problem? What has Dumaka Lant done?"

Emia smacked her lips while studying me. She then carefully adjusted her shift, fluffing the collar with the tips of her fingers. "Dumaka Lant is not content to let the Waki'el species die a natural death. He follows a cause, but who leads the cause, I cannot say."

"What do you mean when you say Dumaka Lant is not content to let the Waki'el species die a natural death?" Hadrien said.

She pointed to the ceiling. "A people should not outlive its sun. That's far too long, at least in this dimension." Emia paused to sit down heavily in a straight-backed chair. "We should be reabsorbed into the creation energy before that happens. In fact, the process has already started. There has been a drastic reduction in Waki'el births. The eggs have all been cracked upon delivery. This signals the beginning of the end as far as many of us are concerned. But Dumaka Lant thinks he can cheat the belligerence of the universe. He's a stupid creature who has convinced other stupid creatures. Unfortunately, those who ally with him are in positions of power."

"Such as Felis Bray'el?" Hadrien said.

"Such as he. And that abomination he calls a clutch sister."

"Mann Re."

"Yes. She has been behind much of this shift in Waki'el attitude."

"We were under the impression that she does as she is told. That she has no real power."

"She has as much as Felis Bray'el has granted her, which is considerable. Mann Re is feared by N'galia."

"Why?"

"She is one of the treasures."

"Pardon?"

"Treasures. She is N'galia born into a Basira family. It happens on occasion but is rare for one to be birthed into the most affluent house on Arif. I don't believe I've heard of it happening before."

I pulled the interview back a wee bit. "What is Dumaka Lant trying to do that will cheat the universe?"

Emia stood up again and paced the area before us. "When a Waki'el is born into the material realm, the creation vibration takes on a particular energy signature. It is what brings on the individual tone."

"The individual tone?"

"Yes. We resonate at a certain frequency. We have a particular tone or wavelength on which our energy resides. Dumaka Lant has challenged this precept."

"How?"

"By using human hearts," she growled. "By cutting into a Waki'el and replacing old, worn-out parts. When he changes parts, he corrupts the energy signature. The creation flow coming into us is segmented and weak."

"You sound like you've seen him do it."

She stopped pacing to stare at me. "I was once a temple assistant. I tended to his every need, made him comfortable so that he might devote his time to unraveling the mysteries of life. He experimented on aliens, and when he was sure they could be of no more use, he started working on Waki'el."

"Are you saying that Waki'el who receive new heart parts are being forced into it?" Hadrien said.

"Some. The newer people born after the war don't ascribe to the old ways. They foolishly believe the drivel dished to them by the Sen'Tal."

"What about the Acu-Sen'Tal?" I asked.

She shrugged. "Ineffective. N'galia always are."

Hadrien leaned forward. His arm brushed my thigh

when he did. "Emia, can you tell us about the concept known as an affair of the heart?"

"It is a taboo in this society to speak of it, but since I no longer care about such things, I can tell you this: It is an immolation of spirit, and it can be done in many ways. Dumaka Lant's tinkering with the natural order of things can be considered an affair of the heart."

23

When we finally returned to the Kourey, Hadrien took two showers. I could hear him through the flimsy hatch cursing the trickling flow of water—calling it British shit. It made me smile. The day Theo's ancestor took over the world had always been a sore spot with the Americans. They once more became a colony of the crown, obedient only when they were given the responsibility to maintain the peace across Sol System.

I sat down before my charts and logos, but I just wasn't interested. At that moment, I didn't give two tits on a boar hog about finding Lundy's killer. My thoughts about Eric kept whipping me until my brain was bloody from the abuse.

His work with zero-point gravity had taken him into parts of the universe that echoed the beliefs of the Waki'el. He was certain about the contiguous flow of energy throughout the dimensions. For him, what happened in one causal plane rippled through each of the planes, including those based in pure vibration and those that were denser and filled with corporeal life. For all we knew about zero-point gravity, it was still a mystery—an application of a theory that boggled the human mind. It had not changed from an exploration of something created from nothing.

"Are you somewhere out in the universe?"

Hadrien's voice floated into my awareness, drawing me back into the room. "I beg your pardon, governor?"

He grinned. "Vacant stare, drool dripping from the corner of the mouth, slow breathing, the occasional grunt. Looks and sounds like a hyperspace trip to another world."

I dabbed at the corners of my lips. "I am not drooling."

He chuckled. "But you were doing the other things. Care to fill me in?" He sat on the couch to study me.

When I didn't respond, he filled in the information himself, and quite well, I might add. "Let's see. You've given the night over to your grief. All this talk about energy and death has tricked you up. You're caught staring at the inside of your belly button without a clue as to how you got there."

"I have a feeling that what goes around comes around."

"What's that supposed to mean?"

I rose from the table and sat down beside him, careful not to touch him in any way. The last thing I wanted to do was provoke his testosterone. "I made a vow that I would find out who killed Eric. I think that vow is coming home. What is put into the world circles back until it bites you in the arse. I think in this case, I might be the revenge on a round rosie of political murder."

He lost any smile he might have had. "What do you think happened?"

"I think Eric got off on some high-horse principle and threatened to undo Theo. I knew it then, and I know it now. The energetic forces of manifestation will use synchronicity to balance the scales."

"And you see synchronicity in these events?"

"Yes, I do. Eric espoused the same things that the old Waki'el female did."

"You're kidding? It doesn't even make any sense."

"Yes, it does. Actually, what she's talking about is a form of slow light."

Hadrien frowned, and for a second I worried that I might outmatch his scientific understanding and in doing so, drive him away. Away from what was the question that begged asking but, of course, I avoided it. "Slow light is an old concept discovered at the end of the twentieth century. Normally, light moves through space at three hundred million meters per second, but scientists managed to slow down this same pulse of light to only seventeen meters per second. Sound routinely travels at three hundred meters per second through an oxygen atmosphere."

"So the light moved slower than the speed of sound," Hadrien said.

"That's right."

"How'd they do it?"

"They used sodium atoms cooled to fifty-billionths of a degree above absolute zero. That forms a cloud known as a Bose-Einstein condensate. The millions of atoms acted as if they were a single atom, and the light pulse slowed down because it exchanged energy with the sodium atoms present in the cloud. Once the light escaped the cloud, the normal frequency was restored, and the photons moved at their regular rate of speed."

Hadrien pulled a deep breath that flared his nostrils. "All right, what does that have to do with what the Waki'el was talking about?"

"We generally regard the creation energy as composed of photons. Eric believed that when the vibration passes through the denser planes, it's slowed as though it were passed through a filter. It's also segmented and, spread within the field it passes through, it continually exchanges energy. In this way, light fills up the dimension, corraled as it is by the limitations of the causal plane. Here, in our dimension, it manifests in corporeality or denser material. In another dimension, it could be simply a single vibrational quality known as thought."

"And the Waki'el believe they are conductors of light."

It was my turn to grin. "That's what it sounds like."

He thought about it a second more. "Actually, they would not only conduct light, but they would also serve as a conduit for the vibration."

"In that, we all are—human or Waki'el. Once the atoms in our heavier bodies stop exchanging energy with the photonic vibration of the creation energy, we die. The energy no longer feeds us. It's a well-known fact that energy doesn't dissipate. Because of this, our soul or vibrational quality must go somewhere. The interplanetudes suggests it returns to the source."

"How does it do that? By traveling along the same transmission route?"

"Perhaps. No one knows for sure. That theory has never been adequately proven." I sighed, almost afraid to voice my next idea. "Until a little while ago, I thought of it as a door swinging shut, as though we each encapsulated a small part of the creation energy, confining it until there was nothing left to confine. But what if we don't confine it at all? What if it flows through us and into other dimensions where it creates more patterns of life?"

He studied me for a moment, but his answer was interrupted by the hatch buzzer. "Come," he growled, twisting around on the sofa to see who entered.

It was Cornelius Paul, looking as imperious as Theo himself. "I have been ordered to inform you that another member of the imperial family has died under suspicious circumstances."

"Who?" I asked.

"Prince Marcus," he said.

That was a startling blow. Marcus was the fourth in line for the crown and a humanitarian from his head to his toes.

Paul wasn't finished with us yet. "The emperor wishes me to inform you that if you don't find the killer, there will be serious repercussions when you return home."

24

The next evening we were forced to hire a jitney bus to take us from the city into the countryside. It was a noisy, bumpy ride, powered by a diesel engine that pushed fumes into the cab of the conveyance. We huddled in the back corner of the taxi for over two hours staring at a dry, scrubby landscape and burnt-orange colors before arriving in the town of Kangla'il where we found Zebrim Hast, the leader of the Acu-Sen'Tal. He seemingly was home alone at his temple, a place that, while still primitive by Earth standards, was by and far more luxurious than any building we'd seen in Nald'eken.

Unlike the other temple, perched high atop the ziggurat, this cloister spread out in a fashion similar to the old abbeys and monasteries so popular in Earth's history. There were no smoking braziers here, no hanging mobiles of some strange god, no one screaming for me to leave. That, in itself, gave me cause to worry.

The temple was elegantly supported by pillars of white marble delicately veined with silver. Glancing down, I noticed the floor was tiled and shiny. It gave me the feeling that I had stepped inside of some kind of weird spaceship. There were no candles or torches illuminating this place; instead, optimum use had been made of recessed lighting. I listened but heard no hum of a distant generator. Electricity obviously buzzed through underground feeders.

"You'd think they'd put some windows around this rub-a-dub," I said.

"Waki'el don't seem overly impressed by fancy surroundings or wonderful vistas," Hadrien answered. He paused, watching as a Waki'el wearing a linen cowl approached us.

"You are the astrologer," he greeted, shaking my hand. Flipping back his hood, he studied me before clasping Hadrien's wrist and introducing himself. "I'm Zebrim Hast. I was informed by messenger this afternoon of your arrival. Please, come into my chambers. I have refreshments." He spun on his heel, his sandal squeaking on the floor. In the wake of that little noise, he was off toward the door, animatedly talking about astrology.

"The interplanetudes is an amazing science. Simply amazing."

"Then you believe?" I asked.

"I believe in the old Waki'el ways, which never put limits on possibilities." He looked over his shoulder. "We have similar ideas about the consistency of the universe. We understand and accept the principles of physics. No one here will deny the truth about the way everything works."

This was certainly a change from our Sen'Tal interview. It made my nose itch with the stingy spice of distrust. Hadrien obviously shared my suspicions, because he stood his ground and spoke out.

"We didn't receive such warm courtesy from your counterpart."

Zebrim Hast stopped in midstep and turned to stare

at us. "The Sen'Tal is not the Acu-Sen'Tal's counterpart. Besides, they have no manners." With that, he was off to the room beyond the door. We followed and found more surprises.

His private chambers were spacious. They were also filled with all manner of treasures: Louis XIV chairs, Corrigadairian photon holograms, a complete suit of armor that would fit a Sumerek, floor pillows, velvet couches, a well-stocked mahogany bar, and a state-of-the-art computer sitting proudly on a Farellian claw-foot table.

Hadrien frowned, threw me a confused glance, and sat down heavily upon the luxurious sofa. I joined him while Zebrim Hast poured beverages taken from a small fridge behind the bar.

"You're surprised by the opulence," he said matter-of-factly as he flashed us an engaging, white-fanged smile.

"Well, yes. Nald'eken looks like a bomb hit it."

"You might say that. At one point, it had been hit by several bombs. The war leveled it. Completely leveled it." He grunted. "Nice place to put a spaceport, huh?"

"It seems that the tourists like the rustic ambience of the city," I answered.

"I think the Sen'Tal built the city to deter tourism, but it obviously backfired. It does appear that alien visitors rather enjoy the degradation, filth, and overcrowding." He shrugged, and his bony shoulders poked at his cowl like tent posts trying to raise canvas. "It makes no sense to me. Take this town, for instance. We pride ourselves on cleanliness and civility, and yet most humans never venture this far outside of the city."

Hadrien used this admission as a springboard. "We were told this town is mainly comprised of N'galia Waki'el. Is that true?"

"Yes."

"Do you have Basira or Tus administrators?"

"Yes."

"And how do you feel about them?"

"Personally? I don't have much use for them. The Basira and Tus try to force their theories of lack and pain upon the population. It's the only way they can truly dominate the rest of us, because the members of other castes are very many in number. If only clans in the caste of N'galia joined together, then we could remove the Basira and Tus from political and social domination." He paused, shook his head, and lost his endearing smile. "It won't happen, though."

"Why not? In-fighting between the clans?"

"Oh my, no. Tus and Basira are warriors. The rest of us are not."

"Why?"

"Because our brain structure is different." He walked around the end of the bar and offered us each a glass of yellow juice.

"This has no alcohol in it, does it?" Hadrien asked.

"No. Alcohol destroys the memory. Can't have that."

"That's not all it does," he muttered.

I leaned forward, concerned more about Zebrim Hast's previous statement than Hadrien's nervous system. "Please tell us how the brain structure is different between castes."

"Evolution," he answered. "Of course, that's the easiest assumption. All three hundred and sixty-five castes are comprised of different Waki'el species. We're not a subspecies of the high and mighty Basira as they maintain to all alien cultures." He returned to the bar and poured another drink, stopping his explanation to sip at the contents of the ceramic mug. Wincing, he took a moment to settle comfortably into a wing chair. "We're as intelligent as they. Probably more so."

"Then how do your brains differ?" I asked.

"We have different posterior lobes."

"That doesn't mean a lot to me."

He took another sip and then leaned forward, span-
ning the space between us. I smelled his musky odor. It
threatened to make me wank, but I held in the nausea,
sitting back quickly.

Zebrim Hast must have sensed my discomfort because
he frowned before pushing deep into the chair. "As I
said, Tus and Basira are warriors. They are grounded in
the physical realm due to the configuration of their posterior lobes. They haven't a single thought of spirituality."

"And everyone else does?"

"We have different levels of understanding. The
N'galia are the most enlightened due to the size and
shape of our brains."

"Do you download energy from another dimension?"
I asked flatly.

Zebrim Hast squinted and then studied me for another
thirty seconds before answering. "Why do you ask it like
that?"

"I'm just trying to put a spin on the Waki'el that I
can easily understand."

He indulged in a little species bigotry. "I wonder if
that's even possible."

"Try me," I growled.

I could tell he delighted in this bit of superiority. "We
dip from two different wells."

"Pardon me?"

"That's right. We don't hail from the same afterlife
dimension."

A memory tickled at my own gray matter, but I
couldn't put up the right amount of brain neurons to it
to make a whole thought. I let it slip away when Hadrien
spoke.

"How do you know this?"

"How do you know whence you came?"

"I don't. We have the interplanetudes, but the science
is based partially on supposition and inference through

the alignment of planets, asteroids, and stars. We've never actually conveyed in physical form along the creation energy circuit into another causal plane."

I smiled to myself. Hadrien knew more about the interplanetudes than he fessed up to.

"The N'galia Waki'el and our brethren who do not define themselves as Tus or Basira come from a plane of pure spirituality. The Tus and Basira come from a plane heavy with the vibrations of emotion. It's why they are efficient warriors and we are efficient thinkers and doers. We regard peace and harmony to be the highest order of the day." He stopped speaking to raise his palms in an attitude of submission. "It's a fact and has been for millennia. N'galia Waki'el are simply not fighters. That's why we're not on top, overseeing the Basira-Tus activities."

"What about the strange phenomenon of N'galia Waki'el being born into Basira families?" I asked. "What's happening there?"

He dropped his hands, and they made a plopping sound when they contacted his knees. "I don't know. We've often wondered if there was not some sort of mix-up in the energy generation."

"You mean transmissions from your spiritual realm get tangled with Basira-Tus emotional frequencies somewhere along the broadcast band between dimensions."

"It's the only explanation that seems logical."

"So, you're saying that the members of the Sen'Tal are capable of murder, but those in the Acu-Sen'Tal aren't," Hadrien said abruptly.

Zebrim Hast laughed. "I don't believe I said anything of the kind. It's true about you humans. You're lightning fast in the brain department. You are also very good at twisting words." He stopped, wet his lips with the tip of his tongue, and then asked, "Or perhaps it's my use of Intergalactic. Am I not making myself clear?"

We ignored his statement, and he didn't seem inclined

to push it. I polished off the rest of my tiddlywink before standing up. Then I took a short stroll around the room for closer inspection of the art pieces so neatly displayed.

"You know we're here about the murder of Imperial Prince Lundy of Earth," Hadrien said.

"Yes, I do, but I don't know why you came to me."

"Was Dumaka Lant a former member of the Acu-Sen'Tal?" I blurted.

"Yes, he was, until his true nature began to show."

"And that was?"

"I discovered that he'd been born into a Basira family. His parents threw him out with the garbage, so to speak."

"Why?"

He shrugged. "I don't know." Pausing, he studied his own knuckles for a second. "Dumaka Lant has too much fierceness in him. It was evident from the start. He had too much of his sire's warlike vibration running through him, and there was no way he could pass for N'galia when he reached breeding age. The drive to mate singled him out among us, though for a while he was perfectly content to identify himself with a lower caste."

"Who is his sire?" Hadrien asked.

"I thought you knew that."

"No, we don't."

"He's a clutch-son belonging to Felis Bray'el's father, Io'wetar," he answered. This response made both Hadrien and me frown. Zebrim Hast noticed. "What's wrong?"

"We were told that Dumaka Lant and Mann Re were lovers."

"Yes, so?"

"Don't you have any taboos about interbreeding within clutches?" I asked.

"No. We've never had such problems."

"Are you sure? After all, you're getting N'galia born

to Basira parents. It sounds like a bit of cross pollination in the gene pool, and every once in a while a throwback shows up in the nest."

It was the priest's turn to frown. "Interesting hypothesis. I've never heard anything so ridiculous, though."

Hadrien moved the subject over a tad. "What was your relationship with Dumaka Lant?"

"He was my student, nothing more."

"But did you have a traditional Waki'el alliance?"

"Most N'galia have one type of alliance. We are masters at indulging various forms of transformation, and of those, there are many. Since I was his mentor and he my student, our relationship was one of clarity in thought communicates interference in creation energy."

Waki'el, even when they tried to be clear about such things, made no sense. "What does that mean?" I asked, turning to study him.

He sighed and shook his head. "Dumaka Lant sought to find ways to overcome the sorrowful situation of his birth by transforming his personal power through applying his mind. I helped him understand how to direct his clarity of thought, but he built his destiny by abusing our alliance. It happens. I'm sure it occurs in humanity."

"We're experts at it," Hadrien answered. "We understand that you may be the only friend to Mann Re on this planet."

Zebrim Hast winced. "That's probably true."

"She's a member of a household belonging to the Sen'Tal. Are you allowed to converse?"

"Of course."

Seeing how vacant his gaze grew, I thought he'd slipped into his memories and wouldn't venture forth again any time soon. He fooled me. "Mann Re became expendable the moment she was born. If that is not a circumstance that screams for transformation, I don't know what is."

"Is she abused by her family?"

"I'm sure of it. She was abused because of what she represents. Her father's association with Theo forced her to compromise herself and bear children to a human. I understand Belinda-Agnes was born from an egg but had mammalian traits, such as the need to incubate within the mother's womb for a far longer period."

"Why are you a friend of Mann Re?" Hadrien asked quietly.

Zebrim Hast drew a deep breath before answering. "Because I love her as much as Dumaka Lant loves her."

As my mother used to say, he was rolling a load of old cobblers. Though well-versed in genuine affection, Zebrim Hast was nonetheless trying to slip us up by shooting a marble off in a new direction. I was having very little of it. After meeting the Sen'Tal priest, I doubted he could care for anyone, especially Mann Re. "Do your alliances allow for love?" I asked. "They seem to be built on emotional polarities."

"Well, surely you understand that love transcends all things."

"Yes, but is your definition of love and my definition of love the same?"

"That I can't say."

Hadrien roared off down the cricket court by reaching into his pocket and pulling out the blue stone found stuffed neatly inside Lundy's heart. "This has the mark of the Acu-Sen'Tal and is apparently a piece of jewelry worn across the sternum ridges. It was the murder weapon used to kill the prince. We were told that it has something to do with a Waki'el concept known as the affair of the heart." He handed it to Zebrim Hast and waited for a reaction. It wasn't long in coming.

The Waki'el set his glass on a nearby end table and rose slowly, opening his hand so Hadrien could place the stone in his palm. His attention never left the blue bauble, though his speech reflected obvious concern. "This has nothing to do with the Acu-Sen'Tal."

"What then?" Hadrien asked.

Zebrim Hast curled his fingers around the stone, taking a minute to study us in turn. "It would seem that someone wants the Acu-Sen'Tal to assume the blame for this human's murder." With that, he squeezed his hand into a fist.

I heard the stone crack and pop under the pressure he applied. I'd not realized that Waki'el were so bloody strong. When he opened his hand, I understood immediately that I'd attributed him supernatural powers where none lay. In the middle of this tiny artifact, I could clearly see the prongs of a computer chip.

"What is it?" I demanded, taking a step up to him.

"It's Dumaka Lant's invention—a pacemaker for the heart."

25

According to Zebrim Hast, the Waki'el concept of an affair of the heart was a taboo subject for Acu-Sen'Tal, and he personally did not know what it meant. He described it as some Sen'Tal idea instituted by the new thinkers in his society that, apparently to him, made the whole thing suspect. Basira and Tus baked their share of pork pies when it came to twisting the truth on age-old esoteric wisdom, and as much as he didn't want to admit it, Zebrim Hast knew the ovens stayed hot.

Public transport across Arif was practically nonexistent and, after we left, we were forced to find a Waki'el who had his own lorry to rent out. The truck was a lumbering piece of metal that when designed had incorporated everything bad about twenty-first-century hydrogen technology. It skimmed across the scrubby desert, but unfortunately, the driver seemed to have a sixth sense about where the bumpiest air currents could be found. So, like a Tasmanian devil biting a whirlwind, we bounced off thermals until my backside was dappled in bruises. Hadrien finally clamped his arm around my shoulders and pulled me close. Whether he just liked the feel of me against him or not, it served the purpose of rooting me to the spot while raising my need for long-overdue emotional comfort. This was silly, a juvenile reaction to a handsome man, and I was thoroughly trapped by it.

I was glad when Hadrien engaged the pilot in a conversation, because it pulled my attention on to other matters.

"I'll bet you don't see too many humans this far from the city," he said.

The Waki'el grunted and tapped on the plexi-dome of the cab before replying. "This taxi has housed many of your kind, ferrying them to safety over this rotting landscape."

"Really?"

"Yes. Just a few weeks ago, in fact. I drive for those who wish to consult with Zebrim Hast. It's a great honor and I earn nuggets for my effort."

I tried squirming a bit in Hadrien's embrace, but he pulled me tighter without a thought. "Do you remember who they were?" he asked.

"They were very important," he answered. "Zebrim Hast commanded me to clean the inside of the cab. Yes, very important. I received a good fee. Took them down the river route. Flying over water lessens the thermals, you know. The ride is smoother. But it takes more energy, and the engine works harder. It costs half again what I charged you for this route."

"Now he tells us," I muttered. Then, louder, I said: "Do you remember any names?"

Our pilot negotiated a dry waddi before piping up with an answer. The bumps pitched me hard against Hadrien, who glanced at me with a devious smile.

"I don't know names. I don't listen to the conversation unless I'm being paid to."

"Speaking of names, what's yours?" Hadrien asked.

"Imu'ula."

"Were you being paid that day to listen, Imu'ula?"

From his reflection in the rearview mirror, I could see the cabby frown. "Why does it matter?"

"It might matter to us a lot. What if we give you half again your fee, and you tell us what you remember over-hearing?"

If I thought this alien was going to give us any trouble, I was in for a sweet surprise. "All right," he said. "What would you like to know?"

Hadrien was up to his hip parts in surprises, too. He reached into his cammie pocket and pulled out a paper photograph of Prince Lundy. Leaning forward, he flashed it in front of the driver's nose. "Was this one of the people you ferried?"

The Waki'el glanced at it and nodded. "He was with the one called the executioner."

It was my turn to be surprised. But the pleasure was cut short.

Imu'ula slammed on the brakes suddenly and almost threw me over the front seat. Standing in front of us was a large white beast the size of an elephant. It glowed eerily in the moonlight, and judging by the way it held its ground, it knew it was superior to the little flyer. The driver swerved hard to port, dragging me away from Hadrien's embrace. I grabbed the safety strap on that side of the car and held on, glad not to die from being splattered like cooked cabbage against the monster. I was even more grateful to put a little space between Hadrien and me.

We recovered, narrowly missing the animal. "Kichen'el!" Imu'ul barked. "Entu Bali needs to rein in his livestock at night." Once back on the bumpy track, he returned to Hadrien's question as if we'd not almost made a fatal detour. "The man with the dark hair and the executioner were discussing a Waki'el female."

"Did they say who?" I asked.

"No. I got the feeling they were talking about someone with rank. Maybe a Basira female. I couldn't tell for certain. She was important, whoever she was."

"Why do you say that?"

"They were very concerned that she was approaching the end of her life cycle."

"How did they know that?" Hadrien demanded.

"For one thing, the man with the dark hair said that there had been a change in her honey. That is a sign of advancing age. She was apparently an amber carrier. That's rare. She would be worth spending money to keep her alive."

"Were they going to see Zebrim Hast?" I asked.

"Yes."

"Were they going to request his help?"

"Most assuredly."

"In what way?"

"I do not know."

"Did they mention anything else about this female?" Hadrien said.

"Only that she could sense the creation energy withdrawing."

I took a deep breath and it spilled into a sigh. Hadrien glanced at me. He studied me for a minute before asking the question I was thinking. "What is it like when the energy withdraws?"

"A person feels weaker with each passing day. Vision becomes cloudy and hearing disappears. As the day gets closer, the hide begins to show a change in hue, and there is a definite disorganization in thinking. I have heard though, that there is a lightening of spirit, an almost rapturous commotion present to entertain the mind and take away the worry of passing completely into the vibration." Imu'ul shrugged at the rest of his explanation and shifted gears, gunning the engine to make it over a rise in the landscape.

"Were these two humans in harmony?" Hadrien asked.

"No, not one bit. If I were to chance a guess about their alliance, I would have to say they fell somewhere between success and failure completes worry's design." He paused to consider his words. "Yes, that's it, all right."

I pulled on the strap and grabbed the greasy headrest of the front seat. "Are you saying that one was positive and the other one was negative, and together they worried the problem?"

"Yes, that is correct, if I understand what you are saying."

"How the bloody hell did you get that out of his word puzzle?" Hadrien asked.

I smeared him with a sneer. "I'm good. I'm so very good."

He grinned, and for some reason I had to turn away, afraid I might give up evidence of my fondness for him.

"They argued a great deal," Imu'ula said. "Well, I think they did. They switched to a language I didn't comprehend, but from the pitch of their voices, I believe they hated each other."

"How long did they visit with Zebrim Hast?" I asked.

"A few hours. He's a good teacher. It didn't take him long to impart wisdom and truth. Now, I can't say that it did any good for the visitors."

"Why?"

"They continued to argue until I dropped them off at the spaceport." He paused, gave me a curious look, and asked, "Do all humans fight so much? They remind me of Basira and Tus when they go at it."

"We've got warlike natures," I answered.

"Then that explains it. You are probably an offshoot of Basira or Tus."

"An offshoot?"

"Yes. You are probably one of the original species to be seeded by the Star Gatherers."

Hadrien stepped in on his response. "Let me guess.

The Star Gatherers would be the nomadic people who colonized worlds across the galaxy by interbreeding with the indigenous population."

Imu'ula glanced at him in the mirror. "I suppose we are talking about the same thing."

"Don't the N'galia include themselves in this gene pool tampering?" I said.

"That is a vile, disrespectful statement," Imu'ula snapped. "Of course we don't. N'galia and only the N'galia are pure-caste descendants of the Star Gatherers. Everyone else on this planet and across the galaxy are a permutation of us."

26

We got back to the Kourey **just as dawn blos-**somed under the light of a scarlet sun. The sepia shadows of night blended into the rusty shine of day. The moment we stepped into our cabin, I decided the oppressive burnt colors of Arif had affected my optic nerves, which had in turn pushed depression into my entire body. Hadrien picked up the pouch of honey he'd bargained for from Rash'nal's seller and headed off to the sick bay to have Omar examine it along with the cracked pacemaker. I was secretly glad for the solitude, however short. I closed the door to my sleeping cubby in hopes it would turn out any thoughts I might have had about Hadrien's virility and my need to experience it.

I removed my clothes, took a shower under a trickling water spigot, and then went to my valise to scrabble for a bottle of jeela oil. I then curled into the lotus position in the center of my bunk and held the bottle to the light, shaking the alien mixture slightly.

A friend of mine had flipped on the old light about this blend, assuring me that the first time I used it, it would sensitize my nerve endings. Combined with deep meditation, it took the experience from ritual to mystical by opening up the physical body to the merest change in the environment around it. The trick was to release complete control so that the ethereal and corporeal merged into illuminated understanding, providing the individual with take-away wisdom like the pearl of enrichment from a Chinese fortune cookie read at the end of a satisfying meal.

I slowly dabbed on the jeela oil, luxuriating in the burn that it brought to my skin. I hit the meridian points along my body: the throat, the breasts, the solar plexus, the pelvis. The astringent quality made my pores snap and my nerve endings vibrate. Once done, I capped the bottle and tossed it onto the bed before closing my eyes and taking a long pull of recirculated oxygen. This simple action spread the effect of the oil to all parts of my body. Drifting, I tried to clear my mind of irritating thoughts so that the gold dust of clarity could fall gently over and through me.

When a human meditates, the cells of the Leydig glands found in the genitive system begin to stew up a bit. They send out energy along an internal path known as the Appian Way. Like an ancient Greek seeking the solace of Mount Olympus, the force rises in the body until it encounters the pineal center in the brain. From there, it splashes out to fill the meditator with transcendental bliss.

I had always found a jeela meditation a sensual experience, unlocking my own sexual ferocity. I had avoided jeela since Eric's death, and I wasn't sure why I used it now. My mind kept centering on the investigation, and so I floated with it, my first curiosity being the supposed differences in Waki'el brain structure. As if on cue, unbidden questions about how the secretive Waki'el used the creation energy to find spiritual and emotional growth through their posterior lobes surfaced to fill my reflection.

Tracing my hands down over my hips, I enjoyed the tingling sensation they brought to my skin. This mediation was just a little lolly, a bit of human extravagance in the midst of alien madness. Unfortunately, it bobbled up my desire for Hadrien, and that bit of attuning was totally uncalled for. I nipped in another deep breath and ran my thoughts off. Unfortunately, they kept circling me, dropping in to remind me that I was sitting on a world full of dirt, smoke, and harsh colors.

I have spent my days dealing with things that are supposed to happen, but once in a while it becomes a scheduling nightmare. Yes, it's true, we have free will and no astrologer worth his bread and jam would say that the science of the interplanetudes is completely accurate.

Still, my calculations about Prince Lundy had to be correct. Even with one eye closed, I couldn't have missed it by that much. Or had my error been the beginning of the truth for me, a day in the past when the reality of my talents as well as the effectiveness of the interplanetudes would be tested and found failing?

Lundy had passed the point where his death would have occurred at a young age. He should have continued on to make a reasonable contribution to humanity. His time, figured by the interplanetudes, suggested he'd signed up for a period of seventy-seven years and five months. How had that been scraped away?

The jeela oil steamed into me, bringing tingling feelings of the air currents moving about my body, and it lulled me into deeper relaxation. I imagined photons like flower pollen bursting from my dark mood to explode in light all about me. When the fantasy showered me in illumination, I had one of those lustrous pearls of insight drop into my naked lap.

One of the laws of the interplanetudes states that while in the next dimension awaiting transition back into the material realm, we decide how many years we need to accomplish our mission in the corporeal state. The length of time carved from the creation energy is guided by the incarnate's desire to join a particular species. Humans have a lingering life span. With the help of medical miracles, we have managed to reach two hundred fifty years old as an average age. Waki'el, on the other hand, count themselves fortunate to make it to sixty. Such knowledge could prime someone toward black-hearted envy that would produce an individual who might act out of a sociopathic jealousy.

Depending on what the Waki'el believed of the afterlife and the existence of dual nature, how appropriate would it be to kill, extinguishing both the body and the soul? Metaphorically, it could be seen as blocking the flow of creation energy and diverting it back to its source. It might be a reason for these aliens to murder, while justifying the heinous act as though it was a martyr mission, part of a holy jihad.

Taking another deep swig of air, I tried to follow a hazy path toward understanding the meaning of the pacemaker found inside Lundy's heart. Was it only a symbol of the killer's belief or an integral part of the death? Had the pacemaker activated upon insertion, massaging the prince's heart with some force we didn't understand?

I tried to focus on this line of inquiry, but my resources were limited, and I ended up forgetting about it all by floating aimlessly with the pleasant euphoria produced by the oil.

I don't know how long I stayed in the spot, because I was swept away. The world sparkled around me and I melded with the material nature of this dimension at the same time I touched the superconscious state of disembodiment. Just as the oil melted through my inhibitions, I sensed a change in the room but, caught by my own mind, I ignored this new shift in the atmosphere.

Suddenly, there was a pressure on my lips, and seconds later I imagined a kiss—gentle at first, and then becoming more insistent and probing. I went with the experience, manifesting thoughts of Eric, before dismissing them because there was nothing familiar about this touch. Realizing this, I opened my eyes to see that the kiss hadn't been of my own creation. Hadrien was with me, and here I was sitting with my sprigs hanging out.

He held me close, and I pulled from his lips to glare at him. "How dare you invade me privacy? I'm in me friggin' fancy suit."

He backed a few inches from my space to let his gaze trace appreciatively over my naked parts, and then he smiled. "Yes, you are in your friggin' fancy suit, and I'd say it's a designer original."

His words wicked me off. So I drew back my hand and slapped him hard across the face. The force I'd packed into my smack knocked him backward. He staggered slightly, giving me a confused look.

I slid from the bed and stalked around the room until I found my robe. Hadrien stood his ground, rubbing his chin and watching me. After I was dressed, I finished him off. "If you ever come into me space uninvited again, I'll rip off your Tommy Rollocks at the roots and stuff them up your pony trap."

27

Hadrien waited for me in our little sitting room, lounging lazily on the small sofa. The minute I stepped from my cubby fully dressed, he spoke in a husky voice. "I'm not sorry I kissed you, and I don't think you're sorry I did, either."

I rolled my eyes in an attempt to downplay the incident. "I should have demanded a separate cabin."

"There weren't any, remember?"

I sighed. "What did you want?"

It was his turn to sigh before answering. "I wanted to tell you that Mann Re wants to see us."

"How? I thought Paul put her off limits to us."

"Paul isn't on board the *Kourey*. He's at the royal villa or something. She's waiting for us right now. That is, if you can rip yourself away from your meditation."

I took a step to the hatch and headed down the corridor without further conversation. He was beside me in only a moment but said not a word as we walked to Mann Re's cabin at the far end of the ship.

It was quiet and dark along the corridor and, surprisingly, there were no guards at her door. In fact, there were no crewmen anywhere near her quarters.

Hadrien tapped lightly on her hatch. His knock was answered immediately by a tall, thin female Waki'el, who wasn't wearing anything other than her own fancy suit. In the ambient light of the cabin, I was startled by her iridescent hide. I found myself searching the length of her arm for strange tattoos. I saw nothing.

"You are the Earth investigators?" she asked quietly.

"That would be us," I answered.

She stepped aside and pointed with an open hand into the cabin's interior.

Unlike the peach petal that Paul quartered in, this space was a silver palace of fabrics, tiles, and carpets; even the lighting had a frosty flavor to it. I glanced at the female, and she practically glimmered in the color. She marched toward a nearby hatch and, leading us within, presented us to Mann Re.

The mother of Princess Belinda-Agnes sprawled upon a day bed in all her naked glory, but her age showed in the dustiness of her skin and the sagging muscles of her thighs. Silver bangles at her wrists and ankles accentuated the golden ties crossing her sternum ridges and added to the glitter in the room. She stood regally when we entered, bowing at the waist far enough for me to see the jutting peaks of her spine. "Thank you for coming. Please have a seat."

She waited until we'd situated ourselves on a small settee that brought me in close proximity to Hadrien; in fact, we were squeezed like a couple of jackie kippers. He gave me a smug look before settling his attention onto Mann Re.

"This is my daughter, Ne'el Zara," she said. "She will participate in this conversation."

Ne'el Zara slid liquidly to a large floor pillow. "My mother has concerns."

"About what?" Hadrien asked.

"About what truly happened to my daughter, Belinda."

"Unfortunately, we don't know," he answered. "We aren't being given much to work with. People seem reluctant to extend information." He stopped, leaned forward, and squinted at her. "Unless, of course, you are so inclined."

"I will try to answer your questions if you promise not to speak to Cornelius Paul about my cooperation. I fear for my children's lives."

"Why?" I asked. "They are heirs to a vast fortune on Earth."

"Yes, but I don't trust Paul."

"Why?"

"Because he's in love with me."

What kind of fife and drum was this? Did everybody love this aging female? "Why does he love you?"

"I don't know why. He has since I first went to be Theo's wife."

"Has he had sex with you?"

"No. Never. Our relationship is one of communication manifests objective by designing commitment."

Hadrien cut me a look. "Go ahead, me mistress. See if you can translate."

"That's easy," I answered before turning back to Mann Re. "You are talking about the fact that you and he share the same objective and he has sought to win your commitment in this matter?"

Mann Re narrowed her eyes, sizing me up. "Yes, that is correct."

"What is the objective?"

"My daughter, Belinda-Agnes."

"And the commitment?"

"To protect her from harm. He was ineffectual, to say the least. My daughter suffered under the auspices of human science. I couldn't convince Felis Bray'el."

"Why?"

"Because Paul is a traitor of the heart," Ne'el Zara growled.

"What's that?" I turned toward her.

"He has lied to my mother," she answered indignantly. "He told her that there were no experiments being performed on Belinda-Agnes. Yet Belinda told me of them herself."

Mann Re interrupted. "Paul had no choice. He does only what Theo tells him. But I'm sure that Felis Bray'el does not know the extent to which Belinda suffered. He could not. He would denounce the liaison between our planets."

"Are you sure?" Hadrien asked.

"I'm sure."

"Do you know the parameters of Theo's association with Felis Bray'el?"

"Do you mean the terms of the marriage dowry?"

Hadrien frowned. "A marriage dowry. There was such a thing?"

"Of course. It was an arranged union. But, since you ask, I can't say. Theo and my brother had many secret negotiations, and being who and what I am, I had no right to ask what they were."

"So, it is possible that Belinda-Agnes was born just for the type of scientific exploitation you mentioned."

Both Waki'el females stared at Hadrien. It was Ne'el Zara who spoke, sounding disgusted and incredulous all at the same time. "How can you even entertain such a thought? That would be an offense to the gods."

"As we understand it, your other uncle, Dumaka Lant, has no problem using people in the aim of science," I said.

Ne'el Zara shook her head and pounded the rug with the flat of her hand. "Don't mention that creature's name in the presence of my mother."

Hadrien crossed his arms and rested the butt of his hand on his holster. "Why not?"

"It was he who suggested the union between Mann Re and Theo," Ne'el Zara announced.

"You must really have hated what he did to you," Hadrien said, ignoring the daughter to focus on the mother.

Mann Re sighed. "Life is about choices. My life had none."

I sat back on the settee, and when I did, my thigh rubbed along Hadrien's leg. There may have been a moment that I imagined it, but glancing at him, I'm sure I saw the flare of his nostrils as he took in a sharp breath. I couldn't help smiling, so I covered it by running my hand over my mouth. Hadrien punched back into the interview, saving me from having to speak.

"We were told that you wield quite a bit of power here on Arif. You have your own staff, and you oversee Felis Bray'el's household."

"Shortly before Belinda's death, I was stripped of my staff of servants. I was also released from any responsibilities regarding the execution of my brother's estate. Once more, I have nothing."

"It does sound as though your brother has made provisions for your children."

She snorted. "He has found a convenient way to dispose of them. People do not approve of me, and he's tired of the reminders. It puts a dent in his political agenda, and he will do what he must to maintain his facade of control. My children will never have official rank within the Sen'Tal, either as administrative personnel or ritual priests. They will be unemployable within their caste."

Hadrien leaned a little too far my direction and his hand accidentally brushed my leg. He noticed immediately and slung me a quick apology before turning his questions onto Mann Re. "So you think your children shouldn't have been singled out for this honor and privilege."

"No," she whispered. Then, as though her thoughts gave her power, she added, "I don't like it. I'm tired of being used, and I won't see my offspring suffer as I have."

"Theo thought quite a lot of Belinda-Agnes," I said.

"Yes."

Upon this admission, Hadrien stopped talking, and I picked up where he left off. "What kind of relationship did you have with Prince Lundy?"

"He brought me word of Belinda in exchange for sex."

"Did he love you, too?"

"Yes, I suppose so. I don't really understand this human concept and why every male is led by his hormones to mate with any female who qualifies."

I saw Hadrien smile slightly and knew exactly what was going through that bread box of his. "Do you carry the amber liquid that is so addictive to males of my species?"

Mann Re studied him before answering. "How did you know that? So few people do."

"And your daughter Belinda had this same substance in her body?"

"Yes. But the last I heard, it was changing in consistency."

"Which means?"

"Which means she had some human frailty making something so simple so complex."

"Or?"

"Or she was dying." Mann Re abruptly rose and stretched. The action spread the muscles attached to her sternum ridge and I could clearly see her long heart beating slowly.

Ne'el Zara spoke up. "Bedevilments empower oppression. Lundy saw how my mother suffered. He wished to help her conquer her problems by literally squashing them out of existence. At least, where he could. He made enemies by bringing news to my mother. It wasn't an association that was condoned."

"Why did he do all this for you?"

"He was a foolish male," Mann Re husked. "My indulgence probably killed him."

"Was Zebrim Hast his enemy?" I demanded.

Mann Re shook her head. "Zebrim Hast is everybody's enemy. He would turn the status quo upside down whether it did any good for anyone or not. Such is the outcome of trying to bridle life's futilities. Me? I've done no such thing. I've embraced them."

"How did your brother feel about Lundy?" Hadrien asked.

"My brother doesn't like any member of Earth's imperial family. He doesn't trust Theo."

"Then why is he permitting you and your children passage to Earth? Why is he accepting Theo's offer to make your offspring legal heirs?"

"Because Felis Bray'el will legally own all those rights," Mann Re snapped. "Don't you understand? My children are considered N'galia, even though they were produced from a union with a Tus male. They don't have the brain configuration for the warrior-priest lifestyle."

"You're suggesting that funds will be funneled to your brother?"

"Yes. It's the way things work in our society."

"And you don't want him to have these funds at the expense of your children."

"That's correct."

"I would like to know how your brains work differently," I suddenly said.

Everybody stared at me, including Hadrien, but Mann Re answered within the minute. "I don't know what you mean."

"Are N'galia more telepathic than Tus or Basira?"

"Telepathic? That word doesn't translate."

"Can you speak to each other with your thoughts?"

"Well, yes, of course, when we need to."

I scowled before glancing at my partner. "Well, now we know how our movements are being tracked."

"But," Mann Re added, "this link doesn't cross castes. Our brains are not designed for it."

"The science on this world doesn't seem very advanced," Hadrien said. "How do you know there are differences in physiology?"

"Egg structure, for one thing," she answered. "You don't need medical pictures to know how you think. The creation energy is strong in each of us. We know who we are intuitively."

That suggested a metaphysical understanding that rocketed past a human's ability to perceive. "What exactly do N'galia use their brains for?"

"Healing, understanding, wisdom. We cogitate ideas. The Tus and Basira use these ideas. They are action incarnate where we are the ones who deliver the knowledge."

"You're channels of some kind."

"Yes, I suppose so."

"What do you channel?" Hadrien asked.

"The creation energy. Like every other being in this dimension."

He frowned. "I don't recall channeling anything remotely like that."

"You are alive, aren't you?"

"Occasionally."

She smiled. "Then, occasionally, you channel this force." Mann Re paused, stole a look toward her daughter, and then glanced at me. "The differences in these abilities between Waki'el and humans are simply a matter of evolution. You will be where we are in a thousand years. Maybe less."

It was too bad I didn't know what she was talking about. "How do you call up this energy? Humans do similar things through a method known as meditation."

Having said that, Hadrien swiveled in the tight seat to stare at me, eyes dark with intensity. "That's what you were up to, wasn't it?" he whispered.

I ignored him. "Do you have a certain way to call up this energy?"

Ne'el Zara spoke up. "No. It flows through us, and the heart is the gateway for it to manifest in this realm. Without it, we would die."

"Do you control it in any way?" I demanded.

It took them both too long to answer. "No," Mann Re finally said. With that, she walked to a burled wood locker. Opening the door, she stood there inspecting the contents. "I believe I know what killed Lundy."

Hadrien and I spoke in unison. "What?"

Mann Re picked up a small plastic packet and turned. "This did it."

She handed it to me. It was filled with yellow liquid.

"The fixative," Hadrien mumbled, using his thumb to press on the plastic. "Where did this come from?"

"It was blended in the southern continent known as Penaris. It's made with a mold that is found in the frosty crust near the south pole. It's the only place on this world where the mold can be gathered, and it's very expensive."

"Who blends it?" I asked.

"N'galia Acu-Sen'Tal. They have the secrets."

Abruptly, we were interrupted by Cornelius Paul. He stormed into Mann Re's private chambers with a guard clanking at his heels. Giving me an imperious look, he growled his accusation. "You are meddling in affairs that don't concern you. I told you that Mann Re was off limits. This will require corrective action; be sure of that!"

Hadrien stood up and faced Paul directly. "I think you'd better watch yourself when you talk about punishment. It's liable to backfire, just like a poorly done electro-crucifixion."

28

By law, Paul could not touch us because we were here under Theo's sanction, but that didn't mean he couldn't make the punishment look like an accident. I knew Paul's logos too well; he enjoyed this challenge; he would do everything he could to win it. Unfortunately, it would be a little on the life-and-death side for us.

As we walked to the sick bay to give Dr. Omar the substance for analysis, I had to say what was on my mind to Hadrien. "Do you think Paul was behind Eric's death?"

He glanced at me out of the corner of his eye and increased his walking speed. "Don't you?"

"I'm not sure what to believe. I have me own theories."

"Well, take my word for it. I've spent years dealing with killers. That guy doesn't like you. He thinks your astrology gives you extraordinary clarity." He stopped walking to face me. "Even if you don't."

Yes, my mouth dropped open. "How do you know that?"

"Maybe my Moon and your Sun are up there diddling in the sky. Maybe I'm a better judge of people than you think I am." He started walking again before speaking softly. "You blame yourself for not seeing the danger coming. You couldn't have stopped it. You might be able to read destiny, but you can't change it."

"We have free will," I said.

He snorted. "Big, swigging deal. It doesn't work. Your free will is as bogus as my nervous system. Let go of your guilt, Philipa. I don't think Eric even deserves it. You're as good as you ever were with divining the stars, so stop wallowing in the pity, and get on with your life's purpose."

I have never been so clearly read in my whole life, and my mouth wouldn't work to deny it. It was the truth that I hadn't wanted to hear, because it placed responsibility back into my lap. After Eric's death, I wanted no obligation, because then I could take no blame. My thoughts began to spiral away, but Hadrien dragged them back by focusing on our well-being. It was a strong Virgo at work in him, and it overwhelmed me for a minute.

"Nothing is a secret from you for long, Philipa. Paul knows this. He knows how perceptive you are, and that's what makes him dangerous to you. Don't underestimate him."

I managed a sentence. "If you understand this, then you realize you've placed yourself in harm's way."

He smiled, but when he did, it made me think of knives. "Me dear friggin' fancy suit. Don't you realize that Paul's been behind all the attempts on our lives since we stepped on board the *Kourey*?"

"I don't doubt it. Paul is protecting something, whether himself or Theo."

"Sometimes, it's a pleasure to do your job," he answered. "What starts out as business often ends up as an obsession. I'd say Cornelius Paul is crapped up in the brain. He's a controller and therefore a worrier. Worriers give me a moment's heartburn. They're unpredictable in their actions."

I almost didn't ask the question for fear I would already know the answer. "Do you think this current conspiracy goes back to Eric's time spent on Theo's secret project?"

"I don't know if it has anything to do with it. One thing is for certain, though. If Theo had Eric killed like you believe, and you find evidence of it, Paul's in trouble with the Imperial Senate. It doesn't matter if he acted under Theo's sanction or not. Those old bastards are just looking for a way to crack the emperor's power."

"But why bring us into the fold? I had gone away to another part of the galaxy. I was no trouble to Theo or Paul."

"Is it possible you could be in the future?"

"In the future?"

"That's right. What does your chart say?" Stopping in midstride, he placed his hands firmly on my shoulders. "I know you have secrets about us and our association— our relationship. Why wouldn't you know what's down the star road for other things?"

I squirmed from his grip and continued toward the infirmary. As much as I hated to admit it, I hadn't looked down my own star road in many months. A train could have been waiting to hit me, but grief, unclarified and unresigned, makes you not give a Gypsy kiss to whether you're flattened like a shilling on the track. When I didn't answer, he stalked up to me and stopped me again.

"Are you going to deny that we'll fall in love?" he asked.

I tried not throwing him a butcher's hook, but he conned the truth out of me anyway. He kept talking, though, saving me the wincing pain of having to say it out loud. "We're joined at the hip from the great beyond.

You can't control it, even though you'd try to throw me into deep space to avoid it." With that, he hurried away to Dr. Omar's office.

It took me a couple of minutes to restart my engine. I have always been quick to think of myself as someone who could not easily be duped. Worse, I considered myself better at this than any other person in the world. The whole time I'd been fooling myself.

When I arrived, Hadrien was giving Omar the packet. "We need an analysis on this, if you can."

Omar held the clear plastic to the light and studied it. "This contains mold spores. There's swift atomic movement. It's very active."

"You've got some good eyes, Doc," Hadrien said. "We think this substance may have contributed to Lundy's death." He glanced at the hatch I'd just climbed through and, satisfied that it had shut with a comforting thud, he went on. "What did you find out about the pacemaker?"

Omar blinked slowly and placed the packet into an analyzer drawer. He waited for numbers to start appearing on the digital readout before he answered.

"It would have been very easy for technicians to analyze it as a mere stone. It is."

"That's it?" I said. "Nothing more than a rock? I saw the remains of a computer chip. Are you telling us that Zebrim Hast fed us a load of Brahms and Liszt?"

They both stared at me, but neither asked for a translation. Omar cleared his throat and spoke.

"It's similar to a magnetized lodestone found on Earth, and yes, there is an electronic component present as well. The covering helped to hinder forensic analysis of its true purpose. You see, embedded within the central core of the stone are tachyon filaments."

"Tachs?" I said. "Faster-than-light atomic particles?"

"That's correct. These are laid out into a string similar to what can be found in a ship's tachyon core fibulator."

Hadrien plopped down in a plastic chair. "Wait a minute. Are you talking about the thing in an engine that excites zero-point gravity to allow the ship to move faster than the speed of light?"

"That's right. It creates a field effect around the ship that shifts it into the flow. It is also used to create a stable pocket for zero-point colonies. Very basic stuff, this. It goes back to the time of the Philadelphia Experiment on Earth. Do you know the one?"

Hadrien shrugged. This time I had the answer. "Back in the middle part of the twentieth century. Albert Einstein and Nikola Tesla created a similar field around the USS *Eldridge*, sending it from the Philadelphia Shipyard to the Norfolk Naval Base."

Omar smiled. "Very good. A student of history. That's the one."

"So, what does that small stone do?"

Omar reached into his jacket pocket and fished out the cracked pacemaker. He flipped it to Hadrien. "It's excited by a tight bandwidth of zero-point gravity flow. I placed it into a tach chamber, and the object began to admit photon pulses."

My brain leapt ahead of his words. "Slow light?"

"Precisely. If this is indeed a pacemaker, it doesn't control the rhythm and beating of a heart. It controls the presence of zero-point flux. Once it is aggravated by the presence of the pure vibration, it slows the incoming flow."

"Could that be at the root of Waki'el heart problems?" I asked. "Does a tight bandwidth of zero-point energy flow through them, linking them with another causal plane?"

"I've never heard of anything like it," Omar answered. "But who knows what's possible, especially when you get balloon heads involved?"

29

We returned to our cabin. Hadrien locked us in and then promptly fell asleep on the couch still wearing his side arm. I found sleep wanting, so I sat at the table with my calculator and cards, trying desperately to break through the inconjunct of my Jupiter and Uranus. The planets represented soul and ego and the ability to enact self-cruelty that would make anything Paul might do seem like a toy show. This configuration kept me from acting on anything. It always had—and after Hadrien's speech, I was forced to face it. Still, I drove myself right down Penny Lane and straight on out to the loony house trying to place ideas and thoughts in some coherent chronological order.

It was early evening by the time I finally gave up, and as I pushed away from the calculator, Hadrien spoke up.

"Let it go, Philipa," he said quietly, watching me from the couch.

I jumped, startled that he was awake. "I don't know what you're talking about."

"Sure you do. There's something going on here that defies the interplanetudes. Maybe the aliens are right.

Maybe the science doesn't work on them, especially since they seem to think they hail from completely different incarnate states. Even among themselves."

I couldn't read his expression in the evening shadows cast through the porthole. "How do you know I was working on that? Perhaps I was doing a little forecasting about us."

"And what do you know?"

"I think I'll keep it confidential for a little while."

He must not have wanted to play in the cricket match, because he grunted, slid from the couch, and headed for his cubby, closing the hatch behind him without another word.

The truth was, I had done a bit of work on several charts, one of which belonged to Captain Tara Verena. She was a twenty-year career officer, and according to her records in the ship's database, she was loyal to the people of planet Earth. She'd twice received the Imperial Medal of Valor given by the Senate, and she had been the youngest officer to be given command of a delegation ship. Verena also had one distinguishing thing about her logos: She was heavily influenced by a grand air trine. Four of her planets, including her Sun, fell into air signs and opposed each other in the form of a trine. It meant that Verena was highly idealistic, intellectual, and despite her display of power, she was saddled with humanitarian values. Her loyalty would waft with the wind, changeable, depending on the direction she found justice and compassion in short supply. I only hoped I could persuade some of this breeze to rise past the crusty rinds of earth planets opposing this configuration. So, while Hadrien stewed in solitude, I decided to visit the captain.

I found Verena on the bridge. It was quiet, shadowy, and except for a few techs mulling over the blinking, beeping computer systems, the crew was on stand-down. She invited me into her office, but before she spoke, she stomped over to the viewing porthole and studied the activities in the spaceport. Satisfied, she turned back to me and pointed to the leatherette sofa. "I was wondering when you were going to question me."

"You've heard about the trouble we've had with Paul?"

She joined me, the furniture sighing when her weight hit it. "Yes. You shouldn't cross him, Ms. Cyprion. He doesn't like you."

"So I understand, but that's not what I'm here about. You've made four hundred flights to this world. Is that correct?"

"Yes. It's public record."

"I assume then, you know a bit more about the Waki'el culture than most people."

"I know some things. I'm no expert, if that's what you expect."

"Have you noticed an increase in the presence of zero-p babies?"

She thought a moment and, lowering her voice as though she worried over surveillance, she said, "We've ferried a good many of them in."

"Why?"

"Why? Who knows? The official line I get has something to do with Theo trying to help the Waki'el increase their technology. If you ask me, Theo wants these muggers to ally with Earth in a bad way. I think he expects an invasion to come from some simmering part of the galaxy, and he's concerned he won't be able to defend against it. Why else would he be giving choice positions in his house and in government to these aliens?"

"Just how many Waki'el has he brought to Earth?"

"I have personally ferried at least two hundred. Each one has taken the place of a human worker back on Earth and on Mars. You know they've bought a whole continent on Mars, don't you? Going to build a Sen'Tal religious community. It's like they are waiting in the dog house for something."

"Who do you think might attack?"

"Personally? I think the Veln have sights on our world."

"Why?"

"You know the old cliché. It's a jewel in space. In this case, there is a basis behind the saying." She smacked her legs and rose. "In all of known sentient space, most planets resemble this dry cake of a world. Sol, the Pleiades, over there on Orion's Arm, and the Dogon System are currently the only places on the list where terran-class worlds can be found. That makes them valuable."

"Earth would be valuable to the Waki'el as well."

She smiled and marched over to her window. The room's lighting cast a golden reflection against the glass, and I saw her frown. "Yes, it would," she answered absently.

"But why kill the imperial hierarchy if you were already invited to sit at the same table?" I asked.

"Maybe you're grudgingly invited to sit at that table, and maybe you know it."

"And maybe it would be better if the host wasn't around at all to spoil the dinner."

Verena turned slightly to stare at me. "I think we've given the Waki'el a powerful weapon, but what exactly the weapon is, I haven't got a clue. Do you?"

I shook my head, and the variables rattled around inside my skull. "Did you transport Prince Lundy and Cornelius Paul to this world in the immediate past?"

Verena hesitated but then nodded. "Yes."

"Why were they here?"

"I don't know. I was not in the need-to-know loop."

"Then what do you think they were here for?"

She grunted, flicked her swivel chair from behind her desk, and flopped in it. "I think they were here to get help for Princess Belinda."

"What was wrong with her?"

"Well, the last time I saw her, she looked like hell."

"From all the medical experimentation?"

"From something. Her hide was almost purple, and in some places it was black. I couldn't tell if she was bruised. It wouldn't have been appropriate to study her openly, but I believe she was dying."

"Why did Lundy come on the trip?"

"Good question." She swung her legs under her desk, and the chair squealed. Leaning her elbows on her neatly arranged blotter, she took a deep breath and fed me her own ideas. "Lundy was having a sexual affair with Belinda. He disobeyed his father, initially."

"Theo set her off limits to him," I said flatly. "But his rising fire sign made that impossible. Belinda became a goal to be reached."

She nodded. "Unfortunately, when he chose his winning prize, she dominated him with her power."

"He became addicted to the amber."

"Woefully addicted."

"Did you see such evidence?"

"While aboard this ship, he maintained a Waki'el mistress, and he still had trouble functioning."

"Withdrawals?"

"He complained of not feeling well, and he was listless."

"He wouldn't make a very convincing arbitrator for Theo, then."

"Precisely. Paul knew it, but there was nothing he could do to convince Theo. Lundy has always had a good relationship with Mann Re."

"So he hoped that Lundy might be able to persuade her to convince someone to help Earth researchers to find a way to save Belinda."

Verena nodded. "Obviously, their negotiations came to no good end."

30

When I returned to my cabin, Hadrien was
awake. He sat at the table, studying my cards like he
actually knew what he was reading.

"I thought you were asleep," I said, shutting the hatch
behind me.

"I heard you leave. Who'd you go see? Captain Verena?"

I grinned. "Did you read it in the cards?"

He shook his head. "It's what I was planning to do
next. What did she say?"

"She said that Theo was driving balloon heads in here
to help the Waki'el increase their technology."

"Sounds like he was worried about staying on a budget with that move."

"Why do you say that?"

He rose, and when he did, I realized for the first time
that he wasn't wearing a shirt. His torso was hard and
muscular. Seeing it, I felt my insides whining again. I
slapped the pasties on my desire by dropping my gaze
to the stuff on the table.

"Why a budget?" I asked.

My attempt not to appear obvious about noticing his body was apparently unsuccessful.

He stepped up to me and touched my face with his fingertips. I stood it for a moment, just relishing the touch of another human being. But in the end, I backed off like Ben Hur chased me with his chariot. "Don't do that," I snapped. "Keep your mind on the investigation. Now, answer me question, please."

Hadrien didn't move—not one muscle—for at least thirty seconds. When the countdown was over, he nodded slightly and slipped back into the seat at the table. "The reason I say Theo was trying to do it all on a budget is this: It would have been easier to accomplish this technological push by using computers."

"But most of the planet is without electricity."

"Yes, which means there would be a time factor that old Theo is worried about. It would take about a year to get a hub center up and running. It would involve lots of people knowing about it, lots of contracts, lots of money. If he ships in balloon heads, then he's got his computers for the price of feeding them plankton once in a while."

"When their usefulness was over, he stranded them on this world," I said.

"That, or the Waki'el made it impossible for them to leave."

"How so?"

"Honey."

"Felis Bray'el addicted them to Waki'el females."

"The little bastards have stunted nervous systems. I'll bet honey hits them hard and fast. That's probably why old Ross has his girlie house."

I sat down across from him and wasted a minute by lollygagging in my thoughts. He touched me again, this time on the top of the hand. For some reason, I couldn't pull away. Instead, I spoke softly, for fear that hearing my words at full pitch would scare the wink right out of me. "I believe Eric was part of this particular contract that Theo had going with the Waki'el."

He answered me by murmuring, "Why do you say that?"

"Because one night he came home complaining that the Waki'el thought they were so damned superior to humans. Theo wanted cooperation not antagonism, and it grated on Eric to no end. At the time, I had no idea what he meant by cooperation, but now I think I do. Belinda may have been the model that joined our two species. They were studying her, and the knowledge they gathered from cross-genetic research, they fed to the Waki'el."

Hadrien pulled his hand back. He was all business now. "They fed the info to Dumaka Lant, didn't they?"

"Or Zebrim Hast."

"Belinda was dying, and she knew it."

"She was crying out for help, threatening to cause a commotion."

"Captain Verena said Lundy came to beg Mann Re to find someone to help Belinda."

"But she couldn't, because the only one who could help her was Dumaka Lant."

"As far as I can figure it, he was getting good data from the Earth researchers, and he wasn't ready to turn his hand by helping to save Belinda's life."

"Turning his hand at what?"

I shook my head. "I don't know. Maybe he needed to see what would happen to a crossbreed Waki'el at the end of her life cycle."

"The life cycle being determined by the continued flow of creation energy."

"So they say. I can't figure out if the Waki'el are referring to symptoms of illness when they discuss the energy withdrawal or if they are talking about a pure circumstance of reversing the vibrational flow."

"Can such a thing theoretically be done?" he asked. "Turning energy back around?"

"I don't know, Artie. I'm not a scientist."

"Did Eric think so?"

I shrugged. "I would assume it would be like closing a circuit in electricity. There are so many things we don't know about the interplanetudes that it's surprising we've gotten this far in time and space." I paused to glance at the cards on the table. He'd drawn several, laying them out in a neat row.

Hadrien saw the shift in my gaze and pointed to them. "So what does it mean?"

"Fortune and collaboration build new worlds of anger to synthesize. Did you ask a question?"

"Yes. You won't want to hear it though."

I cleared my throat and stood up, knowing that he'd wondered about our relationship. There was no way on this orange world I would give him the satisfaction of my interest until I was ready. If I did have free will, then, while the planets hurled us toward an inevitable collision, I was going to do everything I could to avoid the crash.

I moved to the porthole, but my mind wasn't on the commotion in the spaceport. "I'm beginning to think that there's not one bit of difference in the Waki'el. The Sen'Tal have used oppression as well as politicians from other planets. Tell your population a lie for a thousand years, and the truth disappears and can never be fully recovered. Even the progenitors of the lie can't recall the reality."

"Do you think the zero-point babies have uncovered something in Waki'el biology that should have been left alone?"

"Well, information can have its price, especially with those irradiated bastards."

"So, what we might be looking at is the N'galia over-running the Tus and Basira castes with selective medical interference."

"Why couldn't the balloon heads be running their own little technology pool with the N'galia? Maybe they are fixing the creation energy so one particular type of egg is hatched more often than not. Maybe they gave that information to Dumaka Lant, and his studies have started breeding in the changes."

"The balloon heads have allied with the Acu-Sen'Tal to beat back the circumstances that Theo and the Sen'Tal have put them in."

"Didn't we find out that the condition needed to create a Waki'el female who carries amber is to be N'galia born into Tus or Basira clutches?"

"So the balloon heads might be seeding the lot on both sides, making life better for themselves here and slowly overtaking the ruling castes through sheer numbers."

"It could be possible, but there might be problems, and that's why amber females are rare."

He nodded. "Such as the shortened life span produced by diddling with the vibrational quality of the individual."

"Yes."

He stood and walked to the porthole to stand beside me. "What do you think?"

"I think we need to talk to our friend Ross. With the right persuasion, he might be able to shed a little more light on this."

"It's almost evening. Do you want to get some rest before we go out?"

I shook my head and pulled my power back to me by walking toward the hatch. "I don't have any sleep in me right now. Let's stop in to see what Omar's done, and then we'll hit the trail."

We headed out right away. Crewmen welded and ironed the *Kourey*, making minor repairs to her interior hull plates. The corridor leading to the sick bay was crammed with equipment as well as men arguing about the proper way to disassemble an oxygen regulator that was about to burst and explode. We cut through the work zone to escape into the quiet confines of Dr. Omar's infirmary, but the moment the hatch closed, I sensed that something was wrong. It was not so much a psychic reaction but a reaction to the stench.

"It stinks like an overflowing yank in here," I muttered, trying to talk while I held my nose.

Hadrien stopped in front of the supply case. Opening it, he took a smelly second to review the contents. He tossed a surgical mask at me, donning one himself before pulling his side arm from his holster and slinging me a muffled command. "Stay behind me."

He had no worries there, mate. I was going to give him all the sherbet on this one. Hanging back, I purposely used his bulk to block me from any trick shooting that might come our way.

We padded silently down the short hall that connected the main waiting room with the examining cubicles. Hadrien checked each space, finding them empty, dark, and uncluttered. The bloody awful smell filled everything.

We finally crept to the refrigeration vault. The hatch was ajar, and when I stepped up to it, I realized the odor issued from within the freezer. Obviously, something had gone rotters.

Hadrien entered, hugging the wall. The place was black, but there was a small sound in the far corner. My partner fumbled for the wall switch, found it, and flooded the compartment with blue neon light.

There, lying on the deck in a lake of his own green blood, we found Dr. Omar. We rushed toward him yet were suddenly stopped by his agonized bellow.

"No! Don't come close. I've been—infected with mold spores. Stay back."

He gripped his chest and squirmed, catching us in his gaze. His eyes were wider than usual with fear and pain. Blood runnels flowed between his fingers and from where I stood, I could see the yellowish stain on his white jacket. "Sirus liver trying to compensate," he croaked. "Smell. Smell. Not good. I'm dying."

"Who did this to you?" Hadrien barked.

Omar took a shaky breath and coughed, spitting his life force in my direction. "Balloon head," he whispered.

Seconds later, the oversized saucers that he called eyes were permanently fixated on the light of the afterlife.

31

According to the interplanetudes, we have daily opportunities to turn the pile of life's manure into fuel that will expand our thoughts, ideas, and attitudes. Transiting planets, the worlds that move through our horoscopes each day, routinely knock up against the planetary alignment set at the moment of birth. They square, oppose, conjunct, trine, septile, and inconjunct. In other words, this movement between the past and present reads like an open book if you know what to look for. My own chart showed Mercury, Mars, and Jupiter septile with my Northern Node. This alone represented an opportunity to take in and learn via the path of least resistance. But farther down the logos, Chiron opposed this same node. Chiron represented my ability to manifest security in my life. This configuration challenged me to blend the two concepts by forming an incongruity in the situation. Unfortunately, my doubts about my own abilities crawled up behind me and bit me in the bum. I didn't know where to turn next.

Hadrien and I spent the following hour asking the workmen if they'd seen any balloon heads float by, but no one admitted to observing anything out of the ordinary. The ship had been sealed to unauthorized personnel; everyone presented valid identification; and we found ourselves offsides at the cricket match. Had Omar tried to tell us something else with his final breath?

The *Kourey*'s security force sealed the sick bay, and we headed away before Cornelius Paul showed up to bugger us with blame. Once we stepped out into the Arifian night, my partner paused to glance up and down the street.

"Do you suspect everyone?" I asked.

"Don't you?"

"No. Only a few people, actually. This is turning into derby day, and we're the horses they're running."

"You feel manipulated, too?"

"More than that. I got me daisy roots in a tangle over this. We've got a ballsy Barney Rubble."

He smiled gently, and I realized that my proper British had slipped into East End slang. "In English, please," he said.

"We've got walking trouble," I answered.

"But we may have a lead," Hadrien said.

I stared at him. "What lead? Omar is dead."

He reached into his cammie pocket and pulled out a short sheet of computer paper. "I found this lying near one of the sick bay analyzers. It was partially wedged under one foot of the machine."

"What is it?" I demanded.

"I think it's the numbers on the fungus. There's something interesting right here." He handed me the paper and pointed to a sentence at the end of the analysis. "See that? 'Substance contains signature properties of atomic alteration. Photon charge corrupted by tachyon particles consistent with hyperbolic stasis created in zero-point gravity. Induction appears to have been precipitated.' " He glanced at me. "I'm no scientist, but I think this means the mold was artificially created instead of all that bunk about being blended in one particular part of this planet."

I almost dropped the printout when I realized what he was saying. "You think he was giving us a clue instead of pointing to his killer."

"I do at that. And I think it's definitely time we visited our favorite pimp." Before I could pose any objection, he stalked away, not even glancing back to see if I followed.

The streets were crowded this evening because another tourist liner had docked from Maya, bringing in a variety of aliens interested in tossing money toward the locals. Every house and hovel on the main boulevard had their charcoal pots steaming by their front stoops, their shingles hung out, and the charm poured on. When we reached Ross's digs, we discovered that the tourists had bought him out of all his girls for the evening. He was alone in his mud-brick bungalow, floating aimlessly in the middle of the room.

He gave us a mean expression that was enhanced by the size of his head. "What are you doing back here?" he growled.

The afternoon's events had plastered a black mood onto my already dark disposition. I walked over to him and, getting close enough to smell the sour onion and garlic on his breath, I spoke in a low, menacing voice slathered with tough East End talk. "Listen to me, you nig nog. We've had a terribly long day. Folks have come up dead right before our eyes, and we know that you and your kind has had something to do with it. We want answers. If we don't get them, then you'll be singing chorus with the Holy Ghost. Do you understand?"

Ross moved his gaze over my shoulder to take in Hadrien. He held back, watching the door for unexpected guests. But he was not so busy scouting that he didn't know the balloon head looked for him to be the moderating influence.

Hadrien chuckled. "In case you need a translation, you'll be toast if you don't answer our questions. My partner has lost all of her patience, and I've seen how effective she can be when pushed past her pleasant personality."

Ross tried the big man routine. "So what? I'm not afraid of you. You don't even have legal authority on this planet."

"Ah, that's where you're wrong," I said. "The emperor of Earth is working closely with the Sen'Tal to find and arrest the perpetrator of the ghastly crimes against Prince Lundy and Princess Belinda-Agnes." I paused for effect, leaning back to run my finger gently over the chair arm controls for his floating bucket. "And now we have another person whose brown bread on us. Dr. Omar, chief physician aboard the *Kourey*. Dead as a doornail with your name on his lips."

"My name? I didn't have anything to do with anybody's death. I'm a goddamned pimp. Why are you harassing me?"

"Because your greed the other night undid your impartiality." To prove we weren't joking, and to make my own guilt about Omar's death set better I flipped the battery switch on his floater. The machine faltered before making a quick descent to the floor. Ross and his bucket hit the deck with enough force to jiggle his big teeth inside his big head. He fought to restabilize his chair, turning on the energy pack. Moments later, he wobbled at me from eye level, his expression full of trepidation. To make matters a little more tense, I did a round about, inspecting all the wires and studs decorating his metal world. "I don't usually like to screw with the dimensionally challenged, but I suspect I could do you quite a number if I pulled one or two of these connections free."

"Please," he blubbered. "I'll tell you what I can, but

honestly, I'm nothing more than a slug to the Waki'el, a human computer. That's all."

"What did you sell out for?" I asked.

He shook his enormous head. "For the chance to manifest an ego."

"What?"

"Life in a zero-point colony is orderly and boring. We're all alike, with very little differences in our brainpower. Didn't you know that?" He stopped speaking to drive his little cart away from me. When he was safely across the room with his controls guarded by the far corner, he continued. "Zero-point gravity affects the intelligence. We're all geniuses, but not one of us can outdo the other with our smarts, and we're all pretty much the same in the emotional department. It's a built-in inhibitor, and why the cells form in a clonelike manner is still a mystery. By coming here, I thought I had a chance to be somebody different."

"Yeah, you've done real well," Hadrien said.

"You Earthers judge everything by outward appearances. And they say you have the imagination of the universe. Bah. You're slow, dim-witted, and given to violence."

I ignored his snide remarks. "When you got here, you discovered that you couldn't make enough wonga to buy your way off this rock. Isn't that right?"

"Your emperor lied to us."

"Theo? Nice chap like him? Doesn't seem possible."

"Are all you Earthers blind? He's a maniac. So is Felis Bray'el and so is that butcher they call a priest."

"Dumaka Lant?"

"Yeah, him."

Hadrien stepped away from the window to pull up before the floater. "When you got here, the Waki'el immediately fixed you up with females. Females who were loose with their kisses."

Ross's nostrils flared, and then he flapped one of his

fins at Hadrien. "I didn't even realize what had happened until it was too late. I was trapped by my own desire." He stopped speaking long enough to sigh. "It happened to each of us, I suppose. We have the perfect nervous systems for it. The addiction was practically instantaneous."

"Why did the Waki'el hire your services?" I demanded.

"When they first approached me, they wanted me to do meteorological work."

"The weather?" Hadrien said.

"Yeah. If you haven't noticed, it's bone dry on this world. No rain for about three decades. If it hadn't been for the alliances that your emperor helped set up between Earth and the Waki'el, this race would have dehydrated—literally."

"They wanted you to predict weather patterns or something?" I asked.

"That was part of it. Mostly, they said they wanted a solution to the problem. They thought the creation children could solve their dilemma and help them with their dependence on outside water sources."

"Obviously, you zero-p kids couldn't pull it off," Hadrien said. "Arif is still a dust ball in space."

Ross flicked at one of the switches on the chair, fine-tuning a setting that I'd obviously misaligned. "You see, therein lies the big, fat problem. When I arrived, the Sen'Tal changed their request. They wanted me to do theoretical analysis of interdimensional amplitude."

"The last time we spoke with you, you told us that," I said. "Stop jacking us around with big words. What's it mean?"

"I helped figure the flow rate of creation energy into this dimension."

"Why?" I asked.

"How the hell do I know? I suspect they wanted to

know how much of the stuff they could channel. They didn't like the news I gave them."

"Which was?"

"The flow rate is inconsistent. There are leaks between the dimensions."

"What kinds of leaks?" Hadrien demanded.

"Do you understand the interplanetudes?"

Hadrien pointed at me. "Talk to her."

Ross nodded, and his huge head bumped against the back of his chair. "You realize that the dimensions are like bubbles situated one beside the other. The only thing keeping them separate is a universal membrane of time and space. When you access zero point, you burst through that membrane via the gravitic energy exchange."

"So?"

"So, the walls of dimensionality get thin in spots."

"How many leaks did you calculate while doing this work?"

He hesitated, but then he answered, "Hundreds of thousands."

"What do you think is causing it?"

He snorted. "Personally? I think it's caused by each and every Waki'el living in this dimension."

32

Instead of giving us everything we wanted, Ross decided to shift our attention by leading us to the hovel of a fellow balloon head by the name of Skelley. I became instantly suspicious, because back on Earth in the bejeweled isles of my homeland, the word *skelley* meant storyteller. What kind of bloody bunk were we going to hear now?

Skelley had a couple of Waki'el females fulfilling his needs when we arrived. They moved about his hut in the harsh light of two battery lanterns, one Waki'el sweeping at the red dust on the worm-eaten wooden floor, the other tending to a pot of stew bubbling over a fire in the hearth. Skelley himself was so shit-faced that he could have floated without the help of his chair. His big, bulb-shaped head lolled on his shoulder, and he drooled onto the collar of his stained linen shirt. A repugnant odor hung heavy in the air. It took me a moment to realize it was the smell coming from the dinner pot.

This was nothing compared to the sight of seeing a big-eyed Corrigadaire lounging on a chair in the corner, watching us silently but intently.

Ross ignored the other occupants in the room to skim over to his friend. Using the end of his flipper, he smacked Skelley across the lips. The balloon head responded with a grunt before stirring himself enough to look around. Ross glanced our way as we hugged the side of the room nearest the exit. "Sorry about his condition. Old Skelley was one of the best before the honey got him." Smacking the bloke again, he finally woke him up.

"Whadya' want?" Skelley slurred.

"Got a couple of investigator types from Earth who want to ask you some questions."

"Why?" Skelley asked. "I ain't got a friggin' thing to say to a couple of clampers."

"Yeah, well you'll do it for a few guild pieces, now won't you?"

One of the females called out, interrupting the conversation. "Yes, he will, Ross. We have little food in the larder, and he hasn't done anything to remedy the situation. Just sits there slobbering on himself." She stopped sweeping to aim the end of the broom at him. I thought she might use it as a long pointer. Instead, she used it to bat Skelley across the back of his huge head. "Wake up! Make yourself useful."

Skelley bellowed a curse but settled down instantly, and the female returned to her cleaning. The zero-p baby swiveled his chair to take us in with a cockeyed gaze. "So? How many guild pieces are we talking about?"

Hadrien stepped forward, halting a good meter from this slimy ball of goo. "We'll start with one."

"Two," the female said.

Hadrien looked her way, and from where I stood, I could see him smile, but I could also see that hooded, dangerous expression slide over his face. "All right, two." He dug into his pocket, produced the coins, and then flipped them to the female before switching his attention back to the wretched reject. "Mr. Ross here tells us that you worked with Dumaka Lant on his creation energy experiments."

Skelley glanced at Ross. "Where the hell did you dig up that crap from, mate? It was Zebrim Hast I worked with."

"Zebrim Hast?" Hadrien said. "What did you do?"

"What didn't I do? Blue-hided son of a bitch. I hope his heart falls off of him, and he drags it through the mud before he realizes it." Skelley paused to dab at snot running down his lip. Then: "Marika, give us a kiss."

The female who swept the floor stopped to glare at him. "You've had enough. No more for you tonight." Turning to her compatriot, she added, "Don't let him touch you this evening. Do you understand?"

The other female nodded at Marika's command and busied herself setting the table with wooden bowls. Skelley settled in easily with defeat, focusing again on us. "What did I do for Zebrim Hast? I computed the angle and trajectory of the zero-point gravity flow coming from the causal plane where the N'galia Waki'el hail from."

Hadrien blinked at him and then shrugged. "Philipa, do you understand any of this?"

I stood there for a minute before answering him, because I was doing a bit of blinking myself. Finally, I managed a sentence. "Plotting an angle and trajectory would require starting coordinates."

"Yeah, so?"

"You're saying that Zebrim Hast provided you with this information?"

"No. His predecessor, Fangor Jaban did."

"How?"

"The creation energy continually flows between each Waki'el and the next dimension. They know instinctively their anchor position in the material realm, and by placing up their descriptions to known frequency flow rates, I was able to pick out their dimensional origin."

I didn't know whether his words were confused by the honey, because my brain only had enough computing power to grasp the image that the balloon head presented. Hadrien stepped off the space between us and faced me, speaking quietly. "Theo is in the glitter, isn't he?"

I chuckled, despite myself. Glitter was a pretty way to say our emperor and our planet were being sucked down the toilet through the other end of the dimensional pipe. I ignored his question to pop one at Skelley.

"Why did Zebrim Hast want you to compile this data?"

"Old Zebrim Hast wants to wrestle the power away from the Sen'Tal. He can't stomach them, and I can't say that I blame him. Dirty beggars." He glanced at Ross. "They diddled us, old man; diddled us hard. Ain't right."

"I know, Skelley. Trapped the whole lot of us, they did."

"What did Zebrim Hast do with the data?"

"He helped Fangor Jaban control the direction, source, and flow of the creation energy." Pausing, he squared me with his beady eyes. "Fangor Jaban made Mann Re."

"Abomination," Marika grumbled loudly.

"Why did he do that?"

"To see if he could control the influx of N'galia born to Basira and Tus clutches. You might call it selective genetics at the photon level."

"Photon level?" Hadrien asked.

Ross jumped into the crowd. "You, me, everything that you see in this dimension is just a play of photonic activity. When it comes down to it, the essence that defines you is nothing more than light."

"So, this bloke, Fangor Jaban, was trying to take over the established norm by overpowering the Tus and Basira at the energetic level," I said.

"Yeah," Skelley said before rotating his car toward

his two alien lovelies. "Come on, Marika. Give me a kiss. I'm suffering here."

"No," she snapped. "Continue to answer questions."

"Nasty bork, you are, Marika. I should put you out of your misery."

"And what would you do, you drooling, big-headed fool?"

"Soni will always take care of me, won't you?"

The other female whispered something, but I didn't quite catch it. Whatever she said seemed to satisfy Skelley, because he turned back toward us, aiming his car like a matador facing a bull. "Fangor Jaban manipulated countless other Waki'el. He knew that his dinking with the product created certain permutations within females. Namely, amber."

"How does Zebrim Hast fit into this?" Hadrien demanded.

"Zebrim Hast invented the zero-p gravity regulator. It was an offshoot of Fangor Jaban's deceitful practices."

"What's a zero-p gravity regulator?"

"It controls the photon wavelength by slowing down light."

"The pacemaker, Artie." I said.

Hadrien nodded. "I thought Dumaka Lant took credit for that invention."

"Bah. Dumaka Lant is a butcher. He found the material for Zebrim Hast to experiment on. After the war, they had a good old time working on aliens. Don't let these blue-skinned bastards fool you. They know more about you than you know about them."

"Then, how did Dumaka Lant get credit for building the regulator?" Hadrien asked.

Skelley chuckled and a spit runnel formed down his chin when he did. "How else do you think he got credit? He stole it and then sold it to Felis Bray'el in exchange for a commission in the Sen'Tal." With that, he spun his chair away so we stared at the back of his enormous head. "That's it for the interview. If you want to know more, talk to Fangor Jaban. I'm outta the question and answer business."

"Well, how do we find this Fangor Jaban?" I asked.

Surprisingly, the Corrie stood up and stepped from the shadows. "I'll take you," he said. "For a price."

33

The Corrigadaire called himself Chuuk, and he
assured Hadrien and me that he would lead us to Fangor
Jaban. It would take a day or so to arrange the meeting,
and with that, he left. We departed soon after, walking
through the sepia shadows cast by the moon. Hadrien
wedged me close to the walls of the buildings like he
was worried about a drive-by shooting. It was near
dawn, and the greedy Waki'el merchants had rolled up
the sidewalks, bagging their guild pieces and going
home to eat bread made of dust and breathe air that was
mostly smoke.

"Slow down, Artie," I said. "Me lungs hurt."

He halted to study me, as though the shadows helped
him to see. "Are you all right? Do you think you sucked
in some of the fungus spores?"

I shook my head and tried to sound nonchalant. "I
think I'll live. It's just this blasted pollution. I feel like
I've puffed down a couple of me daddy's oilers."

"Oilers?"

I sighed, more in an effort to oxygenate my blood than
to show impatience. "Oily rag—a fag. Cigarettes."

A cold breeze launched down the street, making me shiver. Dust devils abruptly birthed in the middle of the lane and spun down the boulevard to break up a clot of Waki'el standing on the corner.

Hadrien took a step onward, waving me into action. "Let's get back to the ship. I want to wash off the grime and put some food into my stomach."

We returned to the *Kourey*, and my new partner did just that. Hadrien was a meticulous sort, and try as I might, I couldn't find evidence of it in his chart. As he took care of his needs, I sat down on the salmon-colored sofa and stared off into space like I might be able to see straight through to the afterlife.

It had been a day manifested with the dark energy of Mars and Saturn. Omar was dead, and the harsh truth was leaking out onto the ground all about us. Perhaps the worst thing was to find out that maybe we Earthers had been bested in the science of the interplanetudes. For all our ideas and imaginative applications of zero-point gravity, we were latecomers to the scene as far as the Waki'el were concerned. If they could, indeed, pinpoint themselves in time and space and experience the creation energy flushing through them, then it could well be said that the differences in their evolutionary path had made them far superior. Theo, it seemed, had blundered into a plot that had taken many years to see to fruition. As it now stood, we still didn't know who killed Prince Lundy and why.

Hadrien waltzed into the room smelling soapy and clean. He wore nothing more than a pair of silkies, dark blue trousers that shimmered when he moved. Instead of nestling into the couch, he stood where he was, studying me.

"What's the matter?" I asked. "Has me lung popped out through me side or something?"

"No. How do you feel?"

"I'm okay. Especially now that I'm topping off with relatively clean air."

"Good." He kept staring at me.

"What is it, Artie?"

He blinked, frowned, and shook his head before heading toward the tiny fridge compartment. As he rifled through the contents, he said, "I feel bad about Omar."

"Yeah, me, too."

"I never thought I'd hear myself say that."

"Why?"

"Because I always punched myself above aliens. As far as I was concerned, humans were at the top of the heap."

"It's rotters to be wrong, isn't it?"

"It's rotters to feel guilty about it." He pulled out a large box of frozen macaroni and tossed it on the table. It hit with a thunk. The noise vibrated through me, filling me with a sense of finality.

For six months, I'd been avoiding death. I'd refused to look at it. In the last four days, I'd been exposed to so many violent endings that I'd grown a callous layer over my soul. It's what I'd been missing ever since Eric had died so brutally.

The door chime sounded, drawing off my reflections. Hadrien stepped to it and glanced through the peephole. "It's Paul," he murmured. Turning away, he headed for his cubby, leaving me to answer the summons.

Paul stormed into the room with two burly guards just as Hadrien returned from his bunk room. I backed toward my partner.

"What do you want, Paul?" I asked.

He straightened the collar of his black robe and glanced around the cabin before answering. "We've been sealed by the Sen'Tal."

"Sealed?" Hadrien said. "What does that mean?"

"That means, Lieutenant, no member of this crew or delegation may leave the *Kourey*, and the *Kourey* may not leave the spaceport." He shifted his weight slightly to make an expansive movement. "And this peach-colored petal of a room is where you two will be confined."

"Confined?" I said.

"That's right, Philipa. Confined. The Sen'Tal is raising questions about your presence. Apparently, the emperor didn't clear your investigation with the government here, and protests have been placed with several senators back on Earth. Of course, that's just like Theo, isn't it? Everyone gets burned but him."

"We haven't harmed anyone," Hadrien said.

Paul smiled slightly, and therein I saw pure evil pleasure. "Someone tried to assassinate Mann Re this evening."

"Who?" I demanded.

"We don't know, but she is to be protected at all costs. That's one of the reasons Felis Bray'el had the *Kourey* sealed."

"I reiterate: We've harmed no one."

Paul held his arms out in pseudosubmission. "What can I say? While here, I am ordered to obey the Sen'Tal's wishes. And Felis Bray'el wishes you two to be locked down."

"He can't do that to us," I insisted. "You can't do that to us. We were fully sanctioned by Theo."

Paul clicked his tongue in amused admonishment, and it ticked me off so badly that I tried to stop him on his retreat to the hatch. I grabbed the flimsy fabric of his robe. Underestimating my strength, I ripped his sleeve from shoulder to elbow. He stopped with his arm raised to strike me, but Hadrien put the kabonks on it by pulling his side arm. It had apparently resided snugly in the waistband of his trousers since Paul's entry—cold steel against warm skin. He pointed it at the executioner's head while Paul's guards met him match point by raising their own guns. Hadrien played it tough the whole way through.

"Touch her and I'll plug you through the bean, old man. I'm not joking or jiving or spitting honey."

Paul stared at him with an expression that barely contained a tornado of hate. He lowered his hand and yanked at his torn sleeve. It took him a moment to turn on his heel, and in that time I was presented with another piece of the puzzle: Zigging up Paul's arm was the tattoolike lightning bolt similar to the ones we'd seen on the Waki'el females.

34

Moments after Paul's abrupt departure, sirens started sounding. The noise rang eerily into the cool, dawn morning, and it forced us to the porthole to see what the problem was. It took no fast draw with a brain cell to see that not only were we locked in, but we would be socked in as well. From our vantage point, we were able to see the city as it smoothed out to the horizon. A sandstorm blew in as if the Sheik of Araby was leading a thunderous horde across the desert. The wind rattled through the spaceport, and small pebbles blasted against the *Kourey*. Within minutes, the sand had obscured all the scenery.

I stepped away from the porthole, reached over the table, and pulled the heat tab on the macaroni dinner. "Thanks for offering to plug that monster through the cranium for me," I said quietly. "But I can take care of meself."

"I know you can," he answered. Hadrien moved up behind me, so close that he whispered in my ear.

I didn't move, not because I was afraid of stepping on his toes, but because I truly longed to hear some comforting word. I was afraid that if I jigged just a little bit either way, those words might not come at all. The joke ended up being on me.

Hadrien took a deep inhale before murmuring: "We are a half-hour from execution, and we still don't know with any clarity who killed Lundy. I'd say we need some bargaining chips in the worst way."

I could have smacked him for speaking the truth instead of some soft nothings about how much he wanted me. "What do you propose we do?"

"Get out, now."

"What, in the middle of a sandstorm? We'd run head-long into trouble without seeing it coming."

"Paul won't expect us to make a mad dash in bad weather. If nothing else, our disappearance will piss him off so bad the big vein in his neck will stand up."

I'd seen that jagged tattoo shadow running up Paul's arm, and Hadrien's words made me consider an insane possibility. But I dismissed it to angle my gaze his direction. "Where in the bloody hell are we going to go if we manage to get shed of here?"

"Right across the spaceport to that Corrigadaire tourist liner."

"You want to book passage?"

"Well, actually, I'm thinking our little friend Chuuk might help us for the right price. Didn't he mention that he was a below-decks mole?"

I thought back to our short visit at Skelley's. "I believe he did."

"He might help us lay low for a couple of days until we start reeling in a fish on this investigation. I don't think the Waki'el want any fights with the Corries, do you?"

"Well, then, Artie, eat your macaroni so we can pack our glad rag bags and haul our boats over to the next jetty. I just hope we don't get lost en route."

"I just hope we can get out of the cabin," he answered as he headed for his cubby.

Paul had seen to it that a guard was placed at our door. To save our pencil necks, we had to first get past him with the minimum of effort and alarm.

We packed our clothes in a couple of rucksacks, hoisted them over our shoulders, and then stationed ourselves to either side of the hatch. The door cycled when opening and slid back on runners, disappearing into the bulkhead until a sensor determined that a person had entered or exited. It was simple hydraulics, kicked into action by a small impulse board. Using the scalpel Hadrien had pinched from Omar's sick bay, I cut through the wall to expose the housing controls, trying to be as quiet as I could. The plastic-board didn't fall away as expected, so I was forced to dig my fingers into the trench cut by the scalpel and paw it free. Dust exploded into the air, covering my dark blue cammies. I sneezed like a longshoreman and was forced to scrabble for a handkerchief so I wouldn't sling yellow submarines all over Hadrien while loudly exposing our plan to the guard outside the door.

He placed a forefinger to his lips and, pointing at the impulse board, he whispered, "Are you sure you know about that thing?"

"Yes," I snapped, suddenly irritated. Turning to the small unit, I took a moment to study the boards. My father had at one time been a locksmith and, in some fit of madness, he decided that each of the kids should learn as much as they could about the fine art of opening doors. He drilled the lessons into us at the end of the school day, making us parrot answers to his questions before we'd get to fill our tums at the dinner table. I dreamed of sequential computer locks. It was part of my soul.

Hadrien grunted and checked his wristwatch. His movement knocked me clear of my reverie, and I turned my concentration back to the board. Selecting the number-two bank, I wedged my fingers carefully into the unit. Glancing at Hadrien to see if he was ready, I tugged on it.

The hatch cycled and slid open. I smiled when the sentry threw a look my way. He stepped inside the room, and Hadrien smashed the bloke over the head with a heavy glass ashtray. The strike made a horrible, squishy thump, and the guard tipped backward right into Hadrien's waiting embrace. While I returned the board to the unit and closed the hatch, my efficient partner gagged the guard before strapping him to the steel shelf inside one of the cabin's closets. He shut and locked the door behind him before signaling me to pop the lock again. Seconds later, we escaped our peach-petal prison, selecting the darkened hallways of the *Kourey* that were closed for maintenance and repair. Our trip led us to an auxiliary hatch in the ship's belly bay, a dim place of pipes and air venting conduits. There were a few engineers manning the bay, but they were half-hidden by a bulkhead, busy welding a fitting. Our passing went unnoticed, and we thought it was going to be boiled bangers and hot taters for dinner after that. Unfortunately, we discovered that the access hatch needed a key.

Hadrien cursed and slapped at the bulkhead in frustration. "We'll have to go clear across this tub to find another exit. That's taking a big chance. The duty officer is going to be along any minute to find that guard missing."

"I agree." Turning, I studied the blue sparks cascading from the welding torch, and then, emboldened by our success with the guard, I approached the workmen.

One of them noticed me and nudged his partner. The man stopped burning through the metal facing to raise his visor. "What are you doing down here?" he demanded.

"I'm ship inspector Jan Whiteston. My partner and I are doing a surprise evaluation."

The man dropped his torch. "Damn! I wish they'd stop with this shit. I can't get anything done for showing you people around."

"I don't require you to show me around. My partner and I need to check the seal on the belly bay hatch. We want to know how the ship and the seal are holding up to the sandstorm outside. We need the key."

He snorted and ripped his visor completely off his head before adding it to the pile of equipment. Running a dirty hand through his greasy blond hair, he grumbled, "You're joking, right? There are rocks the size of my grandma's head flying around out there. You'll get yourself killed."

I put on a superior tone. "Let us worry about that. Now, do you have the key, or do I need to speak to someone else?"

He sighed and then shook his head. "There's no key. The bastard sticks."

I upheld my end of the play. "Why hasn't it been repaired?"

"Because no one will answer my request and issue a hinge inhibitor. And I'm not paying for it myself."

"Understandable. Can you pry it open?"

"I can pry any goddamned thing open." With that, he marched toward Hadrien, who tossed me a cautious look as I joined him.

The maintenance man wrapped his fingers between the hatch and the bulkhead and popped the door. "Just gotta know which emergency stud to hit."

"What's your name?" I asked.

"Blake," he answered. "Richard Blake."

"Well, Richard, I'll see what I can do to get your supply requests answered. Thank you for your assistance."

He grunted and swaggered away, fully aware, no

doubt, that the bureaucracy wouldn't change over a simple act of courtesy.

"Ready?" Hadrien said.

"As ready as I'll ever be."

We stepped through the hatch, allowing it to cycle closed behind us. Pulling our hoods up over our heads, we started off, clinging to each other as the wind and sand pummeled us straight on. It was impossible to see jack-squat. Hadrien yanked me in what I hoped was a straight line, but when we reached the other jetty, we found a sand wall raised. It was the steel bulkhead that shielded the Corrie ship from its neighbors at the dock.

We stopped suddenly, then followed it in the same direction that the sand swept through. I had to pause once, unable to get any kind of breath at all. Sinking to my knees, I wheezed until I was certain that I spat blood.

Bless him for his concern. Hadrien fell to his knees beside me and, like a magician, he produced a handkerchief. He helped me tie it around my head before bodily lifting me to my feet and dragging me around like a rag doll.

I was certainly stronger than this. Why then did I let him do most of the work on this escape? I let him lead me around to an aft opening in the sand wall. Once inside the slight protection offered by the fence, I pushed off, standing under my own power. Hadrien didn't seem to give me a second thought. Instead, he immediately walked over to the hatch and banged on it. Seconds later, a Corrie crewman appeared. Hadrien said something to him before the monster nodded. My partner turned toward me and waved me inside the liner.

35

Chuuk was more than happy to help us out for
the right price. He quickly led us into the filthy, greasy,
dark bowels of the ship, which was known as the
Tru'lant. He stowed us in a cubby that had two bunks
with flat mattresses and no pillows. Rats—yes, the generic Earth kind—had spread throughout the galaxy, and
some had found sanctuary aboard this vessel. One of the
little beggars scurried along an overhead pipe to disappear into a large hole in the bulkhead above it. Hadrien
grunted when he saw its race toward safety, but instead
of speaking, he barred the grimy steel door and threw
his pack onto the cot.

"Can you breathe okay?" he asked.

Despite sucking in a tonsie of grit, I was all right. "I
don't know how many more days I can stay on this
planet. Goddamned Mercury is still retrograde."

He rifled through his bag and tossed out a question.
"What does Mercury have to do with it?"

"All plans are forfeit to the whim of the gods."

"Gods? Philipa, what are you talking about?"

"First tell me what you're looking for."

"A sock." He found one the next moment and dragged it free. It was a thick, woolly thing, the same gray color as the bulkheads. He climbed on the bed and, grabbing the pipe, he hoisted himself upward to jam the sock into the hole. After he was soundly on his feet again, he shrugged. "I hate rats. And I don't think that's going to hold them for long."

I nodded, suddenly more weary than a trog after a bad day at the races. My arse hit the cot with a thwack and drew Hadrien's attention right to me. He sat down next to me, so close that his thigh touched mine. Yet again, when I thought he might try to put the make on me, he drove the moment away.

"There's something about this investigation that you are not telling me."

I sagged in response. It was almost as if all the grief, anger, and futility of the last year descended on me like a curtain of black. Now, when the only thing that I really wanted was my jollys rocked, I couldn't even ask for it. Instead of answering immediately, I slid away from him and plopped on the other bunk, stretching out on the smelly mattress. Hadrien didn't move; he just watched me, silently coaxing me into an admission with his intense gaze. I finally spoke up, surrendering the thoughts that had bothered me for the last couple of hours.

"There was an older scientist who worked with Eric. His name was Isak Mura. He was me husband's mentor of sorts. Supposedly a brilliant man. Mura held an interplanetudes theory that he called ingested time, and Eric boldly supported his views. According to his calculations, there were inherent inconsistencies within zero-point gravity where the creation vibration was collapsed through irregular expansion and contraction of time. His hypothesis figured that ingested time was an integral part of the incarnation process because it toughened the skin between dimensions like repeated kneading toughened dough."

Hadrien blinked. "So? What does that have to do with the Waki'el and Lundy?"

"His analysis had proven that energy trapped in the discarnate state couldn't find the creation pipeline."

"The afterlife is a crowded place of light displacement."

"Yes. And this theory did not sit well with Theo."

"Why?"

"Because it suggested that once we die, our consciousness does not convey through the dimensions simply because it can't."

He squinted. "Our egos remain firmly trapped in the corporeal dimension."

"Yes. And they remain here like vibratory vessels. Eric thought that when the energy from the afterlife trickled through the dimensions, it was necessary for it to connect with an available energy source—an unfilled ego force still residing in this plane at a quantum level. He referred to it as the point when creation's force animated the life field."

"What happens to our consciousness while we're waiting to be filled again with new energy filtering in on the zero-point vibration?"

"Nothing. Eric thought the energy might have converted to a state of celestial suspended animation."

"In effect, you have reusable consciousness."

"Yes." I shook my head. "Eric opened his mouth and fought for Mura's theory. He never knew when to take it lying down. It was a bad mistake, I think, especially with the emperor."

"Why should Theo care?"

"It places the responsibility of the soul squarely on the ego. The ego is essentially trapped in this dimension, and it is the link that centers us in the corporeal causal plane. The discarnate energy or what is called the soul essentially becomes nothing more than a spark to ignite the kettle waiting to steam. What we do with each incarnation through our thoughts, words, and actions affects the discarnate energy by converting the vibration ever so slightly. When the body dies and the soul escapes to the afterlife, it takes these changes with it where it infuses this altered frequency with the generic host."

He nodded. "What one ego does affects all the other egos through dispensation of the energy field."

I smiled at him. "You're some smart guy, there, gov." I paused to stretch, feeling the tingle surge through my sore muscles.

"Did Theo believe Mura's conclusions?"

"Yes, he did. On top of that, Eric's statements professed a belief that the nature of the universe was more variable than we'd first suspected. Theo suddenly felt like he lacked control, and this possible truth scared him fore to aft."

"And then along come the Waki'el."

"That's right. Mentors of light. Beings who instead of having to fill a heavy consciousness trapped in this realm, apparently manifested corporeality by the constant influx of zero-point gravity. They are, by all accounts, the true creation children."

"Then our stay in this plane is not calculated by the amount of time carved out in this dimension by the returning entity."

I sighed. It was the very thing that the interplanetudes had been based upon. Now, lying here in this slimy hole, I had to admit that it had indeed been the joke of my life. I had spent years learning to calculate the movements of the planets in accordance with theories inherited through our collective desire for our continued existence. We all wanted to believe in an afterlife that remained true to our understanding. From the old ideas of Heaven and Hell to the new thoughts about soul manifestation in the next causal plane, it was all very likely wrong.

Hadrien still wandered over the rough terrain of my explanation. "Theo was threatened by this idea. He's a bloke who needs control, and he identifies himself with the materiality around him."

"Yes. If I remember me history, it wasn't long after we ran across the Waki'el that the emperor began plying them with treaties. It would have been all right if Eric hadn't stirred the soup by jumping up and arguing for Mura's theory. I just can't see how Theo would let the bear out of the bag. He thinks he owns the world. Nothing can interfere with his reality."

"He talked Mann Re's father into delivering her to Earth so he could actually study a crossbred child and maybe gain something on the Waki'el and every other alien species out there."

"Theo is a stinking yank, he is. He will do anything to keep himself in power, including lying to humans about the origin of their souls. It's something emperors have been doing for a long time, starting with ancient Rome. Reincarnation was a widely held belief until the Council of Nicea overseen by Emperor Justinian made it against the law. Old Theo wants to make sure this new concept doesn't get out. He doesn't want people to believe that they are more than they are."

"Now you know what his downfall will be."

I glanced at him. "I suppose I stumbled upon the possibility more through dumb luck than anything having to do with the interplanetudes."

"What's this?" he asked gently. "Shaken faith? Maybe our dimensionality doesn't work like the Waki'el's. Maybe Mura's theory was a bad load of elephant manure."

I didn't answer because I couldn't. I didn't have enough energy to even discuss the idea. It was then when I was at my weakest and most vulnerable that Hadrien made his move.

He moved to my bunk, balancing on the edge. There was nothing hurried about his actions, and he spent another minute just sitting there staring out in the middle distance. Finally, turning his head slightly, he let his gaze roam over me before he whispered, "You were right about us. The planets brought us together."

With that, he leaned forward and kissed me in a most insistent manner. It was a pleasure to let him.

36

Two days passed before the sandstorm wound
down. During this time, I huddled with Hadrien, content,
at least for the moment, to be safe in his strong arms. It
was an illusion, true, but one I'd not indulged in since
Eric's death. I rather fancied the thought of having a
partner again. Of course, I knew it was my Libran lean-
ings that swayed my desires. Venus, the planet of love
rules my eleventh house, making me wish for friends
with which to share my ideals. That was a good excuse,
anyway.

It was late in the evening after the storm blew through
when Chuuk came to take us to see Fangor Jaban. As
we left by the ship's aft gate, the Corrie tried to up the
ante.

"You are wanted by the Waki'el," he said, picking at
filth between his fingers. "If I get caught, I will lose my
job and my life. What have you done to make Felis
Bray'el so upset?"

"How did you find out about all this?" Hadrien demanded.

"It is not a secret. No, no, no. Not a secret."

I glanced at him and saw those photon mincers of his glowing in the dark. "Has anyone been aboard looking for us?"

"Yes. The one called the executioner."

Hadrien blew out a hard breath. "Again. Tell me, how do you know about this, being a below-deck mole?"

"News travels. And I saw him. Yesterday." He paused to clomp down the chipped concrete steps leading to the street level. Once at the bottom, he added a real stinger to the conversation. "Executioner is volatile."

"Yes, we've figured that," I said.

"He has a bad nervous system."

Hadrien stopped abruptly. "What do you mean?"

"I can see it. Bad nervous system. Works strange, even for humans." Chuuk studied Hadrien with those pie plate eyes of his. "You have the same kind of nervous system he does, but your energy flows free. His is blocked along the big canals. Pressure builds. Energy explodes. That's what it looks like, anyway."

"Do you think Paul has got a rev problem?" I asked Hadrien.

He shook his head and waited for a tourist to walk by before answering. "When we first met with him, he drank alcohol. I don't see how. Maybe it's something else." He started walking, changing the subject. "How'd you find out about this priest?"

"Old Fangor Jaban. Yes, yes, I know him from a long time." He ran his hands down the greasy jumpsuit he wore. "Fangor Jaban hates the Acu-Sen'Tal."

"He probably has good reason," I said.

"Yes, yes, probably. An old priest. Been around for a long time."

Hadrien glanced at me and jumped into the interview as we exited the spaceport and stepped onto the street. "How old is he?"

"Oh, some say he is seventy years old. Very old for

a Waki'el. These people aren't supposed to live that
long. Least, that's what they tell you."

"You don't believe that?"

"I don't believe anything. I go by what I see, and I've
seen some old, old Waki'el. When they get too old, they
either die or they run away to ballon head country."

"They take up residence in a creation colony?"

"Oh, yes. Time isn't much of a factor there. I met a
Waki'el at Lykosol Station last year. Said he came to
zero-point gravity when he was forty-two. Figured he'd
been there four decades by his reckoning. Those big-
headed boys know how to use the creation energy to
refit a person."

"You mean they have a zero-point process that
strengthens the person?"

"Yes, yes. So I'm told. Very expensive though. And
really—who wants to live with the zero-p babies, anyway? You might add years to a frail life, but is it worth
it? They are so ugly they offend the membrane that
covers my eyes." He stopped walking and drew us close.
"You know that Waki'el whose kids are taking over for
the dead Earth prince?"

"You're referring to Mann Re and her children?" I
asked.

"Yes, yes. Mann Re. I heard that she was going to be
taking a berth in a creation colony, but I guess she
changed her mind, since she's going to Earth now. She's
real rich, you know. One of those who can afford it."

It was my turn to glance at Hadrien. "I thought she
was at the beck and call of her brother—without power
or property."

Chuuk laughed, and it sounded like a tinny dog bark
to me. "She's rich. Powerful, too. Felis Bray'el claims
he owns her out loud, but if you've ever been near her,
you know she has a mind of her own. She is very close
to the executioner."

I hadn't gotten that impression. "How do you know her?"

"Had to clean up her cabin when one of the top-level janitors was detained."

"She's taken a trip to Corrigadaire aboard your ship?"

"Often. Yes, yes. Nasty beastie. I don't like her. She was busy consorting with a human when I came to polish the deck."

Hadrien moved on this information like his britches were on fire. He dug through his pocket and pulled out the photo of Lundy to show to Chuuk. "Is this the man?"

Chuuk abruptly clammed up like a mussel from Briton Beach. "It's dangerous. Yes, yes, very dangerous."

It was a first-rate bilk. All the shivering and sweating reminded me of my old Uncle Benny when he'd come home to face Aunt Margaret's leather bobbie club. I fumbled through my pocket until my fingers found a guild piece. "Will real metal bring you a little more courage?"

He clawed the coin out of my hand. "Yes, yes, that's the human. That's the prince. Right?"

"Yeah," Hadrien said. "Did you see anyone else when you came to clean?"

"Only the daughter."

"Daughter?"

"Yes, yes. The daughter. The one they call the Alien Eater."

"The Alien Eater?" I said. "Are you talking about Ne'el Zara?"

"Yes. She has helped the butcher."

"The butcher being Dumaka Lant?"

"Yes. They are lovers, and she has gladly experimented on prisoners, so I hear." He pointed at my chest. "If you get caught by them, they will experiment on you."

Chuuk nodded and slipped the gold piece into his pocket. I didn't get another word past my flappers before he took off down the street quickly, refusing to answer any more questions.

He led us down a dark alley in a grimy neighborhood west of the ziggurat. Here the charcoal pots didn't burn on front porch stoops and the orange glow of hearth fires didn't filter out into the street. It was a dilapidated conglomeration of mud, stone, concrete, dust, and shadow—and some of the shadows moved. I heard Hadrien curse before he drew his side arm.

"Shhh," Chuuk hissed. "Dangerous part of city. Many balloon heads here."

"What makes a balloon head so dangerous?" I whispered.

"It's the size of their brains. Too much brilliance. Too dangerous. Especially in this society. It frightens the natives."

"Why?"

"Because Waki'el are not that smart."

He shut up then and led us to a narrow walkway between two buildings that was covered by a cracked, arched ceiling fashioned from cobblestones and crumbling mortar. We picked our way along this path until we came to a low-slung door at the dead end of this conduit. Chuuk tapped on it lightly, and a moment later it was answered by a wizened Waki'el. A crackling hearth fire silhouetted him, and I could see he was bent from age. Instead of a vibrant pitch of colors in his hide, he was the same shade as dried cranberries. The old geezer nodded. "Come in," he finally murmured.

Chuuk backed away. "I'm done. No need to come in. No, no, no." He glanced at me. "Return to the ship by the aft gate. You will be admitted there."

Before we could thank him, the Corrigadaire turned and hurried up the cut back toward the alley. We went inside, surprised that the accommodations were a comfortable blend of softness and heavy wood. Paper books lined one wall, their spines cracked from use. A small battery-operated lamp shed gentle light across a table strewn with what appeared to be an unfinished calligraphy project. I stepped over to the work to study the parchment documents, seeing only the scrawling text of the Waki'el language. The priest joined me, sliding into the straight-backed chair. He picked up a pen and, dipping it into a clay cup filled with ink, he let the tip soak up the substance before he spoke. "I am in charge of the library palmpiset," he announced.

"Why not input the information on a computer?" I asked.

"These are religious documents. The law requires that they be transcribed by hand. Electronic process causes interference in the energy surrounding the texts."

"As if paper has a life of its own," Hadrien said wearily as he plopped onto a green sofa in the hovel's sitting area.

"Everything has an energy signature," Fangor Jaban answered.

"Tell me something," I said. "Is my energy corrupted because I'm an abomination?"

Fangor Jaban frowned. "Who told you that?"

"Dumaka Lant."

"Like he knows. Pissant."

His attitude immediately grabbed Hadrien's attention. "You don't like him. Why?"

"He's N'galia Waki'el. No matter what he does or says he is, he's not Basira."

The priest dropped his pen on the table and turned in his chair to give me what I thought was a disapproving gaze. He screwed up his mouth and frowned. When he again spoke, it was in a quiet tone, nothing like the meaty response I expected. "No, you're not an abomination. That idea started just after your emperor wed Mann Re. It was to prevent other heads of household from selling their females into human bondage."

"We were told you created Mann Re," I said.

"That is not something I would admit to. Such a thing could get a person killed, and since I've lived so long, I would like to continue doing so."

"So, I take it you didn't approve of Mann Re's marriage to the emperor," Hadrien said.

"I don't believe I've given you any indication at all. It is none of my business. Besides, I would hardly be one to have a problem with cross-species induction—if you believe the rumors you have heard about me."

I switched gears on the trolley. "Can you explain the Waki'el life cycle to us?"

"We are connected to the creation energy. It flows through us. It stabilizes us within this dimension."

"How?" I demanded.

"In the same way it flows through every living creature. The difference with the Waki'el is how our brains convert the energy. We're connected to the dimension that humans call the afterlife."

"So are we," I answered. "Creation energy dominates us like it does all corporeal beings."

He shook his head. "You misunderstand. We are not dominated by creation energy. We have the ability to inspire this power."

If my eyeballs had been marbles, they would have popped out of their sockets and rolled around on the floor. It took me a moment to put words into my mouth. "Do you mean that aside from the time concepts of birth, aging, and dying, there is something else you can control?"

"I believe that is what I said."

Hadrien sat forward to turn slightly my way. He frowned. "What am I missing?"

I worked at getting my mouth back into motion, because my thoughts thundered down alleys that led to the past. Eric had been certain that zero-point gravity required nothing special to manifest that, as Saint Thomas Aquinas maintained, zero-point gravity had always been and always was. Our abilities to calculate its existence didn't change the true nature of the energy frequency itself. If we only could find the valve, we could channel this force to create something from nothing. Since we are all essentially a by-product of this vibration, then we should be able to harness it at an individual, physical level. His theory had sounded so impossible that I'd laughed at him for being such a wet doily about the mysteries of life.

"There is a problem," I said quietly. "Because of certain permutations in your species, you can't control the whole creation energy vibration. You have trouble directing it."

The old priest placed his pen on his table and stood up. He stared at me with hazy blue eyes before turning toward a large clay smoking pipe that leaned on a metal rack by the fireplace. Pausing, he flipped open a red box and, taking out a small spoon resting upon a bed of black powder, he filled the pipe's bowl. He replaced the spoon, closed the container, and then, taking an ember from the hearth, he lit the powder but didn't suck in the sweet-smelling smoke. Instead, he handed the pipe to me.

"It's nothing that will hurt you," he announced. "It merely confines the space in the room so that when we continue our talk, we don't risk interference or invasion."

I had no idea what he was suggesting, but I did remember my manners and trusted him on his word. Inhaling on the pipe made me cough. I passed it to Hadrien, who shook his head.

"I can't," he said. "I don't mean to be rude, but my nervous system is a mess. I'd better not sample the concoction."

It must not have been of prime importance, because Fangor Jaban simply took a breath of smoke and proceeded to explain the things that had been eluding us in this investigation. "You are correct about our limitations.

It's one of the reasons that as compared to other species, we are short-lived. This creation vibration streams into us from what you term the next dimension. It moves into our hearts, filling our bodies with life-giving energy, but first it floods through different receptors in our brains. Its strength is converted so that we can adequately assimilate the incoming vibration. N'galia Waki'el have a very gentle energy. It is much lower in intensity than that of the Basira and Tus." He paused to take another hit on the pipe before continuing. "When the stream stops, we die."

"But Dumaka Lant has solved that problem with his pacemaker," Hadrien said. "It keeps your heart pumping."

Fangor Jaban croaked a laugh. "Oh, he solved it all right, but not in the way you're thinking. He has done experiments—he and that thing he calls a mentor."

"You referring to Zebrim Hast?"

"Yes. A creature I had once called friend." The priest spat the word with such vehemence, I was certain some had landed on me. "He was the one with the idea for the regulator, not Dumaka Lant."

"So, Zebrim Hast should hold a bit of revenge against Dumaka Lant."

"It depends on their alliance. I don't know what their relationship is, but I suspect it is power raises power. That would preclude revenge."

Fangor Jaban set down his pipe on the rack before answering. When he did, his voice barely reached a whisper. "Most people can't control the flow of creation energy coming into their bodies. These new N'galia can. I saw to it."

"Can you tell us what the Waki'el concept of an affair of the heart is?" Hadrien asked.

"At one time, such a thing was the domain of the gods," he answered. "But Dumaka Lant figured out how to make it the concern of normal Waki'el by using the regulator Zebrim Hast created."

"Please explain it," I said. "We are ignorant of the process."

"It's quite simple. The incoming energy is blocked at the heart level. As it can no longer proceed through the organism, it is bounced back to its point of origin, in this case the next causal plane. Once there, it is then trapped because the channel between dimensions is closed down due to the change in the frequency. When the flow stops, the person dies in the physical realm."

37

Astrologers theorize that in the course of an un-
folding destiny, there are points of no return, places
where free will can do nothing to change the choices,
circumstances, and situation. You tumble toward an ir-
reversible outcome that transforms your life and leaves
you melting in a puddle of your own wank. If I'd had
the courage to check the board during the time Hadrien
and I dallied, I might have noticed a pattern that would
have screamed loud and clear at me. Stupidly, I preferred
to run along blind.

We left Fangor Jaban's hut, deciding to look up Yana
one more time before we returned to our hideaway to
decide on our next plan of action. We moved with the
shadows, concealing our mugs by pulling up our jacket
hoods. Once more, Hadrien used his bulk to block me
from the street.

I suppose it's usually awkward after a professional
duo succumbs to passionate sex. Hot upon the lingering
kiss, there is always that question of how one heart feels
about the other. Being here on this decimated world surrounded by the biggest hearts in the galaxy, it was hard

to avoid the subject. I was glad when Hadrien opened the discussion.

"If humans are a flood of creation energy that has filled empty ego receptacles by matching the force atom by atom until life animates, then why don't we remember our former lives? Once the union is complete, there should be some sort of memory remaining."

"I don't know. I don't even know if I believe it."

"Amazing thing—light."

"Yes, that it is."

We walked along in silence for a minute. After stepping around a charcoal pot, he glanced at me and asked a new question. "Do I seem familiar to you?"

"Familiar?"

"Yes. Like you've known me before."

Deja vu? "No, Artie," I answered softly. "I'm sorry."

He shook his head and grinned. "That's okay. I don't remember you, either."

I chuckled. "I do agree with you, though."

"On?"

"On how we were supposed to come together. You're going to have to trust me on that."

"I don't have to trust you. The truth just can't be denied sometimes." With that, he dropped the subject of our exclusive pairing with a loud thunk of finality.

I let his answer go, and when we turned the corner to Yana's house, I stopped him by grabbing the sleeve of his cammies. "You better hold your head down so that the rock-throwing Waki'el doesn't aim for you again."

He frowned but complied. Unfortunately, it did little good because we were greeted at Yana's door by Foran herself.

Hadrien stepped back, almost falling off the porch. I grabbed him by the wrist and yanked him into balance, even as I addressed the Waki'el. "We don't wish any trouble. We only came to speak with Yana."

She studied us like we had the bubonic plague. I

stared in return, sure I saw the Waki'el version of a
screeching fishwife. But it was an evening for surprises.
Foran pulled away from the door, inviting us into the
dusty hovel with a flick of her hand.

"Where's Yana?" Hadrien asked.

"He's gone," she answered quietly, moving to a small,
smoking fireplace. Stirring the embers, she shook her
head and tugged on the collar of the linen robe she wore.

"When will he return?"

"He won't be returning. I've been gifted with his personal effects. I'm trying to sort through them now."

"Did Yana die?" I squeaked.

"He might as well have. He was summoned to the
temple by that bastard Sen'Tal."

"You're referring to Dumaka Lant?"

"Yes. Yana was called this morning. They will execute him to take his heart parts. He still had a good
pumper, but the energy level was down. That happens
when a person grows old. It used to be that when one
grew weak with age, people would consider you a body
who'd lived long enough to acquire wisdom. Now it just
means defeat." She pointed to Hadrien. "He told me you
shared a blood clause with him. Is this true?"

Hadrien was fast with the lie. "That's right. He's got
a hanky full of my red stuff."

She shook her head. "I own the blood clause now. It
transferred to me. I'm required to help you in whatever
way I can, and you are required to help me, though I
don't expect that will ever happen."

"I'm honored," he answered.

She grunted. "It's not that I want to, mind you. I just
have to." She suddenly forgot the fire to turn to the table
to fetch an iron pot filled with water. She then carefully
dug a trough in the embers with the bottom of the pan
before placing it snugly in the heat.

Hadrien used the wall to lean against, and I took the
one available chair by the door.

"What do you want?" Foran demanded, leaning toward the image I had of the fishwife.

"You don't like the Basira, do you?" Hadrien asked.

"No. They are ruining everything with their highbrow ideas. The Sen'Tal has changed, especially since they started inviting in aliens to trample through our world. That, and taking on N'galia as priests of the heart."

"We understand Dumaka Lant is doing great things for the people," I said. "We were told that he's expanding the life expectancy of the average Waki'el by using donated human organs to reinvigorate failing parts."

"No one asked him to do that for us," she barked. "It's not necessary."

Hadrien turned the conversation abruptly. "Does Dumaka Lant randomly choose people for his heart operations?"

"I doubt that there is anything random about it."

"Why was Yana chosen, then?"

"Because he helped you."

"Are you afraid that you'll be called because we're here?"

"No. I'm Tus. He doesn't touch Tus or Basira. He's only interested in N'galia Waki'el and especially those abominations of N'galia born to Basira families." She stared at me. "I've seen one such egg. You would think it was encrusted with gems."

"I thought it was bad form to have someone like Mann Re born into a ruling caste."

"Who told you that? Females fetch high prices for marriage dowries because of the amber."

"What about the males born into this circumstance?"

"Males? I don't think I've ever heard of a male N'galia appearing in a Basira clutch. No, not all. If it were to happen, I would think the offspring would be killed."

"Why?"

"They might be too powerful and take over the house. Couldn't risk that."

I glanced at Hadrien. "Sounds like Fangor Jaban was trying to turn a few shillings by focusing on the female moneymakers."

"Well, if he made any wonga, he's hidden it. I'd say he's living on rocks instead of gold bars."

"Fangor Jaban?" Foran said.

"Yes. Do you know him?"

"Everyone does. He is scheduled to lead the priesthood when they relocate to a planet called Mars. Have you heard of it?"

I smiled. "Yes. It's Earth's neighboring planet."

"Your planet has much water, doesn't it?"

"Yes. We have things called oceans."

She nodded, but her expression was stuck in a frown. "Fangor Jaban has promised us that he would bring back water from Earth."

When she said it, I felt Hadrien stiffen. "They're seeding Earth's imperial government to make it easier to overtake the planet."

It took me a moment to grasp the severity of the situation. "They could knock out the whole imperial family."

"And I'd say they're halfway there already."

"Why do they need to take people's hearts?" I asked Foran.

She shrugged. "I don't know."

My next question was cut off by the tootling of horns and the bang of drums mixed with a triumphant cheer. Hadrien and I both moved toward the door, opening it to find a parade of Waki'el moving down the street. They wore shiny white cloaks and yellow feathered headdresses that were trimmed in sparkling colors. People stepped onto the streets to applaud these mummers, and Foran, like the good little Tus she was, barged by us to stand on the stoop and offer her own rousing salute.

"What's going on?" I demanded.

She glanced at us before answering me. "This is the Parade of New Warriors. They will be taken back to the temple for transformation."

38

Foran didn't explain this newest Waki'el ritual
any further, so Hadrien and I decided to tag along to see
where the whole thing took us. I should have reminded
my partner that both our Saturns were opposing Pluto,
and it was likely going to be a grand old time at the
villa tonight, but I kept wondering if I was anywhere
close with my feelings of foreboding.

We clung to the shadows and disappeared into the
crowd as the parade moved toward the ziggurat. Halfway there, we stumbled upon our old comrades John
Trainer, his wife, Mary, and Randal and Nina. They
stood on a street corner, each nipping from a small flask
while watching the Waki'el file by. We stopped with a
quick hello.

"Do you know what's going on?" Hadrien asked.

"It's some sort of fancy-schmancy ritual," Randal
said. "Heard them talking about it at the pub."

"What's it all about?"

Mary shoved her way into the conversation. "Well,
apparently, certain N'galia Waki'el got what it takes.
They make good warriors, though I ain't for certain

how." She turned toward Nina. "Did you get the plunk on the barkeep's explanation?"

"As far as I can tell, they are special-designed folks," she answered.

"You mean they've had their DNA tampered with?" Hadrien asked.

"Something like that, I suppose. The barkeep said they were folks born from special eggs."

"N'galia Waki'el born to Basira families?"

"Could be. Don't know for sure. They're kept in a special compound of the Acu-Sen'Tal where they grow up. When they're ready, they come and do this ceremony."

"How many of them are there?" I asked.

"The barkeep says they do this thing right often," John said. "At least a couple of times of year. I'd say that would give them quite a crowd of warriors."

"Is the ritual open to the public?"

"Naw. It's held somewhere inside that bloody awful building they call a temple."

Hadrien drew me aside as the old blokes started hitting a gin flask hard. "What do you make of this? Do you think they've got a factory turning out these special Waki'el?"

"I don't know, but it does sound like Felis Bray'el and the rest of the Sen'Tal are aware of the advantages that Fangor Jaban sewed into his creation energy beings."

Nina stepped over to us. "I heard that this ceremony transforms them. It binds up their power. Does that make sense to you?"

I shook my head and stopped talking to watch the parade pass, my thoughts beating along with the drummers. Obviously, the priests worked together, though they had opposing religious viewpoints. The strange polarities of their alliances might have been the reason they did cooperate, restrained in their actions by cultural ide-

ology. It certainly made an unusual mix of unrequited
vengeance.

I let my concentration fall away then, finding myself
mesmerized by the chanting that abruptly swelled from
the marchers. The sound was at once melodic and fierce
and vibrated through the mud-brick and concrete canyon
of the city. Waki'el bystanders responded to the noise
by adding harmony to the chant, their voices rising like
Sunday morning devotions sent to the emperor and to
God.

The ruckus hurt my ears and made my eyes water.
But as abruptly as their song began, it ended, sparing
me more discomfort. Glancing at the parade, I saw we'd
come to the end of the party. Here, being hoisted in a
litter of velvet fabric perched beneath an awning fashioned with gleaming gold guild pieces was the guest of
honor. He was a large, iridescent blue Waki'el, his skin
color dramatized by two paper lanterns hanging from the
overhead drape. He wasn't naked, like most of the
Waki'el. No, this bloke was dressed like a dog's dinner:
feathers, sparkling sashes, and shiny silver lamé britches.

"Who is it?" I asked Hadrien.

It was Nina who answered. "That there is Felis
Bray'el. Right spiffy for a leader, ain't he? Theo should
take a lesson and put on a show like this. It'd be worth
all that value-added tax we gotta cough up every few
months." She paused, took a breath, and yelled at Randal, "Hey, you old sot, are there going to be fireworks?"

Before her beloved spouse could answer, Mary interrupted him with a shout. "Looky yonder! That there is
the executioner, ain't it?"

Hadrien and I both stiffened and, stepping forward in
the crowd, we tried to see who the woman was pointing
at. Riding in a litter directly behind Felis Bray'el's conveyance, I saw Mann Re, her daughter, Ne'el Zara, and
Cornelius Paul.

We took our leave of the tourists, following the procession up the street and around the corner, lingering just out of Paul's line of sight. From a vantage point, we could see that he was familiar with Mann Re. He touched her often, and she touched him back. Ne'el Zara looked angry, baring her teeth as a human strayed too near her litter.

It was at least an hour before the route took the parade toward the base of the ziggurat, and another thirty minutes for the crowd to be dispersed enough so that the mummers could come to some sort of formation. When all were properly stationed, Felis Bray'el dismounted, followed after a minute by Mann Re, Ne'el Zara, and finally Cornelius Paul. The executioner immediately sought out Felis Bray'el and, leaning close, they shared some private joke that caused Paul to bark with laughter.

An inconspicuous door at ground level had been flung wide. Torches blazed in stands by the entrance, casting more orange in this firelit world, but we still edged as close as we could. From where we stood, I could count the number of pinfeathers in the Waki'el headdresses.

Felis Bray'el growled an order in the Waki'el language, and in unison the marchers turned toward the door and began to disappear inside, their sandals smacking loudly against the ziggurat's stone floor. The leader followed, tenderly escorting his sister by offering his hand. Ne'el Zara and Paul pulled up behind them.

There were no guards, and the last blokes through pushed the door closed behind them. Hadrien took a chance to rush for it, catching the heavy brass handle at the last second. Despite all the folks milling about as well as the blaze of light from the foul-smelling torches, Hadrien and I silently decided that we were invisible, and in we went.

39

The door concealed a long hallway illuminated by the ever-present burning torches. In such close confines, the scent of steaming tar nearly undid me, so I was grateful when Hadrien stopped short to hide behind a huge statue. I caught my breath while he ran his hand over the carving, letting his fingertips linger upon the gold veins running through the black marble. The statue was cast in the image of a Waki'el holding a long staff decorated with a jagged design.

It was my turn to run my fingers over the lightning bolt impressed in the stone. I pulled Hadrien around to inspect it. He shrugged before gently pushing me down the low-ceilinged corridor.

I have claustrophobia. It's as simple as that. Being inside the belly of the pyramid oppressed my power of concentration, and I found that I had to keep touching Hadrien just to feel better. He finally realized my discomfort at the thought that tons of rock hung directly above our heads, and he touched my shoulder to guide me along.

The last of the participants slipped through a large,

heavy wooden door. It contained a simple locking system that used an old-fashioned key. Hadrien was forced to prove his own resourcefulness at breaking and entering. He dug through his uniform pockets until he came up with a tiny laser scalpel.

"How many of those things did you steal?" I whispered.

"A whole set," he murmured. "I thought they might come in handy."

Hadrien hunkered down to eye level and, pressing the wand's activation stud, he burned a nice hole around the lock. Grabbing it with his fingernail, he dug the circle out. He leaned forward to peep through the opening.

"What do you see?" I asked.

"Nothing. It's dark and quiet." He stood and slowly turned the knob. The door swung open on creaking hinges, and when he pulled it back, I smelled the strong, eye-watering odor of disinfectant. He noticed it, too, because he grimaced and grunted. The shadows cast by the smoldering wall torches picked up his expression and gave him a rather appealing, demonic look. It took me the odd moment to get back my perspective.

Hadrien pulled me onward into the next hallway. It was lit by small, glass wall sconces decorating the far end. As we rolled up to a distant door, we discovered that the lights were electric and that the line was stapled to the mortar between the bricks. We followed its course along the edge of the floor until we came to another door. My partner pulled up short before trying the lock.

It was all wrong. Even I could sense it without need to check a logos or consult my cards. Where were the guards? Did the Waki'el have no need to protect their secrets, or did their feelings of superiority make them reckless?

The door was unlocked. Hadrien opened it, wincing when it squeaked. Once done, we were presented with an incongruous sight, for the entrance led to a white-washed, Sheetrock hallway softened with a dense-pile blue carpet. It was harshly illuminated by overhead fixtures of fluorescent tubes.

Hadrien stilled himself, eyes narrowed as he listened. The hallway swung a corner about ten meters ahead, and in our silence, we heard a humming sound. We moved quietly toward it.

Turning the arc in the corridor, we were halted suddenly by the appearance of a glass-walled surgical theater, its exit door standing slightly ajar. The bright lights drove away all the shadows, and we dashed for the cover of a tiny, rounded alcove formed at the juncture of the corridor and the operating room. Several moments ticked by as we squeezed into the space, trying to still our breathing while we listened for approaching footsteps. The sound did come, but it was produced by commotion taking place in the operating unit.

We watched as a female Waki'el was marched into the room by two male attendants and ordered to lie upon the gurney. One of the nurses adjusted the table, swinging a side piece clear. Locking it into place, he took the female's hand and, situating it with palm upward, he secured it to the extension with surgical tape. They then both stepped back to make room for another Waki'el coming through the door. Imagine our surprise when we saw that it was Zebrim Hast.

Hadrien glanced at me with a frown, and I mirrored his look back to him. Then I turned my attention to the scene in the operating theater.

Zebrim Hast wore not one glad rag to spoil his beautiful, glittering body. Nor did any decorations span his sternum ridges. His heart beat strongly and slowly, and the major artery traveling from his pumper vibrated as the blood passed into the rest of his body. I was caught staring at this peculiar part of his anatomy, trapped by fascination as well as confusion.

One of the attendants handed him a beaker of yellow

liquid. Hadrien touched my shoulder, mouthing the word: *fungus*.

Yes, it was the same stuff that had infected Lundy and Omar, and now Zebrim Hast boldly swabbed it onto the Waki'el's wrist. He spoke to her while he did, using Waki'el words that we couldn't quite make out.

When he was done painting the patient, the priest handed the jar back to the attendant, who offered him a small laser scalpel that was just like the one Hadrien had used to file away the lock. Zebrim Hast ignited the cutter before leaning over the Waki'el's hand. I watched, transfixed, while he sliced her wrist open at the artery. I was stunned to see that the Waki'el didn't bleed. The yellow fungus juice seemed to prevent it.

I leaned farther from the alcove to grab a better look. Hadrien held onto me at the waist, a comforting action in the midst of a strange and abnormal situation. His fingers dug into my side, though. I could feel his tension translating to me.

Once Zebrim Hast was done filleting the Waki'el, the attendant took the scalpel and handed him a small blue object. He paused before returning to his patient, holding the object toward the light. The moment he did, I saw that it was a pacemaker just like the one found nestled inside Prince Lundy's heart.

Assuming his position over the Waki'el's hand, he slid the pacemaker into the slit he'd just made. The attendant brought him a suture pen, and he made some connections within the musculature on the patient's arm. She groaned slightly. A few minutes more, and Zebrim Hast moved away from the table to allow the nurses to untie her.

I pulled back, trying to get clear of Zebrim Hast's view. Unfortunately, the glaring electrical lights spoiled all hope of concealment, and Hadrien and I were found out—not by the Waki'el surgeon-priest but by a guard who came out of nowhere, brandishing a staff decorated with the jagged symbol.

"Abomination!" he bellowed. "The pyramid has been desecrated!"

His shout grabbed the attention of those in the surgical unit, and they launched toward the door to help the sentry detain us. Hadrien pulled his gun, firing over the guard's head to stop him. When the bull kept coming, he pumped a round straight into his heart.

40

The Waki'el sentry stopped, shuddered, and then glanced down at his own chest with a surprised expression. Seconds later, blood traveled from his heart to his mouth, running like a tropical waterfall over the points of his sternum ridges. He collapsed in a rag doll heap, burbling his final good-byes.

Hadrien and I bolted for the exit, but it was a pointless exercise, because we were headed off by a detachment of guards led by Dumaka Lant. My partner grabbed me to pull me close, muttering something about me not carrying a side arm on a goddamned, smelly, alien planet.

The guards formed an impenetrable wall of sharp, pointed spears. Raised against Hadrien's gun, the situation suddenly turned into a face-off that spanned more levels of technology than I wanted to count. Dumaka Lant pranced bravely down the middle of it all. He didn't realize that I could grab him by his imperious attitude and break his neck with a simple chi movement. I did pause a moment to wonder why I didn't.

He stopped before us and settled his gaze upon me

for a full minute before speaking. "Your interference here tonight has created a tragedy, one that the Waki'el people will not appreciate should they find out. If I were to put this information to the people, I can guarantee that you would not reach your ship in one piece."

"What are you talking about?" Hadrien barked. "We didn't interfere in anything. We've done nothing but walk through an open door."

One of the guards leaned close to his master to whisper in his ear. Dumaka Lant nodded and then smiled. "Open door? On your world, I believe it's called breaking and entering. My sentries have already found the door you burned the hole through." Dumaka Lant ended his sentence by frowning at me. "Because of you, astrologer, this tragedy has occurred. And because of you, more tragedy shall follow."

I'll admit it: The hair crackled along the back of my neck at his ominous tone. "What is that supposed to mean?" I whispered.

"The ritual you watched being performed demands the highest of manifestation vibrations. You are an abomination. Your energy has corrupted the sanctity of this temple."

His answer nicked me off, and I snapped nasty on him. "Why don't you stop lying to your people, Dumaka Lant? There's nothing wrong with me energy. It's a big lie to keep yourself in power and control. I'd say it's a good bet you've duped Felis Bray'el as well."

Like an actor stepping up to a good cue, the leader of the Sen'Tal pushed his way through the pack of guards to stand beside Dumaka Lant. He stared at us with a hateful expression on his face. When Felis Bray'el finally spoke, his baritone growl made me jump.

"Your government has not been honest with me," he thundered. "We were told that you were under house arrest aboard your ship."

"Tit for tat," I answered, facing him down with a bold stare of my own.

He leaned close to me, and I could smell his sour breath. "What is that supposed to mean?"

"It means that if you are dishonest with Theo, then he is dishonest with you. Come on, Felis Bray'el, we know you're trying to weasel your people into Earth's government. You're trying to take over through attrition. The only problem is you're blatant about it. Not good. Not good at all. Especially when it concerns the emperor. You may have, indeed, met your match."

My big words didn't faze him. "The old humans of the Imperial Senate will do nothing to change the course of our aggression. They are too fat and lazy to do anything. I'm not worried. As to Theo, he may not be around to defend your glorious empire." That threat spoken, he spun on his heel to address Dumaka Lant. "Fix them up. Make sure their capture serves some purpose for our people."

The priest smiled and nodded. Bowing to his sovereign, he waited patiently for his liege to stalk away. Once gone, he transferred his lizard look onto us, again happily focusing upon my supposed abominable self.

"The law dictates that each candidate who would have accepted the regulator this night will now be executed because your energy has corrupted the whole temple. Their hearts will be ripped off their chests and the parts burned. You see, we can't use them at all. No other Waki'el should be made to accept tainted organs."

I might be full of splatty, salty emotion, but I like to think I don't show it. Unfortunately, my mug must have resembled the mud slide at Glastonbury after the deluge of 2116. He picked right up on my instant regret.

"That bothers the humanity in you. You Earthers think that every culture should abide by your silly ideals of spiritual supremacy. Not all people are created equally."

"Who gives a bright green piece of shit?" I managed

to growl. "What are you going to do with us?"

He used another minute to assert his authority by calling his guards to attention first. Then, returning to us,
he finished up his power play. "You shall serve as experimental subjects. What we discover about you will
fuel a program of conquest. Who knows? There might
be some secret about humans that only you can provide."

He flicked his wrist, and a guard stepped forward to
aim the point of the staff at Hadrien's neck.

"I wouldn't consider any frivolous action. The ends
of the staffs are dipped in poison. One prick from the
magic wand, and you're dead. Please don't give my sentry justification to kill you. That is my right, and I do
grow irritated when it's denied me."

We were promptly marched to a small stone room and
tossed inside. Once the wooden door was shut and
latched, we found ourselves huddled in total darkness.
If I expected Hadrien to react immediately about his im-
prisonment, I was in for a surprise. He pulled me along
until he found a wall, and then we both slid down to the
cold stone floor.

"Did you see where Zebrim Hast buried that pacemaker in the Waki'el female?" he asked.

"It was hard to miss. Right in the wrist. The yellow
juice seemed to prevent bleeding."

"A stabilizer of some sort. Lundy's murderer must
have used it to keep the prince from bleeding all over
the friggin' floor."

"What if it does something else?" I whispered.

"Like what?"

"Like stabilizes the person's energy field."

"Is this some interplanetudes concept that's going to
be hard for me to follow?"

"You won't have a bit of trouble with this."

He reached out and touched my arm. "What kind of
energy are we talking about? An aura or something?"

"An aura is generated by the person once he manifests

in this dimension. It's a signature of the person while he's alive in the flesh. There is a concept in the interplanetudes known as Crimper's Law, which states that life is bedeviled by its expansion."

"You're saying that energy that manifests life in this dimension has a built-in fail-safe system in case the species makes a hop, skip, and a jump ahead of itself."

"That's right. Think of it as blowing the natural selection process all to hell. The creation energy flows at a specific megahertz into the corporeal plane. That's one of the ways scientists measure its existence. They know that this force contains several piggyback vibrations that attach themselves to zero-point gravity like sucker fish on a shark. The thing about it is this: The creation energy can pass through the dimensional tissues easily, but according to Crimper's Law, these lesser stowaway vibrations don't pass with the creation energy, even though they affect it by changing the manifestational frequency. These vibrations are trapped in the plane of origination and become a function of time."

"Just how many different planes are there?"

"Unknown, and that's not the point. We assume that our life forces are individual frequency vibrations that attach themselves to the creation force."

"But the Waki'el don't believe that," he said. "They think they *are* the creation force."

"It might be a matter of semantics."

"Or they just might be wrong. Maybe that's why they keep experimenting on people. They just might not have a clue in hell what they are doing."

"With the help of the balloon heads, I'd say they've got a good idea."

"So you're saying that they've reversed the process. Instead of the stuff getting crimped off in the plane of origination, the Waki'el are crimping the life force on this side, stopping it from flowing through with the creation energy."

"Makes sense. In effect, they are regulating what frequencies pass through the individual."

I heard Hadrien take a big lungful of air. Having oxygenated his system, he sighed. "Omar saw heightened photon activity in the yellow fungus juice. He found tach threads in the Waki'el pacemaker. So the pacemaker can control some of the vibrations riding the creation frequency by slowing down the light, but it can't control the energy itself."

"I don't think any man or beast can control something like that. Not even zero-p babies. I also think that's how they killed Lundy."

Hadrien sighed before whispering, "Well, for whatever the idea is worth, it won't do us a bit of good stuck here."

"Paul is obviously working with the Waki'el," I announced. "In fact, I think he might be one of them."

"What does that mean?"

I leaned my head against the stone wall before answering. "Artie, I'm sure he's been fitted with a regulator."

41

My claustrophobia started kicking up the instant I remembered we were wedged in a small, dungeonlike space. The air suddenly became hard to breathe, and it was all I could do to remain calm and not give away my fear to Hadrien. He had enough to deal with on his own.

One of the theories concerning the application of astrology has to do with the fact that a person can draw on the combined strength of the planets. If Mars is an active component in the logos, it can ignite the flames of aggression. Both Hadrien and I had substantial Mars energy. This fact kept coming home to remind me that our anger and indignation might fuel the fire into a full-blown war against a species who wouldn't hesitate to execute all of humanity to get to the paradise we called Earth. With the weapons they possessed, humans were as good as dead.

We sorted through our game plan for escape while we sat in the darkness, and by the time our captors came to fetch us, we were ready. As the door creaked open, we steeled ourselves, coming to a stand and taking our weight low in the calves. A smoking torch preceded the visitor. Like a young hyena going for the jugular vein of the unsuspecting antelope, Hadrien charged forward, grabbed the burning punk, and yanked it out of the Waki'el's hand. He then swung the business end around and clobbered the bloke. The fire caught on the guard's linen shift. He forgot all about us as he beat the growing flames.

His companion pushed him away, grappling for me when I bolted through the door behind Hadrien. He was slow, and I took advantage of it by kicking him in the head. He yelped but recovered enough to chase me. I stopped again to face him, and he launched his spear in my direction. It was easy to duck his lumbering maneuver by spinning toward the wall. I took a couple of more steps, retrieved the staff, and turned it back on him.

The idiot punched forward like he thought I wouldn't use his weapon. I was in no mood for this scrap, so I took careful aim, and when he moved upon me, I drove the point between his sternum ridges and through his heart. His chest exploded in color, covering me with his sticky blood. The guard dropped, dead before he smacked the floor. I tugged the spear free, turned, paused to gather my bearings, and then called out for Hadrien.

He responded with an urgent bellow. "Hurry!"

I did as he instructed, flying around the corner to find him holding two more guards at bay. The tiff had energized me, and I used the power to toss the spear, hitting one of the sentries in the abdomen. There was enough force behind my throw to impale the bastard clean through. Seeing my lethal aim, the other Waki'el remounted his efforts but did so a tad too late, because Hadrien hooked him behind the ankle with his foot and brought the beast down on his backside. His spear clattered away. The guard twisted to reach it, but my partner was faster. He stomped on the alien's chest, bringing down all his weight by jumping on him. I heard the

Waki'el's sternum ridges crack, and the next thing I knew, Hadrien was covered in as much blood as I was.

He turned toward me, grinning demonically. "These boys are made of papier-mâché."

"But there are a whole lot of them," I answered, heading off down the corridor. "Do you remember how we came into this maze?"

"No." He stalked to a torch wedged into a brass fitting tacked to the wall. He broke it free and waved me into action.

We ran as fast as a couple of old sots heading for free booze, finally coming to a four-way junction that did not look at all familiar. We hustled for another fifty meters before we turned a corner and realized we'd straggled into a dead end. Unfortunately, it wasn't a wall we'd run at, it was a guard unit.

Despite all our biting, hitting, and kicking, we were woefully outnumbered and finally subdued. They did the unthinkable by splitting us apart. Hadrien was dragged away, roaring a foul-mouthed protest at his captors. I simply surrendered to avoid more bruises. The guards carried me to a new cell, this one large and well lit by overhead fluorescent tubes. I was not alone, either. The room was filled with lonesome-looking Waki'el, one of whom happened to be Yana.

The sentries dropped me like a bag of taters, and I hit the floor with a thwack. Still angry, I flipped to my feet and kicked at the knee of the nearest guard, my heel connecting solidly. I heard a loud crack even before I saw the bone pop through his hide. Yes, Hadrien was right. These blokes were made of papier-maché.

One of the guards slapped me hard across the face and knocked me back toward Yana. The old Waki'el broke my fall by catching me in his arms. He dragged me back to his comrades, while the sentries pulled their injured comrade clear and slammed the door behind them.

The people in the room gathered around me as I tried to dislodge the ringing noise in my head. My mouth hurt, my ears hurt, and I was truly nicked off that I didn't know what was happening to Hadrien.

"Are you all right, Astrologer Cyprion?" Yana asked as he knelt beside me.

"I guess I'll live. For a while, anyway. Where am I, and why are you here?"

"This is the death room," he answered.

"Death room?"

"Yes. We come here to wait until we are called for execution."

I glanced around at the lot. They were sorry beggars for the most part—old, dingy, and bent—yet they showed me kindness by bringing me a drink of precious water.

"We are allowed liquid in great quantities," one of the ancients announced. "It is the blessing they give us before we are sacrificed for the good of the people."

I sat up and accepted the cracked cup, the mention of liquid making my tongue ache from lack of moisture. Slugging it, I nearly choked. It was ice cold.

"I have been here for two weeks," someone said. "Tonight was to have been my time to go, but there was some disturbance that postponed my fate."

"I'm afraid I'm part of that disturbance, mate. Sorry if I inconvenienced you."

The Waki'el approached me, towering over me in all his cranberry-colored glory. "Inconvenienced? I do not want to die, human. None of us do."

"And how is your death connected to the warrior ritual?" I asked.

Yana answered for them all. "We are not connected with the new warriors, only the ones who have served for a specific length of time."

"Why them?"

He shook his head sadly. "Because their service to the Waki'el people weakens their hearts. We are used to correct these problems. Like it or not."

42

I remained with Yana and his friends for only a short time before guards returned to hustle me off. Yana made his fast good-byes, he and his comrades bowing low at the waist. Seeing that, I had a bad feeling that Saturn had just contacted my Uranus, and I would be in for a long term of suffering.

The guards led me down one long hallway after another until I was finally deposited in the operating room. The captain of the unit shoved me onto the operating table and, despite my struggling, managed to get a pair of clampers around my ankles. Trussed up like a Christmas goose, I figured I was already cooked. It then went from fridge to fire, because who should walk in but Cornelius Paul.

He was alone, and he was as naked as a scrawny, lily-white jaybird. I glared at him, refusing to make any to-do about his glory hanging out. Instead, I let my gaze fall upon his arm. He wore no gauntlet, and I could clearly see some sort of round implant in the underside of his wrist as well as the jagged pink trail running up his arm. Paul noticed where my attention lay and smiled sardonically. He raised his arm to show me better.

"You're one of them, aren't you?" I growled.

He laughed but sobered quickly. "How long have you been living in a fantasy? What? Do you think I'm some kind of mutant created by Fangor Jaban's fiddling in the creation energy?"

"I don't know. Why don't you tell me?"

"It's all a big pork pie," he said flatly.

"What is?"

"Fangor Jaban's assertion that he could manipulate the creation energy. He's a crazy old fool who shouldn't have lived as long as he has."

"So what makes you such an expert?"

He paused to pull up a plastic chair and mount it pony style. "It simply cannot be done. This is according to our friends the balloon heads. The Waki'el are lying to themselves and doing nothing more than pumping up their alien egos."

"Then how do you explain the appearance of N'galia Waki'el born to Basira and Tus parents?"

"Genetic. Actually, it's cyclical."

"You mean this happens at a predictable rate throughout their history? How do you know this?"

"I've studied their culture, Philipa. How else do you think I know this? The Waki'el refuse to believe that a genetic retrogression can be possible. From what I've read, there's a significant shift in population numbers about once every thousand generations. The pendulum swings back and forth as pretty as you please."

"Then why don't they believe it?"

"It's Felis Bray'el and his Sen'Tal who refuse to believe it. Bad form for the government, you see."

"You killed Lundy, didn't you?" I snapped.

Paul didn't answer right away. Instead, he studied me thoughtfully before delivering his zinger. "I killed your husband, too. But then, you already knew that."

His words stung me like a poisoned arrow, and I just

lay there, staring at him. I suppose my gaze made him uncomfortable because he explained. "He had discovered something that Theo wanted kept quiet. A similarity between humans and Waki'els."

"How did he find all this out?"

"Through his studies on Belinda-Agnes."

"What similarity?"

He raised his arm, showing me the jagged line. "Actually, he discovered this."

"What is it?"

"Well, essentially, your brilliant husband discovered that buried in the myelin sheath surrounding many of the nerves in the human body, there is a layer composed of photon particles that he associated with the zero-point gravity force. Eric also found that these particles are present in the brain neurons, as well as strong evidence that they float freely in the spinal fluid. Mix all this together, and the combination acts as a conveyor of the creation energy within our bodies. This layer of particles also connects us directly to the causal plane from whence we have each sprung. I believe he said that people who suffer from debilitating nerve dysfunction have lost the resiliency of the gravitic energy. The force is blocked within them. Fascinating, don't you think?"

Not just fascinating, but something that I never expected. "The Waki'el have learned to use this photon layer."

"Yes, they have, and they've made remarkable strides since your loudmouthed husband went around Theo and informed Felis Bray'el of his extraordinary find. The Waki'el have long been allies of the balloon heads. You get enough of those thinkers together, and you can figure out anything."

"But Theo shipped them in. I got that word straight from Verena."

He shook his head and smiled. "No he didn't. I did. Theo knew nothing about these monsters. He didn't even realize that he'd footed the bill for research that would eventually collapse his government and bring the people of planet Earth to their knees. So much for bureaucratic efficiency."

"You're saying Theo didn't order you to kill Eric?"

"No, of course not. It was necessary to silence him for my own survival. You see, he was planning on telling Theo all about me."

"And what did he find out? That you're a traitor to your own kind?"

Paul shrugged. "That and the fact that I am a confirmed honey addict. Actually, amber, if you want to get technical."

"Just like Lundy."

"Yes. We were both pegging Belinda-Agnes, you know. I believe your husband had a go at her once or twice but didn't find the amber to his liking." He stopped speaking to squint at me, obviously trying to gauge my reaction to word of Eric's infidelity.

I refused to give him the pleasure and remained monotone in expression and voice. "So, you were fitted with an experimental regulator by Zebrim Hast. How does it work?"

"Amazing things these balloon heads can do with slow light. By shifting the speed of the photon layer in my nervous system, I am able to indulge in Waki'el females and still remain active. You see, on top of my addiction, I do have a rev problem. The regulator took care of most of my difficulties."

"That's sick, Paul."

"Yes, it is, but it's the best I can do. I got myself into trouble, but I also got myself out of trouble and into a very comfortable space between Earth and Arif."

"Why did you have someone kill Lundy?"

"Because his affair with Belinda-Agnes had grown serious. He was also a favorite of Mann Re's. She was angry at the treatment of her daughter as was Belinda herself."

"So, in exchange for amber, he sent word between mother and daughter, using the biowaste deliveries as a cover-up."

Paul clapped and laughed. "You always were a fast one, Philipa. Mann Re could have caused me infinite trouble, so I cut off the source of her information."

"Did you kill Belinda?"

"Yes. Not willingly, you understand. It had to be done. I could not afford for her to stir up trouble before Felis Bray'el had his warriors ready."

"You mean assassins who are prepared to undertake an affair of the heart."

"Yes."

"Tell me. How did the pacemaker placed in his heart kill Lundy?"

"Oh, come, you've already figured that out."

"Once activated by photon energy, the regulator slows the light to the point that it starves the layer in the myelin sheath."

"It's as though this action closes the door between the dimensions, effectively shutting off the flow of the creation force. Once the energy stops traveling through the organism, the organism dies. You might say we turned the lights out on Lundy. You might also say that this method of execution scrapes away a person's time in this dimension by trapping his life source in the plane of origin."

"Why did you place the regulator in his heart?"

"The heart is a check valve of sorts. It has many nerves and is the hub of photon particles. Besides that, it hurt Lundy like hell, and I wanted to make sure that it did."

"How did the killer place the unit in his heart without disturbing the tissue and bone?"

He pointed to his wrist. "A properly inserted and activated regulator can create a dimensional vortex. We are nothing but light, Philipa. You cannot imagine how easy it is for us to move between causal planes just by being able to control the rate and flood of photon particles flowing in from our source." Paul stood, studied me, and then smiled. "You shall get your chance to find out all of this firsthand. That is, if you survive the insertion and activation of the regulator. Your partner is in the next operating room, receiving his now. To amuse myself, I'm going to make you watch the process."

43

*It appeared that once more my abilities to chan-*nel complete understanding from the rise and fall of the planets had failed me. While I had suspected Cornelius Paul to be Lundy's killer, I'd not read anything in his logos that suggested he was capable of committing high treason to further his own personal gain. I simply had not seen it, and now whatever happened to Hadrien and me was completely and utterly my fault.

I was dragged from one surgery unit to the next operating theater, where I found Hadrien strapped to a table. His arm had been firmly secured on an extension and, from where I stood, I saw that he was oblivious.

"What did you do to him?" I demanded.

Paul smiled. "Oh, just a little kiss was all it took. Now he's a man who has a funky nervous system."

"Why? Why are you doing this?"

"Because the Waki'el have not had the chance to gain enlightenment by experimenting on a healthy human female or a male with a rev problem who does not have an active addiction. I promised them both. Some time ago, actually."

"You were behind this whole thing, weren't you, Paul? You set Hadrien and me up from the start."

He sneered. "I would have thought your precious planets would have alerted you that you two had nothing in common and no reason to be thrown together on this project. He was a perfect specimen, and you—well, I wanted you quiet and out of the way."

"I wasn't causing you any trouble."

"That's because you were still in the painful throes of grief. But how might that change once you were thinking clearly? I couldn't take the chance that you could actually read the future."

No worries there. "You're going to kill us with these alien devices."

"That might happen, yes. It is more likely you will survive, though, and be kept in this compound and monitored by the Sen'Tal for the rest of your lives. Which could be very short, indeed."

"Why do you say that?"

"Every time you activate the unit to create a dimensional displacement, it shortens your life span. And I'm sure you will be required to do quite a lot of that by Dumaka Lant. You see, he wants to learn to do it on a large scale. He has grandiose dreams, and I'm sure that with your help he'll be able to realize them. It is unfortunate that the effect of the regulator damages the body through nervous progression." He leaned close to me to make his final point, and I smelled mint on his breath. "All your major bodily organs get into the act, especially the heart muscle." He glanced at Hadrien and then slowly brought his gaze back to me. "Him, I don't expect to last but a few weeks. You might go on for a year or so. No more." He stepped back, smiling. "I'm an executioner, Philipa. One of my goals is to prevent boredom in my chosen career. Creative approach this, don't you think?"

I honestly had no response. My brain wouldn't work

in the face of such callous disregard for human life. When I didn't answer, Paul laughed and waved the guards into action. They dragged me to the empty operating gurney across from Hadrien, literally picking me up and dropping me onto the table.

"Don't do this, Paul!"

"It's too late, Philipa. The sentence must be carried out."

With that, I was strapped to the table. Paul receded into the shadows and, after tussling with the guards, my arm was tied to the extension and my cammie sleeve ripped away to expose my wrist. The sentries stepped off, leaving me hanging there. I did my best to break my bindings, but it was like the last-ditch hope of the Light Brigade. In a few minutes, I was joined by Dumaka Lant and Zebrim Hast.

"The moment I laid eyes on you both, I knew you would be perfect for our experiments," Zebrim Hast said brightly. "Yes, indeed. Perfect."

"Please don't do this," I begged.

Dumaka Lant smiled, and I saw the tips of tiny fangs. "It is my pleasure to do this. Why in the world would I give up an opportunity to transform my people through knowledge?" He raised his attention and glanced beyond me. "That would be insensitive, especially since Paul did so much to get you here."

Zebrim Hast took a step toward a steel counter and returned with the familiar yellow elixir. He began to carefully swab it onto my wrist. It burned, and I hissed at him. The Waki'el ignored me, instead explaining about the implant.

"The regulator will immediately mold to your personal frequencies and become an integral part of your system. If you try to remove it, you will die soon after."

"You bloody bastard! I hope you rot in Waki'el hell."

He smiled indulgently but didn't reply. Turning, he walked to the counter, replaced the beaker, and then returned with my very own pacemaker. Holding it up to the overhead light, he studied it before glancing at me. "It's a new design that should allow for increased power in dimensional displacement."

Dumaka Lant suddenly produced a laser scalpel. He flipped it on, and the hum it made sounded horribly loud in my ears. I did my best to fight, but it was impossible to move, trussed as I was like Uncle Lou's hernia. The moment Lant touched the cutter to my wrist, I was sure I would vomit. It would have served him right if I'd tossed my beer and oats all over him, but unfortunately, my stomach flattened out.

My gaze was locked on the procedure. He carefully opened a space at the base of my hand by digging deep into the muscle. I felt a pressure, but no pain. There was no blood, and I found myself wondering where my life force went. If this regulator converted light, was it also transforming my platelets?

Dumaka Lant graciously conceded his space at the table, and Zebrim Hast replaced him.

"Please," I begged.

He ignored me to focus on the regulator. It was smaller than the one that had been found in Lundy's pumper, and it was round and flat. Zebrim Hast secured it with a pair of tiny clamps and then slipped it neatly into the incision his partner had made in my wrist.

Whereas I didn't feel the slice taken out of my muscle, I did, indeed, feel the insertion of the regulator. A spark of pain ignited in my hand. It was so bright I cried out, despite having sworn to myself that I wouldn't give them the satisfaction.

"The pain will stop momentarily," Zebrim Hast said.

I couldn't answer. My throat felt raw and my tongue thick, and breathing suddenly seemed like a lot of work. If a human doctor had been there, he would have surely said that I was heading for a state of shock.

To compound my difficulty, I had thoughts of death—

quick, battering thoughts. Would this strange, alien contraption prevent my soul—my energy—from returning to its source at the time my physical body gave it the old heave-ho?

Dumaka Lant stepped forward again and sutured up the wound he'd caused. I watched with weird fascination as the skin closed neatly over the regulator. He noticed my attention and chose to brighten my day with information. "We have had to leave the stud exposed in the past, so that it could be controlled, but significant pressure against the skin in just the right place will activate the regulator now." He gently touched his fingertip against the bottom of my thumb. "Right here." Before I knew what happened, he pressed hard enough to give me a bruise.

I might have replied had I been so inclined, but right at that a moment a flash raced through my body. I call it a flash, because that is what it felt like. It was as though someone had sprayed my insides with liquid light. I arched against this power, and when I did, Dumaka Lant bruised my hand again. The second he did, the exquisite pain abruptly ceased. It left me bleary but suddenly desiring to experience the flash again.

"The implant has been activated," Dumaka Lant announced.

He took my chin in his fingers and turned my head toward him. "Do you understand me, Ms. Cyprion?"

I couldn't get my lips to cooperate, so I grunted. He took it as an affirmative.

"Good. The tachyon filaments inside the regulator are now reacting to your photon layer. You should feel a tingling in your arm quite soon."

He was right; the burn had started. I whimpered against it, my transforming nerves singing out their agony at being converted, their natural actions corraled and regulated. Centimeter by centimeter, I was enslaved by the very force that had given me life in this dimension.

The burn traced down through my arm and exploded in my heart. My chest throbbed, my lungs ached, and just when I thought the conversion had finally passed through my pumper, I experienced another flash. I cried out, more for the ecstasy it caused than the agony.

"First stage complete," Dumaka Lant said.

"She's handling it quite well," Zebrim Hast said. "It was too bad we couldn't have had this kind of data with the male."

I would have cursed them, though for some reason, I was swamped in a dizzy euphoria and unable to collect my anger and indignation. Following the flash, the burn moved down my torso and into my legs, circuiting back until I could feel it enter my spinal cord. The burn increased, forcing me into a panting sweat as the regulator conquered my mobility, paralyzing me in stages while it ate up the photon layer in the thousands of nerve control centers.

The next thing I knew, I couldn't breathe. My muscles wouldn't push my lungs.

"Be strong, Ms. Cyprion," Dumaka Lant said quietly. "You will be able to breathe in just a minute."

A moment scraped by, followed by another. Abruptly, I managed to draw air, and it felt cold as it rushed down my windpipe.

The burn continued to crawl up my back before passing into my neck. When I felt it hit my brain stem, I was treated to another flash. This one filled my skull, and it was so intense that I was sure the back sides of my eyeballs were melting.

"She's passed the second stage," Dumaka Lant announced.

With that, I lost all focus and felt myself sliding toward unconsciousness.

44

*I woke up in a stone dungeon fixed with an elec-*tric light. The bulb hung directly over the hard cot where I lay, and when my eyes first opened, I thought the pain from the brightness would explode my head. I moaned despite my best efforts to keep my mouth shut. It was then that I realized my entire body hurt.

I burned from stem to stern. The fire worked through me, rising as a wave of pain before ebbing to an annoying tingle. I lay there a long time with my eyes closed, cataloging bits and pieces of my body until I was sure that everything was still there.

Thirst corrupted my thoughts, adding to the toll of my discomfort. I tried desperately to get a widdle of spit on the back of my tongue, but there was nothing I could do. I'd turned to sandpaper inside.

Eventually, I gave up trying to conjure liquid on my own and tried to move my head, hoping that there would be a jug of water sitting near the bunk. When I did, I saw Hadrien.

He stretched out on a similar bunk. His face was turned toward me, and his eyes were closed. He was pale, and his expression wasn't of a man experiencing angelic sleep. I tried to call his name, but my throat would not cooperate. Had this alien insert burned out my vocal chords?

I lay there for several more minutes before I felt as though I might not burst into flame. It was a grand effort for me to turn over and sit up. The moment I did, I was swamped with dizziness. I held my head still, afraid to move it.

I have lived my life in anticipation of what new experience would await me around the next bend in the road. There never seemed to be any room to manifest hatred. As angry as I had been with Theo over Eric's death, I still did not hate the man. I had honestly thought that I was incapable of desiring revenge, but now, after this bloody awful violation by Paul and the Waki'el, I not only despised my captors, I was determined to do everything I could to bring them down in a way that would make them suffer on equal par with me. If only I could move my head without jiggling out the gray pus that had one time been my brain.

I glanced toward the small table at the other end of the room and noticed that we had, indeed, been provided with a bottle of water. It sat there, along with globes of yellow fruit and a loaf of bread. I climbed to a stand, but almost tipped backward from dizziness. Taking one fragile step at a time, I finally reached the table. I tapped the bottle and slugged the liquid. It hit my throat like quicksilver before rolling on toward my stomach. I hacked and gagged as I slurped up the water, greedy to hydrate my system. After having downed half the bottle, I turned slowly to study Hadrien. He had not moved, and I couldn't be sure he was even breathing.

I trudged back to the bunks, pausing to check the pulse in his neck. His heart beat slowly. At least I knew the old kettle drum was still pounding.

"Hadrien," I whispered as I slapped him gently on the cheek. "Hadrien, wake up."

There was no response—no moan, no groan, no sign that he was going to recover with a simple prodding. I sighed, unable to muster much more energy than that. Flopping down on my bed, I studied him, trying to figure out why the universe had brought us together only to kill us in the service of an alien species. I turned over my hand to stare at the place where the Waki'el had inserted the regulator. There was a small red scar from the suture tool. A jagged pink lightning bolt traced up my arm from this point. I ripped open the zipper on my cammies and found that the strange design ran straight to my heart where it stopped, leaving the image of a sunburst upon my chest.

Blast them and their Frankenstein experiments! I stood, reached over, and checked Hadrien's arm, seeing that he, too, bore the lightning bolt.

"Artie, can you hear me?"

Nothing. His nervous system might keep him down for days, and we needed to get out of there. I would not take this abuse without a fight. If Dumaka Lant and Zebrim Hast wanted to study the depth and breadth of power inherent in the human energy, then they would have their wish.

I took another slurp from the water bottle, set it back on the table, and breathed deeply. The air in the room was cold, but it filled my lungs, giving me the extra vitality I needed to make my next decision.

Stepping to Hadrien, I picked up his hand and feeling just below his thumb, I pressed hard. When I did, his reaction was instantaneous. Hadrien arched against invisible power as though I'd turned on a switch. He cried out and for a second, I felt unutterable dismay at harming him in this way. I dropped his hand, backpedaling to watch the effects of the alien implant.

He settled down in the next minute, moaning softly.

Still, he didn't come around all the way, and so I was forced to give him a couple of good whacks across the face. Finally, he opened his eyes.

I forgot all my own discomfort in a flood of relief. Kneeling by his bunk, I tenderly rubbed the red spot I'd made on his cheek. "Are you all right?" I whispered.

He squinted at me. I panicked, thinking that the regulator had futzed up his mind, and he no longer recognized me.

"Artie, can you understand me? Do you know who I am?"

Hadrien opened his mouth, but like me, words would not emerge. I offered him a drink, cradling his head with my arm and feeding him the liquid slowly. He coughed as the water hit his throat, but his choking didn't stop him from pawing for the bottle. When he'd polished off our ration, I removed my arm, and he flopped back down on the thin pillow.

"Do you remember anything?" I asked.

He thought a minute before turning his gaze in my direction. "I died," he croaked.

This statement startled me, yet I let it go for the moment. I helped Hadrien to sit up, but he was so drained, he could barely move. He buried his head in his hands and sighed heavily. It was such a sad sound that it drove me away to the table where I broke open one of the fruits and returned to feed him the moist pulp. He ate a few bites before he wrapped his hand around mine and squeezed gently. Gazing into my eyes, he told me what I knew to be the truth. "I love you, Philipa."

"And I you, Artemis."

He didn't smile at my admission. Instead, he frowned, dropped my hand, and rubbed his arm across his forehead. I waited as long as I could as to not spoil the last romantic moment we might ever have, but I just had to know.

"How do you know you died?" I asked quietly.

He swallowed hard and grunted softly before fixing me with that familiar, dark expression. "Dumaka Lant hit me with some kind of hypo. I went out on a speeding train." He paused to lick his lips. "It was like being sucked into a wind tunnel. My whole body felt like it was being stretched."

"Why did they hit you with the needle?"

"I broke someone's nose."

I couldn't keep a grin hidden. "Good boy. Sinus problems. Serves him right."

He managed a thin smile. "Yeah, well, I paid for it."

"Were you awake for the installation of the regulator?"

He nodded slowly and then glanced down at his hand, turning it so he could see the jagged line running the length of his arm. "I didn't lose consciousness. I was with them right up until they activated the goddamned thing."

"Yeah. That was a bloody jolt. When I got in there, you were down for the count."

"I wasn't down for the count, Philipa. I was gone. I was in a different dimension."

"How do you know?"

"Because I was nothing but thought. My body wasn't with me. It was as if I'd turned into a thousand sparkling shards, each one separate yet complete."

For some reason, I felt a sense of envy when he spoke this. Perhaps I should have felt a kernel of relief knowing for a fact that Eric's soul lived on, but I suddenly felt very little connection to him. The emotion I had was wrapped up with Hadrien. "What else do you remember?"

"I wasn't alone."

"How do you know?"

"I could hear them." He stopped speaking to scowl. "No, that's not right. I could understand them. It was as though there was a veil between me and all these other entities."

"What did they communicate?"

"I can't remember."

"How did you return to this dimension?"

"I was sucked back through. When it happened, I found myself half here and half there. Wherever *there* is."

"Could you see your physical self?"

"Barely. I could see through myself. I shimmered."

My mind hopped back to stories told by the surviving crewmen of the USS *Eldridge*. When they'd phased back onto the ship after the dimensionality experiment, some had materialized within bulkheads and decks. It was as if their atoms had melded with the physicality around them. The same kind of displacement had allowed Lundy's assassin to insert the pacemaker in his heart without damaging tissue, muscle, or bone.

"It seemed like it required a great deal of energy to return to my physical body," he murmured.

"I was told we would eventually die from the action of the implant."

Hadrien shook his head. "It won't be the implant that will kill us, Philipa."

"What do you mean?"

"I mean there will come a time when we'll decide to stay in that other dimension. We will simply choose not to return to our physical bodies."

45

I could recall nothing from my time spent in oblivion, which led me to a new line of thought. Was the afterlife composed of images and ideas but segregated into different experiences, depending upon what the entity believed? Did Hadrien unconsciously seek an afterlife where he was welcomed into the bosom of old friends and relatives? Was his version as real as the blackness I'd experienced? What did that say about my deep-down notions of the great beyond? How could I, as an astrologer, face the possibility that my afterlife would be composed of nothingness instead of a dimension of light and understanding?

Hadrien and I huddled on the bunk, hugging each other more for the strength it provided than any need to show affection. It was quite clear that my partner had suffered from his trip into the beyond. He apologized half a dozen times when he awakened suddenly after having drifted into sleep.

Rest eluded me. The flame of revenge burned inside me with an explosive force that was as snapping hot as the flash that had gone through me when the Waki'el had activated the regulator. When I heard Hadrien's gentle, regular breathing, I knew he'd fallen asleep, so I arose, sliding quietly from the bunk.

Revenge wasn't all that was on my mind. I was determined we were going to waltz out of there. Maybe it was my stubborn Virgo spurring me on, or perhaps it was a death wish struck up by my profound weariness of life. It didn't matter. We were leaving, and I knew how we were going to do it.

Keeping in mind the experiences of the sailors aboard the USS *Eldridge* and the method of Lundy's assassination, I talked myself into believing that I could literally walk through the stone wall. The trick, of course, would be to not lose my grip on incorporeality and materialize within the stone instead of passing through to the hallway beyond.

Standing before the wall, I realized why Paul had been naked the last time I'd seen him; he'd been tripping the light fantastic. I decided to do the same and stripped off my glad rags. It was certain the light would transform me, but not my clothes. Once naked, I took one last look at Hadrien sleeping peacefully, and then, with all the strength I could muster, I pressed the spot below my thumb.

The tachyon corridor opened immediately, and I could feel the transmission of light feeding throughout my system. In a matter of moments, it rose up my arm and into my chest where it stung my heart until I was sure it was going to send me into cardiac arrest. Glancing down, I saw the spot on my chest brighten to a deep red. Another minute passed, and my mood transformed. I was abruptly exhilarated, dizzy with energy. It convulsed through me until it impacted my brain, and I knew I'd found the link between the causal planes.

The moment I crossed this bridge, I knew what Hadrien had meant. I sensed the presence of others. I could hear their chatter in my mind. The noise had not entered through my ears. It flowed through me like a great gush of wind.

Stepping up to the wall, I placed my fingers lightly against the stone. From my vantage point, I could see the sparkling light of my essence. I paused to marvel at how shiny I truly was. I was sparks of lovely light popping like stars in a bright nebula of blue white gas. Then I pushed my hand through the wall.

The bursting stars grew chaotic as the stone reacted to the presence of slowed light. I felt no sensation at all as I swam into the stone up to my elbow. Inside the wall, the shimmering grew brighter and the voices louder.

I stepped through until my whole body was encased by the thick stone. If the regulator cut out or I did something out of ignorance, I would come completely back into corporeality, and my atoms would meld with those comprising the wall. I would be trapped for all eternity.

The thought gave me the jim-jiminies, so I hurriedly moved on through to the other side, emerging into the corridor, right beside a sentry guarding our door. He acted as if he didn't see me, so I paused to run my hand through his arm. The little stars popped and fizzed. The guard didn't move. In fact, he was completely oblivious of my presence.

I stepped away from him and glanced up the corridor. It was lit by electric lights, but there were no other sentries to hinder our escape. Now all I had to do was to figure out how to materialize. I couldn't press the stud because I apparently had no physicality. What did I need to do?

Standing there, I'll admit I had a moment of panic, but then my mind picked up the voices flowing through me. The noise calmed me in a way I cannot explain, and a sense of euphoria overcame me. Yes, Hadrien had been right. If this was death, it wasn't a bad place to be.

They say we Brits are a practical people, and so I

worked off that assumption to find my way back into the realm of corporeality. I imagined the light speeding up again. When I did this, I could suddenly feel my heart! Had it returned to the heavy gravity of this dimension before the rest of me?

The more I concentrated on returning, the weightier I grew until I stood before the guard fully formed. He saw me pop in and stiffened.

"Hello, me fine bloke," I greeted. "Thought I'd go out for a stroll. Care to join me?"

The Waki'el grimaced, growled, and charged at me with his poisoned spear. I easily sidestepped his lumbering attack by knocking the shaft clear with my foot. His momentum carried him into my upraised knee, and he impacted on the sharp side of it. I felt delicate sternum ridges shatter as I drove my body into his. He lurched toward the opposite wall, and I brought my fists down on the top of his spine. It was a killing blow; I knew this before I delivered it. He sprawled where he was hit, his essence already vacating the shell of his body.

I didn't give the fellow a second thought. Instead, I rushed to the door and pulled back the latch. Hadrien sat up on the bunk, staring in my direction. There was surprise and weariness in his expression, but he jumped up the instant he saw who it was.

"Grab me glad rags, Artie. We're going to make things even with Cornelius Paul, and then we're going to have Captain Verena blast off this dusty rock."

He didn't fight me on any of it. It took him no time at all to scoop up my clothes and follow me out the door and down the hallway.

The temple was silent. There were no sentries posted along any of the corridors we tracked down; no sound from connecting chambers. At one point we passed the surgical theater and saw that the lights had been turned off in our torture chamber. We both hurried away from the unit and the memories.

The Waki'el's assumed superiority was their undoing in the end. They lost two of their research animals before the experiments ever began, because there was no one about to oppose us in our escape. We stepped through a side door out into the bright light of the Arifian day.

46

I'd often thought that I was ready for a spiritual makeover, especially after Eric's death, but this is not what I had in mind. Still, the laws of the interplanetudes were specific: What one thinks, one manifests. It is the nature of the universe, and I knew it for a fact. There was nothing to do but play the hand the planets had dealt me when I volunteered to come into my present incarnation. Destiny would not be changed, because it could not be changed.

We reached the *Kourey* unhindered, and walked aboard. A crewman was posted at the entrance hatch, and he simply saluted us as we tracked by. Once we were in the main lobby, I stopped, pulling Hadrien to a halt with a simple tug to his cammie sleeve. He turned to stare at me.

"Go get Verena," I ordered. "I'm going after Paul."

"You should wait, Philipa. We both need to talk to Verena. Besides, we don't know if Paul is here."

I shook my head. "He's here. He doesn't want to attract attention to himself—especially from Theo. I have an account to close with the executioner, Artie. Go, get the backup while I balance the scales of justice."

He didn't try to talk me out of it. "Be careful. I don't want to lose you."

I smiled. "You can't lose me. Our lives are entangled. You know it as well as I."

With that, I started off before I changed my mind and copped out on my fate by allowing another to assume the responsibility of my karma.

The crew ignored me as I walked through the ship. It was as though I wasn't quite visible to them. Before I arrived at Paul's quarters, I wondered if I hadn't left something important back in the ethereal dimension.

Standing before the door to Paul's cabin, I braced myself for the encounter. My anger had grown into a red-eyed rage that fed my conviction to drop him where he stood. I spread my feet wide, taking my weight low in my thighs, preparing myself before I knocked lightly on the hatch.

Paul's attaché answered. I punched him so hard in the nose that I drove the bone back into his brain. He fell in a heap. I stepped over him and cycled the hatch shut behind me.

The executioner rushed from the cabin's bedroom, the black robes of his office billowing around him. His expression gave away his panic, but he managed to calm himself and toss me one of those disapproving looks.

"How did you escape the temple?" he demanded.

"I used me brains, you blooming imbecile. Did you think that by installing this piece of alien shit in me wrist, you were going to be safe from me learning how to use it?" I took a few steps toward him, and he retreated just as many. "What's the matter, Paul? Don't you have the new, improved version of the regulator? Am I wee bit more powerful than you are?"

He didn't answer. Instead, he reached for a lead crystal vase sitting on a side table and aimed it like a rocket in my direction. I ducked, and it impacted with the bulkhead, denting the gaudy wallpaper. This lame defense did nothing to deter me.

Paul turned to flee into the bedroom, but I was on him like a hawk. I used my fury to knock him to the deck, and when he hit, I heard the air rush from his lungs. It took me only a second to use this to my advantage. I added to his breathing difficulty by climbing atop him and banging my fist hard on his sternum. Whatever life-giving oxygen was still present in his system, it steamed out. He struggled against me, but my anger overwhelmed him. Suddenly, it overwhelmed me as well.

I phased. That is all I can call it, because one minute I was whole and sound, the next I saw sparkles, glimmers, and glitters. I had not touched the spot under my thumb, yet my concentration had pushed me into the dimensional bypass where I was not fully in either world. Thankfully, there was still a bit of corporeality to me, and it was enough to cause pain in my victim.

I pushed my fingers through his chest muscle, and he abruptly gathered enough wind to scream, but oddly, he stopped flailing. Continuing on my lethal course, I passed my hand through his sternum, feeling gooey flesh at the same time I experienced the atomic displacement. Paul flopped against the deck and yet, in his surrender, he was fully aware that I was killing him. I could read it in his eyes along with his helplessness. He blubbered at me—words that made no sense. My fingers touched his pumper, and a feeling of joy filled me.

Paul arched against me. "No!" he begged. "Please."

If I commanded myself into complete physicality, would I make a five-inch hole in his chest through which I could pull out his heart, or would our atoms join us like a strange pair of Siamese twins?

"Don't do it, Philipa."

At first I'd thought Paul had said it, but then I realized it had been Hadrien. I glanced behind me, and there he stood with Verena and a contingent of guards.

"Don't do it," he repeated. "We need him alive to present to Theo."

I sat there for at least thirty seconds before my confused emotions settled and I got a grip on myself. I yanked my hand out of Paul's chest. Despite a little spilled blood, the bastard would live to be judged properly.

I turned my attention to him, kneeing the executioner in the groin as I spoke. "My partner is right. Death is too good for you."

47

A week later, Hadrien and I sat in the plush apartments of the emperor, awaiting a face-to-face audience with him. Paul had been arrested for his part in the grisly game. And according to Verena's recommendations, Theo had cut diplomatic and trade ties with the Waki'el.

Hadrien and I had both recovered from the dramatic events on Arif, but we were each in our own way frightened about the future. I had my cards, my calculator, and the certainty of the planets. Still, it didn't seem like enough to guide me through the waters of physical life. Like Hadrien, I kept thinking about the few times I'd walked between the realms. It had been exhilarating, and I had experienced a totality that eluded me in the physical plane. The sheet of corporeality was limiting, heavy, and suddenly cumbersome.

"What will you do now?" Hadrien asked me quietly.

"I don't know. I can't say I want to stay on Earth."

"Why?"

"Just doesn't feel like home anymore." I rose from the velvet couch and strolled to the window to stare out at the view of old Londontown. It was the same as it always had been: foggy, rainy, dank, and dreary. But Eric's ghost no longer resided here, and that meant I was free from the shackles of my grief and pain. "I don't think there will ever be any place in this dimension where I will feel totally comfortable again."

Hadrien slid from the sofa to join me at the window. Angling his face, he studied me. "I'm going through the same kind of dislocation as you are. It's as if I'm no longer a creature of either realm."

"At least we averted a disaster for the people of this planet."

"That we did. And we unwillingly gave up our immortal souls to do it."

His words fell like stones of truth in the silence of the room. We stood at the window a minute more before returning to the couch.

"What will you do now that this whole mess is over?" I asked.

"Well, I won't be returning to Terrapol, if that's what you mean."

"Why not?"

"That life would seem uneventful now."

I laughed lightly. "Right. Nothing could compare to this last investigation."

He leaned back and stretched. "That's true, but unfortunately, we're still trapped in this plane, and we need to do something to support ourselves."

"Do you have an idea?"

"As a matter of fact, I do," he answered. "I've contacted an acquaintance who hires out investigators throughout this arm of the galaxy. He needs a couple of folks to do some work for him—none of it on Earth and none of it too stressful. At least that's what he said. I told him I was interested." Hadrien stopped speaking to grin at me. Then he added, "I told him we were a team. I want you to come along."

I sat there for a minute, knowing the whole time what my answer would be. Touching his hand gently, I interlaced my fingers with his. "Tell me, Artie. How much does this gig pay?"